Camryn paused, eyes widening. "Wait a minute. You *don't* believe me. How could I be so stupid? You said it last night—if. *If* I was telling the truth."

"I do believe you." Will reached out to touch her shoulder. She jerked away from his hand. He dropped it to his side, clenching his fingers. "I do. You didn't have anything to do with the embezzlement, I'm sure of it."

She stared at him. As he watched, the anger seeped from her expression, leaving her face pale, dark circles under tired eyes. "I want to believe you," she said. "It seems like forever since someone other than my family has trusted me. But I don't know if I can."

Slowly he reached out. He lifted her chin. For a moment her eyes remained downcast, then her lids fluttered upward.

He leaned in and kissed her.

Her lips, at first firm and closed, softened, opened. Her breath trembled out, swirling from her mouth to his, warm and sweet. He tasted her sadness, her need, and gathered her in, his arms surrounding her, hoping the press of his body would express what his words hadn't.

Her hips arched into his as her arms wound around his neck and he felt the pull of desire strike deep. She fit him like water in a glass, filling an emptiness he hadn't realized consumed him. Their tongues met, darted, teased, their lips separating only long enough to gasp in a breath before connecting once more.

He'd thought to offer comfort, reassurance. Instead he found himself drowning in sensations that had nothing to do with those tepid emotions. He was fire and ice, she was challenge and surrender.

He was lost.

Crossroads Corner
The Bendixon Sisters: Book Three

Brenda Margriet

CROSSROADS CORNER

This edition published October 2019
Copyright © 2019 Brenda Margriet Clotildes
Print ISBN 978-1-7751542-8-0
Digital ISBN 978-1-7751542-9-7

Cover Art by Steven Cote

Dedication

To anyone who's read one of my books and
then taken the time to let me know you liked it…
this one's for you.

CHAPTER ONE

This isn't the way things are supposed to be, Camryn Bendixon thought, despair making her brain muzzy and thick.

The burly man standing next to her said, "I'll give you two hundred for the table and chairs. And another two hundred for the sofa and end tables."

Said tables, chairs, and sofa were the last large pieces left in the condo she'd called home for the past thirteen months. Everything else had already been Kijiji-ed off, the rooms now hollow and empty of any possessions.

"They're worth five times that," she protested. As the words left her mouth, she realized with a heart-pounding jolt she was still trusting what Anthony had *said* he'd paid. He'd lied about so much. He'd probably lied about that, too. She'd been scrupulous about paying her portion of everything. For all she knew, Anthony had inflated the prices so she'd paid more than the furniture was worth, while he'd pocketed the profit.

"Not my problem," the man—Dave? Dan? She couldn't remember and didn't care—said, his voice rumbling and echoing in the almost empty space.

She simply didn't have the energy to bargain. "Fine," she said. "It has to be out of here by the end of the week." Building management had *un*graciously allowed her to stay until the fifteenth of the month, but it had taken a stern phone call from her lawyer to get them to agree to even that much.

"All right." He extended a beefy hand. She shook it, not even wincing at its clammy dampness, her depression overriding everything else. "I've got to borrow a buddy's truck. I'll call you."

She nodded and walked him to the door, closing it behind him, then leaning against it for a moment, gathering her strength. She felt like she had the flu, her bones aching, chills and heat alternately flushing her skin, a heavy weight in her chest. Until recently she hadn't realized how much her mental health could affect her physical well-being, taking both for granted.

She'd taken a lot for granted. And now she was paying for it.

Two suitcases were ranged against the wall, packed and ready to go. A third lay on the floor behind the sofa. It had been acting as a dresser in the two days since she'd sold the bedroom suite, just as the sofa had taken the place of a bed.

Beyond the living area, the sleek kitchen with its black, high-gloss cabinets and gleaming marble countertop reflected the lights of downtown Vancouver as they streamed in through the wall of windows. Curling into a corner of the couch, she refused to dwell on the day she and Anthony had moved in, yet couldn't help remembering how happy she'd been—a fairy tale princess living in a modern castle high in the sky with the prince of her dreams.

Ironic, come to think of it. Her life had been built on fiction, just like every fairy tale.

Her cell vibrated, rattling loudly on the plate glass top of the end table beside her. The last thing she wanted to do was talk to anyone. But the screen showed the grinning face of her sister, Mattie, and Camryn never ignored a call from either of her sisters.

"Hey! What's up?" she said.

"Hey, yourself. How are you doing?" Mattie's voice was warm and soft, caring.

Obviously, Camryn's forcefully cheery tone hadn't fooled her. Her stomach clenched and she swallowed as a surge of nausea burned the back of her throat. She'd told her sisters that she and Anthony had split up. Since she had also worked with him at the same interior design firm, they'd believed her when she said she'd left her job to avoid him. But she hadn't confessed the whole story.

The story that included embezzlement and fraud. And the shattering of Camryn's self-confidence.

"I'm fine," she said, keeping her voice from breaking through willpower alone. As the eldest, she'd long had the role of leader, the sister that set an example by being strong-willed, smart, successful. Now, she would have to cling to the memory of what she had been until she could find the strength to become it again. "I'm looking forward to seeing everyone soon."

"You *are* still coming, then?" Mattie sounded eager, yet uncertain.

"Of course I'm still coming. I said I was, didn't I? Besides, it's Thanksgiving."

"Yes. But you've said that—" Mattie stopped abruptly.

Camryn had no problem filling in the blank. "I know I've changed my plans at the last minute before. But not this time, I promise." Anthony had never wanted to take the one-hour flight north to Camryn's hometown. He'd only met her parents and her sisters a couple of times in the two years they'd been together. While she would have liked to blame him for that disconnect along with everything else, she had to take responsibility for her own actions. She could have made the trip without him, tried harder to bridge the gap. Not that it mattered now. "I'll see you at the airport on Friday night and we'll gorge together on turkey with all the fixings on Monday."

"It will be good to have you home, even if just for a few days."

"Yes. I'll see you soon. We'll have a good visit then," she said.

What Mattie didn't yet know was that Camryn wouldn't be returning to Vancouver at the end of the weekend. She had only purchased a one-way ticket. What had at first been planned as a short stay, a chance to regroup and rethink and spend healing time with family, was now a search for sanctuary.

A few days later, Camryn ducked out of the airplane's low door and made her way down the metal steps. As she crossed the open tarmac, her coat flapped briskly about her thighs and hard pellets of cold October rain stung her cheeks. Once inside the doors leading to the Arrivals area, she looked up to see Mattie bounding across the concrete floor.

"You're here!" Mattie wrapped her arms around her. She was several inches shorter than Camryn's five-nine, and only some of the height difference was made up by the thick soles of the heavy work boots she wore. Her paint-splattered overalls were partially hidden under a canvas jacket, dark with rain on the shoulders. "It's so good to see you!"

"You, too." Camryn squeezed back, finding comfort in the casual embrace. "How's Marcus? Isn't he home soon?" Mattie's boyfriend was a world-class cellist and had been on an international tour for the past few months.

"Two weeks today. Minus two hours." Mattie's face lit up with anticipation. "I can't wait to see him again."

Camryn couldn't help feeling a pinch of jealousy. Two months ago she'd been in a stable relationship, had thought she might be soon engaged. She should be happy she'd escaped *that* disaster at least. *Marrying* Anthony would have been a failure overshadowing all others.

"Thanks for coming to pick me up," she said as they joined the crowd at the luggage carousel.

"Of course I came. Jo's waiting for you at the house."

The plan had always been for Camryn to stay with Jo, the youngest Bendixon sister, since she was house-sitting the family residence while their parents were driving a motorhome around North America. She, too, thought it was only for the Thanksgiving weekend, but Camryn hoped that arrangement could be extended, at least for a few weeks. She needed some time to get back on her feet, but it shouldn't take her long to find a job and a decent place to live.

At least, she really, really hoped so.

Mattie scanned the bags coming out of the chute. "Which is yours?"

Camryn pointed out three matching cases. She'd packed the personal items she'd salvaged from the wreck of her life into a pathetically few boxes and had begged an acquaintance to store them until she was settled. Everything else was right here, circling around on an endless loop of interlocking metal scales.

Mattie gave her an odd look, but thankfully didn't comment on the fact Camryn appeared to have arrived with her entire wardrobe. They lugged the bags out to Mattie's black, monster-sized pickup, waiting in the short-stay parking lot, and headed into town.

The drive home was quick and quiet, but Mattie barely gave Camryn time to say hi to Jo before she launched into her interrogation.

"Okay, spill it," she demanded. "This is more than a simple breakup, isn't it? What's really going on? Even *you* don't pack three suitcases for a weekend at home."

The three of them were in Camryn's old room, Jo and Mattie on the bed, Camryn methodically hanging clothes in the narrow closet. The room looked nothing like it had when she'd called it her own. It was now a cozy yet impersonal space with pale blue walls, a cream-coloured comforter on the twin bed, and beach-themed artwork and decor. Not even the echoes of Camryn's teenage self remained.

"You're right," she said. "I haven't told you everything." She concentrated on making sure the petal pink silk shirt hung exactly right on the wire hanger as she answered.

"You'll feel better if you get it off your chest," Jo said. "Maybe we can help."

The irony that Jo, eight years younger, was offering such advice was not lost on Camryn. Camryn was usually the one making suggestions on ways Jo could make her own life better—which made it galling that Jo had recently become engaged and seemed to be getting her life in order. Both her sisters were moving forward, finding good men, taking on new challenges. Camryn was the only one flailing around, out of her depth in a mire of her own making.

Choosing another item at random from her suitcase, she sucked in a deep breath, let it out, and forced herself to get it all out in one fell swoop. "Anthony was embezzling from our company. He got caught. Because I was his girlfriend, they suspected I was in on it, even though there was no evidence. They asked me to resign. So I did."

Unwilling to see the looks on her sisters' faces, she turned to the closet and hung the blouse on the rod. The silence behind her vibrated with unasked questions, hummed with unspoken thoughts.

"That scum." Jo's voice was so filled with fury it had Camryn spinning in surprise. Jo took everything in stride, never seemed to feel worry or guilt. She was the last person she'd expected to fire up over this. "I never liked him. Never."

"Jo," Mattie, ever the peacemaker, said, "that's not helpful."

"It's okay." Camryn sighed and squared her shoulders. "He is scum. I just wish I'd seen it sooner. Although I wasn't the only one fooled. After all, the CEO of our company made him Vice-President of Finance."

Mattie crawled off the end of the bed and hugged her. "This is so crappy. And unfair. Why should you lose the job you love because of him?"

"I wouldn't have stayed, even if they'd wanted me

to." Camryn could still feel the sting of sidelong glances, hear the spiteful whispers that abruptly stopped when she entered a room.

"Of course you couldn't," Jo said. She also slid off the bed and wrapped her arms around her sisters' waists, completing the circle, connecting them. For the first time in weeks Camryn felt the ice in her spine thaw slightly. "Let's go to the kitchen. I have something that will make it all better—a bottle of wine and a box of chocolates."

Jo was right. Wine and chocolate did make things better, at least for the moment. But it was having her sisters beside her that really helped. She found herself telling Jo and Mattie the rest of the story. She told them how Anthony had been caught by pure fluke, when his assistant bookkeeper had discovered an anomaly and, instead of taking his query to Anthony, had brought it to the attention of the CEO. How he'd blustered and lied and tried to bully his way out of it. How he'd made snide comments to cast suspicion on Camryn but hadn't come right out and accused her. How in the end she'd avoided charges, but couldn't escape the censure and mistrust of her colleagues and had seen how impossible it would be to continue working with them.

But she couldn't tell them the worst of it. Didn't know if she would ever be able to.

Anthony hadn't just embezzled from the company. He'd also maxed out their joint credit cards, hadn't paid the rent on their very expensive condo for months, and left her tens of thousands of dollars in debt.

Though her firm had given her a small settlement when she left—*guilt money,* she thought bitterly—it hadn't been enough to get her out from under. She'd been certain she'd be able to land a new job, but despite the fact she hadn't been involved in Anthony's crimes, every door had been shut in her face.

Vancouver was one of the most expensive cities in the world in which to live. With no job and no funds to tide her over, she'd had no choice but to come home, soul bruised and battered.

Camryn spent much of the weekend sleeping and watching the home renovation channel. It had been years since she'd been so lazy and unmotivated, but she felt like she was recovering from a bout of illness, and the rest was much needed.

Monday morning, she woke late to discover Mattie and Jo, along with Jo's fiancé, Luke Donwell, elbow-deep in preparations for Thanksgiving dinner. She was immediately put to work peeling potatoes, and over the next few hours had little time to think about the mess that was her life as she obeyed Mattie's orders. It was a relief to have someone else in charge, at least for a little while.

Since Marcus, Mattie's boyfriend, wasn't around, it was easy to forget she had a partner. But Camryn couldn't avoid the secret glances, the casual-and-yet-not-so-casual touches between Jo and Luke. When Jo had told her she was getting married this December, only six months after she'd started seeing Luke, Camryn had worried they were rushing into things. But he was devoutly Catholic—in fact, had been considering the priesthood before Jo came into his life—and didn't believe in sex outside of marriage. Jo had admitted this last with a deep blush, which led Camryn to believe *something* had happened between them. Seeing them now, though, her worries eased. They looked right together. Right in a way she didn't think she and Anthony had ever been.

By four o'clock they were gathered around a table loaded with food. A laptop had been set up at one end as their parents were Skyping in from Arizona, and they'd been joined by their grandfather, Jason Bendixon, and his bride, Lorraine, who was also Marcus' mother.

"It's too bad Marcus isn't home yet," Jo said as she handed a dish heaping with potatoes to Luke. "We haven't all been together since the wedding."

Jason and Lorraine shared a private smile, and Camryn lowered her eyelids to hide the envy rising in her chest. It was hard being the only single person in the family. Not that she wanted Anthony back—the thought made her shudder.

"He wanted to Skype in, too," Mattie said, "but we couldn't coordinate it with the time change and his schedule. The orchestra is on its way to Athens right now."

Conversation flowed, yet Camryn listened to the familiar voices with the unwelcome sense of being an outsider. Thirteen years ago, she'd left Prince George at the ingenuous age of eighteen to attend university and hadn't returned except for short visits. While she'd kept in touch, nothing could replace daily interactions. She'd never felt the distance so keenly than right now.

She was roused from her introspection by Jason clearing his throat. "If you don't mind, there's something I'd like to say."

The chatter died instantly, and everyone's attention focused on him. He smiled at Lorraine, who patted his hand where it lay on the table.

"While Lorraine has made a wonderful recovery from her stroke a few months ago," he said, "the whole experience was a reminder of how precious life is. We've been talking over the last few weeks, and I've come to a decision. I'll be retiring at the end of the year."

A chorus of congratulations rang out from the laptop, Jo, and Luke. Mattie, at Camryn's side, gasped and stiffened. "You can't! I'm not ready for you to retire," she said.

Jason looked across the table at her, a slight smile curving his lips. "You're the one who brought it up first."

"Only because I was worried you were planning something and hadn't discussed it with me." She added in disgust, "Seems I was right."

Jason shook his head, eyes glinting with a hint of devilishness. "Don't worry, I'll be around awhile yet. There's a lot we need to figure out. But I am definitely retiring, and sooner rather than later." His gaze settled on Camryn. Her stomach gave a funny little flip. "I decided weeks ago to make this announcement tonight," he said. "But given what you've told us about the changes in your life, maybe it was meant to be."

She swallowed. "What do you mean?" Camryn had told her parents, Jason, and Lorraine about breaking up with Anthony before they'd sat down for dinner. An abridged version, mentioning only that Anthony had been charged with financial indiscretions at the company, and that she had left her job because it had become too uncomfortable all round.

"I'm very proud of what Bendixon and Sons has achieved over the years," he said. "But the last eighteen months have been tough. Competitors like the Kohlenburg Group"—next to her, Mattie nodded, and Camryn remembered her mentioning the company months before—"have been outbidding us no matter what I try to do. I think it's time for new blood. Mattie knows Bendixon and Sons inside and out, has worked hard to keep us going, but she can't do it on her own. Someone needs to take over my responsibilities. I think that someone should be you."

Everyone's heads swivelled to Camryn. She felt pinned by their gazes, a butterfly on a board. But she also felt the first prickles of hope rushing under her skin.

"I don't know anything about running a construction company," she said. She hadn't told anyone about not going back to Vancouver. Could she avoid that humiliating confession? Could this be the salvation she was looking for?

"You'll have more than two months to learn from me," he said. "With your experience and education, I can't see it being a huge leap."

Mattie gripped her wrist. "Say yes, Camryn." Her voice vibrated with excitement. "Jason's right. This is meant to be. You need a new job, and Bendixon and Sons needs you. Say yes."

Camryn looked around the table. Her parents nodded encouragement from the computer screen, Lorraine smiled, and Jo and Luke offered thumbs up. Identical expressions of hope lit Mattie and Jason's faces.

Could she do it? Could she take over from Jason? The idea was like the warm, bright light at the end of a dark, dismal tunnel. Everything that had happened recently with Anthony had had her doubting herself. It was wonderful to know her family still had faith in her. Of course, they didn't know it was misplaced. Camryn wasn't as smart and successful as they thought she was. But she would be, she vowed. She would be.

"Yes," she said.

CHAPTER TWO

"Hey, got a minute?"

Will Danson looked up from his laptop screen to see Samuel Antoski hovering in his office doorway, a plate of cookies in his hand.

"Only a minute. I've got to get to the open house for the dental office soon."

"Won't take long." Samuel approached with his long, loping stride. He held out the plate. "Want a cookie? Made them myself."

Will waved it off. "Thanks, but I'm still stuffed from Thanksgiving."

"That was two days ago." Samuel shrugged and took a treat for himself. Thin to the point of gauntness—Will had no idea where the many calories he ate went—with blond hair styled in a Caesar cut and a taste for bright colours and tight pants, he was the glue that held the offices of the Prince George division of the Kohlenburg Group together, monitoring the world from his console in the front office. At any given moment he knew where every crew was, whether they were on budget and on time, and what they had had for breakfast.

"We've got a problem with Barrow Hardware." Through bites of cookie, Samuel launched into a complaint over delays incurred because a supplier had delivered the wrong items. "This is the third time they've screwed up. I think we need to look at other options."

"I agree. Make me a list of alternatives. We'll go over them tomorrow." He rose to his feet and hooked his jacket off the back of his chair.

"Will do." Samuel rose with him and together they headed down the hall. "Good luck at the open house," he said, and veered off to his desk.

Will shoved out the exit, taking the stairs two at a time and trotting onto the street through the employee entrance. The wind wrapped icy fingers around his neck and he hurried to his SUV, slamming the door against the bitterness.

He had accepted his promotion to Prince George in a stew of pride and panic, exultation and trepidation. He'd worked for the Kohlenburg family for more than ten years and owed them much for the personal security and professional satisfaction they had provided him. Yet when Wayne Kohlenburg had asked him if he'd take over the new branch in Northern British Columbia his first instinct had been to refuse. His daughter, Laura, didn't take well to even the smallest change in routine, and this was so much more than that. But Will was aware that his chances of advancement if he stayed in Vancouver were slim. The upper management was settled and committed, and opportunities were rare. Since he wanted to continue growing, he made the move. While there'd certainly been major hurdles along the way, he couldn't find it in himself to regret the decision.

It only took ten minutes to get to his destination. He parked in front of the two-story building with depressing grey siding and large windows, the interior hidden from view by gap-toothed vertical blinds. As he pushed open the door, the scent of antiseptic assaulted his nose, and he made a mental note to include a high-quality air purification system in his quote. It was bad enough having to go to the dentist—who wanted to be reminded of needles and pain the minute they entered?

He suppressed a childish sigh of relief that he wasn't there to have anyone scrape and scrub at his teeth. The dental practice had plans to build a state-of-the-art facility at a new location, and they had sent invitations to contractors to attend this open house, a meet and greet opportunity where information would be shared about the project. Will wanted it badly, not just because the plans were a modern, sophisticated design that would showcase their work, but because the dentists were well-respected, prominent citizens in the city, and their endorsement would open even more doors into the business community.

As it was a weekday, the office was filled with clients, and the small space was crowded. An elderly man with a pinched look about his mouth and a woman with a preschooler squirming on her lap sat in hard, plastic seats ranged in front of the reception desk. Another woman wearing bright pink surgical scrubs led a man in a business suit down a narrow hallway leading to the back of the building.

Yet another man—wearing a pin-striped suit and a

boldly-coloured tie, both items Will would wear only under extreme duress—stood at the far end of the room, near two easels holding architectural renderings and blueprint layouts of the new clinic.

"Hello!" he said, stepping around the row of chairs, hand outstretched. "Are you here for the open house?"

"Will Danson, the Kohlenburg Group." He shook the offered hand.

"Abel Quinson, Charette Architects." He gestured at a row of green folders laying on a white-draped table pushed up against one wall. "Feel free to take a package and review it while you're here. I'm available for any questions."

"Thanks." Will took a folder and started flipping through it. A thought struck him, and he looked up. "Charette, you said?"

The other man nodded.

"Aren't you the architects for the proposed development up in College Heights? Crossroads Corner?"

"Yes, that's us."

Will was about to question him further when a rush of cold air swirled in and his attention was drawn to the outer door. He recognized Jason Bendixon coming through the entrance. The older man's company was a long-time player on the local construction scene, but not one Will considered much of a competitor. Too caught up in the past, not forward thinking enough.

The person immediately behind Jason had Will forgetting all about Charette Architects and the folder in his hand.

Later, he wouldn't be able to say what he noticed first. It might have been her hair, the colour of buttered popcorn, shorn so short it hugged her skull in a way that should have looked masculine but only emphasized the delicate bone structure of her cheek and jaw. It might have been how she held herself, poised and straight, or the clear blue eyes artfully yet subtly enhanced by mysterious makeup magic. It might have been the stylish trench coat belted tight at her slim waist, or the long legs encased in burgundy slacks, or the stilt-high heels.

In the end, it didn't matter what it was. Because once he'd seen her, he couldn't take his eyes off her.

Abel Quinson was still talking, but Will had no idea what he was saying. Jason and the woman approached, and Abel turned his attention to them, introducing himself, offering his hand to both.

"This is my granddaughter, Camryn Bendixon," Jason said to Abel. Turning to Will, he added, his gruff voice even more curt than usual, "Camryn, meet Will Danson. Of the Kohlenburg Group."

Was that a flicker of attraction he saw in her amazing blue eyes? Or was it only wishful thinking?

"How do you do?" she said, reaching out her hand.

Will took it, the feel of her warm, smooth skin sending a wave of lust through his veins. He felt lightheaded and dizzy, as if suddenly struck by sickness. His heart beat so hard he could barely hear over the ringing in his ears. She wriggled her fingers and he immediately let go, not sure how long he'd been holding her, curling his fingers into his palm, aware of the loss of her touch.

Realizing he hadn't answered her, he swallowed hard to work some saliva into his mouth. "I'm good. Great. Thanks for asking," he stuttered. "We finally meet. I knew Jason's granddaughter worked with him, but somehow we've always missed each other." Which now seemed a tragic loss. Months when he could have been getting to know Camryn, wasted.

Her eyes widened, but before she could speak, Jason said, "Wrong granddaughter. You're thinking of Mattie. Camryn has been in Vancouver the last several years."

Now that Jason mentioned it, the vision in front of him certainly didn't look like a woman who spent much time working construction sites. Digesting this new detail, Will said, "I'm from Vancouver. Were you in the industry there? Maybe I know the company."

She hesitated before answering, shifting slightly on those towering heels. "Not exactly. An interior design firm."

He was about to ask the company name when Jason said, "Not anymore, though. Camryn's joined Bendixon and Sons. She'll be part of the team from now on."

"Welcome back to town," Abel said, his expression about as starstruck as Will felt. The other man took Camryn's elbow and drew her toward the easels. "Here, let me go over the project with you."

As Abel began his patter, Will did his best to drag his attention to the business at hand. It was difficult to concentrate with Camryn just in front of him. A light, orangey scent drifted from her, and the nape of her neck held him spellbound.

"We're looking for high-end finishing work and strict adherence to deadlines. There must be a seamless transition from this building to the new one," Abel said. He looked at Jason. "I know you are well-respected in the community, but do you have a large enough crew with the skills we need to meet these expectations?"

Camryn answered for her grandfather. "Of course we do," she said. Will felt her low, confident tone deep in his gut. "Bendixon and Sons is prepared to do what it takes to make you happy. As a smaller, boutique firm, we'll work with you, one on one, right from this moment until the final day. Unlike larger firms where your initial contact will, in all likelihood, be replaced by someone else, possibly multiple times during the project."

Will wryly appreciated her not-so-subtle shot at the Kohlenburg Group. This was a woman to be reckoned with, and while his animal instincts might have responded to her sensual beauty, his brain was definitely intrigued by her smooth, intelligent response.

Abel's expression softened, grew thoughtful. "A boutique firm," he said. "What an interesting idea. I'd like to hear more."

Will knew he had to speak up, get the Kohlenburg Group back into Abel's sights, but before he could, Camryn answered. "You won't be disappointed, should you choose us. We'll be sure to get you our bid quickly, and I look forward to working with you."

Jason opened his mouth as if to speak, then closed it again. Will felt sympathy for the older gentleman. Camryn's confidence overshadowed her grandfather's more casual approach. If she was planning on sticking around, Will should be concerned about that. Bendixon and Sons' solid reputation combined with an aggressive and bold personality would be sure to provide a much bigger challenge in future.

He'd have to keep his eye on Camryn Bendixon.

It would be a pleasure.

After the open house, Will returned to the office to wrap things up for the day, but his concentration was shot, his thoughts filled only with Camryn Bendixon. He'd never experienced such an instant attraction to anyone, not even Laura's mother. Exasperated with himself, he stuffed his laptop and folders into his briefcase to work on at home later.

One of the things he liked most about this small city was how close everything was. In under fifteen minutes, he'd be getting a welcome hug from his little girl. His thoughts drifted as he drove, blue-white headlights and siren-red taillights cutting through the early gloom of the autumn evening.

He and Laura had been in Prince George for a year and a half now. At first, it had been as traumatic as Will had feared. Laura woke up screaming from nightmares she couldn't describe and reverted to sucking two fingers, a habit she'd grown out of months before. She'd cried and clung to him every time he left and suffered frequent stomach aches. Her distress was so severe that he'd wondered if they should return to Vancouver, even though giving up wasn't a lesson he wanted to teach his daughter. Her life would be full of challenges and she needed to learn to conquer them. When consulted, her pediatrician recommended patience, and they'd stuck it out, although it had taken many weeks until life settled down. The advent of kindergarten just over a month ago had brought new anxieties, but not to the same degree, thank goodness. Hopefully everything was on the upswing again.

He grinned as he turned onto the wide, tree-lined residential street. It was easy to spot his house. Lights were on in every single window, as well as above the front door, on either side of the garage, and on the peak of the second story gable. Laura was so sensitive to the lack of light that, especially in the darkening days of fall, she would go from room to room, switch to switch, turning every light on. She said it was to welcome him home, and that was certainly one reason. But he also wondered if it was to delay the moment when the dark would take over completely.

The garage door rumbled closed as he pulled his briefcase out of the backseat and went in through the entry leading to the open plan kitchen and lounge area. He sniffed with appreciation, tasting vanilla and chocolate in the air. Corinne and Laura must have baked that afternoon. The lid of the ceramic Winnie the Pooh cookie jar clinked as he lifted it.

A cheerfully scolding voice stopped him. "No cookies until after you eat dinner! I helped Corinne make spaghetti."

Laura stood in the opening leading to the playroom. She grinned and he saw the gap in her top row of teeth. She was only five and he hadn't been prepared for her losing that baby tooth. That wasn't supposed to happen until grade two, maybe even three, right? She was growing up so quickly.

"You have ears like a cat," he said, moving forward to scoop her into his arms.

She laughed delightedly as he swung her around. "No, I don't! Cat's ears are furry."

"I mean you hear really well." Her blue eyes shone, perfectly clear, sparkling with fun. He grabbed her hand and blew a raspberry into the palm. She giggled and wiggled and he had to grip her tightly to keep her from falling. "What else did you and Corinne do today?"

Laura nattered away about a trip to the grocery store as he carried her into the playroom, a bright, airy space just off the kitchen. Corinne Matheson sat on the floor in the centre of an explosion of Lego. The first thing he'd done when he and Laura had arrived in Prince George was start the search for a housekeeper/nanny. He'd envisioned a grandmotherly woman with years of experience and a professional manner, a clone replacement for Mrs. Grady in Vancouver. Instead he'd ended up with a purple-haired, multi-pierced early-twenty-something with a sarcastic attitude.

She made him feel decades older than his thirty-one years, and frightened him, just a bit, with her sheer efficiency. He didn't know what he'd do without her.

"Hi," he greeted her, as Laura wandered off to the corner where a kid-sized kitchen was set up. "Sorry I'm late. How was her day?"

"One of her good ones." Corinne tossed the last of the Lego into a bin and hefted it onto a shelf. "Her teacher says she was much less anxious at school than normal, so I took her grocery shopping."

"Yes, she told me. It sounds like she enjoyed it."

"She did. No jitters at all."

He watched his daughter chatter to herself while stirring an empty pot on the tiny toy stove with one hand. The other hand patted the counter until she found a lid and put it in place with only a small fumble. His heart broke with pride and pain.

His beautiful, perfect daughter was blind.

One day just after her first birthday she'd been irritable and out of sorts. Short hours later he was holding her limp, feverish body, listening in sheer terror as the doctor decreed meningitis. He'd known it wasn't a simple flu, but hadn't expected that terrible diagnosis. Through the long days that followed he'd prayed for her to live, prayed that she wouldn't be taken from him so soon. She had survived, but not unscathed. Discovering the illness had left her blind had been a gut-wrenching blow, but one he'd been willing to accept, if it meant he still had her with him.

Corinne finished tidying and stood next to him. "She really is doing much better. It's been weeks since she had a major panic attack." Absently, she reached out and knocked on the wooden door trim, an old-fashioned superstition Will found charmingly out of character for such a cynical young woman. "We did some Braille training and her spatial awareness exercises, then she helped me make the spaghetti. She cut up the mushrooms."

His eyebrows shot up in alarm and he opened his mouth to remonstrate, but Corinne held up her hand before he could speak. "I gave her a butter knife, and, more accurately, she tore the mushrooms apart. I wouldn't give a *sighted* five-year old a real knife. I'm not an idiot."

"I'm sorry. Of course you're not." Together they moved into the kitchen, leaving Laura to her play. "How's school going?"

"Ugh." Corinne took her army camouflage jacket down from a hook by the back door and pulled it on. "I have a huge project due Monday." She attended the local university part-time, studying social work. He still didn't know why she'd applied to cook and clean and care for a child who was severely visually impaired. But after Laura had thrown screaming fits when introduced to the first two women he'd chosen, he'd been willing to try anyone. He could only guess that Corinne, being the complete opposite of her beloved Mrs. Grady, had been enough of a novelty for his daughter to staunch her homesickness. "I'll pick up Laura after school tomorrow as usual. Anything special you want for dinner?"

"Surprise me. I'll see you later."

Corinne called a casual goodbye to Laura and

clattered out the door. Will opened the oven and found the spaghetti, already mixed with sauce, keeping warm. The work he'd brought home with him was a constant burr at the back of his mind, but for now his evening stretched ahead, sweet and familiar. He'd eat dinner with his daughter, then he'd help her with her bath, and they'd cuddle in bed as he read stories until she fell asleep.

If he wished there was someone with him to share those precious moments, that wasn't a new wish. What *was* new was the uncomfortable certainty that he'd met that someone.

And that she had barely acknowledged his existence.

Crossroads Corner

CHAPTER THREE

Thursday morning, Camryn backed her mother's sedate blue sedan out of the garage and headed toward Bendixon and Sons.

She couldn't believe how her life had changed in just a few days. She had a purpose again, a reason to get up in the morning. She was determined to breathe new life into Bendixon and Sons, saving both the company and herself in the process. And no one was going to stop her.

The Tuesday after Thanksgiving she'd spent with Jason, learning his painfully antiquated filing systems and familiarizing herself with the basic processes of the business. She itched to get her hands on the books, to delve into them, maybe discover inefficiencies and outdated procedures that could immediately turn the company's fortunes around. But Jason didn't think she was ready for that yet, so she'd spent the next morning with Mattie on

31

site at a home renovation, before going with Jason to the open house at the dental office.

"You have to start somewhere," he'd said, blunt as ever, when she'd wondered if it was too soon for her to start meeting clients. "This job is more than just looking at plans and crunching numbers. You have to get out there, meet the people with the projects, build relationships."

She had mixed feelings about how the open house had gone. She thought she'd kept her insecurities hidden, although she was concerned she might have gone a bit far the other direction and been too confident. After all, what did she know about anything yet?

Some of her uncertainty, however, centered around Will Danson. He'd unnerved her with his focus and attention. Not in a creepy, spooky way. She hadn't felt threatened by him at all. But she'd felt his instant attraction, and if she was honest, had returned it. She could see him now—eyes the same maple shade as his hair, which was slightly too long and casually messy, not the contrived look of many of the men she'd known in Vancouver. The creases of his leather jacket were pale, evidence of long wear, his jeans neat and tidy but definitely not new.

Then there was his voice. When he'd spoken, she'd felt the deep bass rumble across her skin like a calloused touch. It was better suited to someone barrel-chested and bearded and didn't match his lean, lanky build and sharp-featured face.

The fact that she could recall so many details almost a day later was more than a trifle disconcerting. She wasn't in the right headspace to allow herself to be attracted to a man—any man, let alone the main competitor of the business she needed to save.

She parked next to Jason's red pickup—*that* was one thing that hadn't changed in all the years she'd been away—and entered the office. The scent of sawdust, old carpet, and breeze block walls enveloped her. She might not have spent as much time here during her childhood as Mattie, but it still had the power to comfort her. The tight knot under her breastbone, her constant companion, loosened.

Helen Fieldstone sat at an aged metal desk facing the door. Her face lit up in a smile. "Camryn! I was that disappointed when I heard you were coming for Thanksgiving, as I thought I wouldn't have a chance to see you. Mel and I had our Vegas trip planned for weeks, you understand. I was that thrilled this morning when Jason told me you're coming to work with us. He talked to me about retiring, of course. We've worked too long together to keep secrets from each other." As she chattered, she rose from her chair and hurried around her desk, wrapping Camryn in a rose-scented hug. "Look at you, just as pretty as ever. I love your cut. Short hair is so flattering on you."

"It's good to see you, too, Mrs. Fieldstone," Camryn said as she awkwardly returned the embrace, flustered at the other woman's effusiveness.

"Oh, go on now, call me Helen. You're all grown up." She beamed at Camryn. Helen had helped Jason run the company since the early days and was an integral reason for its past success. Her blonde hair had turned a beautiful silver grey and Camryn was certain she recognized her bright purple cardigan from years long gone, but her eyes were sharp and clear in her lightly lined face.

Camryn smiled back. "I'm looking forward to working with you, Helen. I've got so much to learn."

"You'll do just fine," Helen said, patting her arm

before returning to her chair. "It's in your blood, after all. Now go on back, he's waiting for you."

Camryn stepped down the narrow, grey-walled hall and entered Jason's office. He sat in a cracked and worn leather chair behind his huge old desk. "Morning," he said, and gestured to the visitor's chair. "Let me finish this email and we'll get started."

She sat gingerly in the aged chair with its dented metal arms and split vinyl seat. She should probably advise Jason to spend time and money updating the entire office. Mattie had assured her they did excellent work on their clients' homes and businesses, but customers wouldn't know it from its rundown appearance. In her experience, clients needed to be impressed right from the start, and they wouldn't be if they ever came here.

He turned from the boxy, beige computer with a relieved sigh and leaned back in his chair. Steepling his hands under his chin, he regarded her steadily. It wasn't an encouraging look, and Camryn's stomach twisted. Had he changed his mind about her? She *knew* she should have been a little more circumspect yesterday, it was just that she was so anxious to prove herself—

"Exactly how much has Mattie told you about the trouble we're in?" he said.

Thankful her fears seemed unfounded—for the moment, at least—she replied, "Enough to know that things are not good."

"We're in the worst position we've been in since the company started," he said, holding nothing back. "I don't know if we'll pull out of it. I sprung this whole retiring thing on you both, and I'm wondering if all I'm doing is tying a stone around your necks and throwing you in the deep end."

The defeat in his tone sent bolts of alarm jolting through her nerves. "Don't think that way," she said, rounding his desk to stand next to him, resting one hand on the back of his chair. "Mattie hasn't given up, and neither will I." Not that she had a choice. Her chances of being hired by any other reputable company were slim, given her connection with Anthony, and she had debts to pay. Bendixon and Sons was her only hope.

When they had moved in together Anthony had offered to make paying the bills his responsibility. "After all," he'd joked, "it's what I'm good at, right?" She had agreed readily, seeing it as an indication of his commitment to her and their relationship. Then, after his arrest, when she'd started seeing the statements herself, she couldn't believe it. He'd maxed out all their cards, making only the minimum payments, and almost every other bill was past due. Stunned and heartsick, she'd spoken to the credit card company and tried to explain the situation. They'd been unsympathetic, and more than a little condescending.

"You are the guarantor on these cards," she had been told. "You signed an agreement that you would be responsible for any debt incurred, no matter who made the purchases. If you hadn't, you would have had recourse. But as it is—" The shrug might have been invisible over the phone, but it wasn't any less obvious.

"I didn't realize I signed anything like that," she'd said, desperate enough to reveal her own stupidity. It hadn't helped.

When it came to the rent, she didn't have any excuse at all. She'd lived there the whole time, completely unaware that Anthony had been taking her half of the rent and squirrelling it away wherever he'd stashed the hundreds of thousands he'd taken from Rosin Interior Design. He'd been an equal opportunity thief, taking all he could get, big or small. Not that the rent had been small. They'd lived in a high-rise, even higher-priced condo, and her portion had been a stretch even with her generous salary.

She was pulled from wallowing in bad memories by Jason swivelling in his chair, causing her hand to fall off the back. "We have to be realistic," he said. "I don't want to push you or Mattie into a corner you can't get out of."

She crouched and put a hand on his knee. "Don't give up hope. You know Mattie will do anything to keep Bendixon and Sons going. And now you have me, too."

"Don't take this the wrong way, but I don't know if that will be enough." He swung back to his desk and reached for a stack of papers. Shuffling aimlessly, he said, "Now, never mind me, girlie. I was just feeling sorry for myself for a minute there. We might as well start working on that quote you promised Abel Quinson. You've set his expectations pretty high."

She thought she heard a hint of censure in his voice but couldn't bring herself to feel sorry. "He was already writing us off. I had to tweak his interest somehow." She meant interest in Bendixon and Sons, of course, but while she might have been a little distracted by Will, she hadn't failed to notice Abel's admiration, too.

Now there was a thought.

If Jason's gentlemanly ways weren't working, maybe it was time to bring a new game to the table. And maybe it was up to her to do it.

The next morning, she entered her parents' kitchen to

find Mattie already there, waiting for the council of war Camryn had called the day before. She certainly looked fierce enough. Her frown threatened to permanently crease her forehead and she wore her worn and torn overalls like a battlefield uniform. Jo was spooning grounds into the coffeemaker, sporting R2D2 slippers, black leggings, and a bright yellow tunic, her long blonde hair hanging loosely down her back.

"Hey, why wasn't I invited to this?" she asked Camryn even before she'd had a chance to wish either of them good morning. "You ask Mattie over to talk about saving Bendixon and Sons, but don't mention it to me?"

Brain still groggy from another broken night—she hadn't slept well for weeks—Camryn said the first thing that came to mind. "I didn't think you'd care."

"Of course I care," Jo said, flipping the lid down on the coffeemaker with more force than necessary. "It's the family business. Just because I don't work there doesn't mean I don't care."

"I'm sorry, I didn't mean it that way." Camryn rubbed her temples in a vain effort to wake up. "I should have said I didn't think you'd have time, since you're at university now." She struggled to remember exactly what Jo was studying. It could be anything from automotive mechanics to zoology, given her sister's wide and constantly changing interests.

"Nice try," Jo said dryly, "but you're just flailing now. Whenever something goes wrong, you shut me out. I'm not a kid anymore. Stop treating me like one."

"I'm sure Camryn didn't mean anything by it," Mattie said, shooting a reproachful glance at Camryn that said she believed the opposite. "If you've got any ideas, we'll love to hear them."

"Fine." The coffeemaker beeped and Jo filled the mugs Mattie gave her, handing one to Camryn before taking the stool next to her. "I could design a website. Bendixon and Sons doesn't have one, and that's a crime in this day and age. Besides, I have a project due at the end of term, and this would fit into my studies. It's a win-win."

Computer Science, Camryn thought in relief. That's what Jo was studying. "That's a great idea. A website was one of the first things on my list." Not that she'd been thinking of Jo at the time. She mentally crossed her fingers, hoping her sister was up to the task. But there was no way she could question her abilities out loud. She'd just have to deal with issues as they came up. After all, something would be better than nothing. As long as it looked professional.

God, she hoped it looked professional.

Mattie was speaking to Jo. "You've already done a lot for the company with the Gateway Crescent project. That really got us through the fall. For now, though, you should concentrate on school, but if the website fits in, that's perfect. If we can keep things afloat, I see a role for you designing home and business automations. I want to be able to compete at the highest level, and it's been like pulling teeth to get Jason to even upgrade to Windows 10. I swear, he's still using a computer from the turn of the century."

Camryn didn't know what Mattie meant about Gateway Crescent, and didn't want to ask in case it was something she should already know. She resolved to find out about it later.

"Jason and I have been going over the financials," she said. "I want to dig deeper today. Maybe I'll see something that will point at why things have gone downhill. Is it possible Jason has been underbidding on projects, so profits are getting cut?"

Mattie shook her head. "I don't think so. I trust him on that. I'm afraid it's simply we aren't getting the jobs we used to. Ever since the Kohlenburg Group came to town, they've been winning pretty much every bid. And they're everywhere. We can barely find a project where they aren't in the mix. The guy they've got running it is really aggressive."

And hot popped unbidden into Camryn's thoughts. She pushed it away. "I met him yesterday at the dental office open house," she said. "He thought I was you until Jason explained. You're not implying he's doing anything underhanded, are you? The Kohlenburg Group is well respected in Vancouver."

Mattie looked like she wanted to say yes, but in the end answered, "No, not that kind of aggressive. He's the new and shiny toy in the market and clients like new and shiny."

Camryn knew that was the truth. Half the clients Rosin Interior Design worked with spent big money on the latest trends, only to switch everything out the next year when those trends changed. Well, now *she* was the new and shiny toy in town, and she planned to work that for all she could.

"I've got to get going." Jo hopped off her stool and dumped the remains of her coffee in the sink. "I'll do research tonight on the website, check out others to get an idea of what we need. See you later." In her characteristic hurry, she kicked off her Star Wars slippers, slipped on knee-high boots, gathered her coat and bag and was gone.

Mattie tucked her phone into the chest pocket of her overalls. "I should get going, too. I'm heading straight to the job site. We've only got a couple days of work left." For a moment her cheerful demeanour faltered. "I hate living hand-to-mouth like this, one job at a time. Everything is so uncertain." She managed a smile. "I'm glad you're here. I just know you'll help turn things around."

"Thanks." Nerves fluttered in Camryn's chest. Anthony had stolen more than her money. He'd stolen her confidence. "I hope I don't disappoint you. Or Jason."

Mattie's eyes widened. "Disappoint us? It can't get much worse after all. Besides, Jason built this company for his family. He's used to me being around. Now that you're joining us? He's thrilled."

The flutter upgraded to a whirling storm as the weight of expectations grew. Camryn swallowed. "I really appreciate your trust in me."

Mattie's smile was a little bit wicked. "Don't thank me too soon. After all, if we can't turn things around, we'll both be out on the street."

CHAPTER FOUR

"Anything else on the horizon, other than the dental office?" Wayne Kohlenburg said, his voice scratching out of the phone's speaker.

Will and Samuel were in Will's office, having their weekly Monday morning phone conference with the president of the company. Will raised his eyebrows at Samuel, sitting across the desk, indicating he should answer.

"There are rumours that a large residential complex called Crossroads Corner is just about ready to request proposals," Samuel said, scrolling on the tablet he held. "It's planned as two six-story apartment blocks, a small retail strip, and a restaurant."

"The architects are the same firm we're dealing with for the dental office," Will added. "I'm willing to take a bit of a hit on that one if it will help us secure Crossroads

Corner."

"Not too big a hit," Wayne cautioned.

Samuel tossed his hands in the air and pointed at the phone, silently but insistently agreeing with Wayne. He'd already expressed his disapproval of that idea. Will ignored him.

"Of course not," he said. "Just enough to make us look even more attractive down the road."

"Do you know who else is bidding on the dentists?"

"Bendixon and Sons was at the open house." Will had found himself thinking of Camryn at odd times over the weekend. Like at the breakfast table when it was just him and Laura, or late at night when he was alone in bed. Bringing his thoughts back to the conversation at hand, he continued, "I assume they'll give it a shot, but I don't think they have much of a chance."

"Did you say Bendixon?" Wayne asked.

"Yes. A local company, been around for years. No real competition, though."

"I was at an industry luncheon yesterday. All the talk was about Rosin Interior Design. Apparently, their chief accountant or VP Finance or something like that was arrested for fraud and embezzlement. I could have sworn they mentioned someone called Bendixon."

Will stopped fidgeting with the pencil in his hand, frozen by the comment. Camryn had said she worked at an interior design firm, and she'd only recently arrived in Prince George. "You mean the accountant's name was Bendixon?"

"No," Wayne answered, drawing the word out as if recalling the conversation. "I don't think so. But there was a connection, I'm sure of it."

"Maybe we should make inquiries," Samuel said. "If

there is something fishy, it would be good to know."

Will didn't want to think about how Samuel would make use of such knowledge, should it be discovered Camryn was involved in the scandal. He was fierce in his advocacy of the Kohlenburg Group.

"Good idea," Wayne said. After issuing a few more instructions, he disconnected, leaving a humming silence behind.

Will's office took up the corner of a suite in a new building in downtown Prince George. The large windows in two walls overlooked City Hall, with its huge spreading elm trees—not quite stripped of their leaves yet—and granite war memorial. Behind it rose an evergreen covered hill. He and Laura had visited the garden on top the past weekend. In summer it was full of scents and textures she could enjoy, but now it was barren and cold. Still, it was good to get out of the house before winter set in for good.

Swivelling away from the view, he looked at Samuel and broke the continuing silence. "Make sure you get your facts straight before you make any accusations."

Samuel didn't pretend to misunderstand. "If Bendixon and Sons is connected to a crime, we need to know."

"Jason is a gentleman, in the old-fashioned sense of the word."

"We're not talking about Jason. This granddaughter of his is an unknown quantity. It only makes sense to learn more about her, even without what we've just heard."

Unfortunately, Will couldn't argue with that. He knew next to nothing about Camryn, other than she made his pulse throb. He itched to call her and ask her to dinner, but when and if he decided to start dating seriously again, it wouldn't be because of simple physical attraction. He'd been burned badly going that route before. No more diving into a relationship without checking for hazards first.

"Don't worry. I'll be discreet. I'll go make some phone calls right now," Samuel said and disappeared down the hall.

Before Will could stew any longer, his computer dinged with the arrival of a new email. He wiggled the mouse to bring the screen to life, then jerked forward in his chair, his throat closing in shock. The subject line simply said "Visit." It was the name standing out crisp and clear in the *From* column that had his skin prickling: Elizabeth Harrow.

His ex-girlfriend. Laura's mother.

A dreadful sense of foreboding lay like a weight across his shoulders. He moved the cursor to the message and clicked it open. There was no salutation, not even his name.

I have decided I need to take a bigger role in Laura's life again. I have booked a flight one week from today and will be staying five nights. I will call after I arrive to arrange visitation details.

He had to read it multiple times before he could absorb it. It sounded just like Elizabeth—brisk, unrepentant, cold. And totally lacking in any consideration for the chaos she would cause in Laura's life.

Springing to his feet, he snagged his coat from the back of his chair and shrugged into it as he strode out of his office. Samuel, sitting royally upright at his desk in the front area, raised his eyebrows at his abrupt appearance.

"Trouble on a site?" he said. "And if so, why don't I know about it?"

"No. I just need some air. I'll be back in a bit. I have my cell." He shoved open the door to the stairwell and took the steps two at a time, swinging around the corners like playing Crack the Whip until he reached ground level. Biting wind struck his cheeks, nipped at his ears. He zipped up his jacket higher, tucked his chin in the collar, thrust his fists in the pockets and headed off down the sidewalk, no destination in mind, just a need to escape Elizabeth's news.

Which, of course, he couldn't.

As painful as the separation had been, he was honest enough to realize it wasn't because he loved Elizabeth. It was because he hated to be a failure. And what greater failure was there than to admit the mother of your child wanted no part of your life? Or the life of the daughter you share?

Elizabeth Harrow had just become the youngest woman ever promoted to partner when they met while the Kohlenburg Group was doing renovation work for her law firm. He hadn't been swinging a hammer anymore—had just moved out of that stage of his career—and was green as grass when it came to dealing with clients. Looking back on it, he'd been just as green when dealing with women of Elizabeth's calibre. She was five years older, blindingly brilliant, sexy, sophisticated, and when she'd made her interest known, he'd been flattered.

Their affair had flashed into flame. He'd been besotted, lustful, dazed by her adventurous sexual nature. At first, he hadn't minded when she'd bought him clothes, told him what to wear to the events they attended together. She moved in elite circles, and he had been thankful for her guidance. Slowly he came to realize what he'd taken as advice was no longer being couched as suggestions. Her demands extended into areas of his life he didn't want to change.

They were only together three months when he broke it off.

A month later she called to tell him she was pregnant.

Last week, Helen had offered to clear a corner of her desk so Camryn could work in the front room, but it only made her feel awkward and in the way. So today she'd forsaken natural light for the buzzing fluorescents of the break room next to Jason's office. It was tiny, with an apartment-sized fridge, small sink, and a counter barely big enough to hold the microwave squatting on it. Her laptop rested on a dinette table, its orange and black vinyl marred with burns and ripped edges. The scent of ancient coffee overpowered the tropical air freshener Helen had optimistically placed next to the industrial-sized container of coffee whitener.

It was about as far from her modern, airy, perfectly decorated office at Rosin Interior Design as she could get.

Pushing her surroundings resolutely from her mind, Camryn focused once more on the bid for the dental offices. Jason had walked her through the process on Friday, explaining how to calculate for hours worked, supplies, contingencies, and a million other details she had never considered before. No wonder most projects went over budget and past deadline. How could anyone keep it all straight?

She'd also spent time with Mattie, whose new passion was accessibility. Between them they worked out a list of suggestions that would take the bare requirements already included in the blueprints and make them seem organic to the design, not simply tacked on due to regulations.

Then, over the weekend, she had taken Jason's boring, black and white estimate sheet and converted it into a sleek

PowerPoint presentation. Using the materials they'd been given at the open house, she blended the hard data with architectural renderings and stock images to create a bid document that was elegant and contemporary.

As she reviewed it one last time, Jason came in, coffee cup in hand. "How's it going?"

Full of pride, an emotion she'd felt too little of late, she twisted the laptop toward him. "Take a look," she said, keeping her tone nonchalant.

He refilled his mug from the bulbous pot resting on the hotplate and took a seat in the arched-back metal chair next to her. Silently he stared at the screen, occasionally tapping a button to move to the next slide. Camryn realized her leg was jigging under the table and stopped it.

"It looks very nice," Jason finally said.

Her confidence deflated. "Don't you like it?"

"I said it looks good. How long did it take you to do?"

Given his lukewarm reaction, she couldn't admit to agonizing over it for two days. "A few hours," she hedged.

"You think making it look all fancy will help us get the job? You think those hours wouldn't have been better spent on something else?"

Camryn leaned back in her chair, the cold metal pressing through her thin blouse and cardigan. "It's all about presentation. The sharper the proposal looks, the more professional we look, the better chance we'll be taken seriously."

"Bendixon and Sons has been taken seriously for four decades without all this." He waved at the laptop, dismissing Camryn's hard work with a flick of his hand.

Before she could think twice, she used the flare of anger lit by his rejection and challenged him. "Then why is the company in trouble? You're retiring. Mattie and I will be doing things differently than you. We need to start now."

His brows beetled low over his eyes and he glared at her. "We need to do good work, not hide behind pretty pictures and frilly words."

"One doesn't exclude the other." Camryn hadn't felt this desperate to convince a client in years. Because that's what Jason was—a skeptical client. She played what she considered her hole card. "I can guarantee the Kohlenburg Group's proposal will be even glitzier and glossier than this one. Maybe it's not fair, but Charette Architects will be judging us right from the moment they see our package. We can't look cheap."

The mention of the Kohlenburg Group caused Jason's eyebrows to lower even further. "I'm still not sold on submitting this bid at all. It isn't a project we'd normally undertake."

"We can only survive on smaller residential projects for so long." Mattie was out on one now, a short turnaround drywall and paint job, the minor renovation from last week already finished. "This isn't totally out of our skill set and will get us in front of a whole new type of clientele."

"I just hope we aren't biting off more than we can chew." He peered at the laptop screen, clicking keys absently. "Oh, what the hell. Send it in."

He didn't sound confident, but Camryn would take what she could get. "Thank you." In childish superstition she crossed her fingers under the table. "Trust me. I know this will work. Just wait."

Will walked several blocks before he broke out of the rage that Elizabeth's email had sparked. When he did, he became aware of his chilled fingers and wind-bitten ears. While his first winter in Prince George hadn't been too difficult to endure, this October was giving fair warning that his second might not be as mild.

Spotting a coffee shop ahead, he hurried up the sidewalk and dove inside. The warm, moist air was a welcome relief, and he breathed in the scent of guilty pleasures—caffeine and sugary delights.

Taking a place in line, he decided on a coffee to stay and a box of doughnuts to go. He'd leave them in the break room for others to enjoy. After he'd taken his own favourite, a blueberry fritter.

Someone joined the line behind him, and he looked over his shoulder casually, to find Camryn Bendixon, blue eyes wide, a hesitant smile on her face.

"Will? Will…Danson?"

He knew he hadn't made as big an impression on her as she had on him, so he supposed he should be thankful she remembered his name at all. How pathetic was that?

She was still looking at him, an expression of uncertainty on her face, and he realized he hadn't replied yet. "Hi! What brings you here?" he said, then mentally slapped himself. Coffee and treats, of course. Why else would she be here?

If she noticed his inanity, she didn't call him on it. She held a twenty between two fingers and waggled it at him. "Mattie called from a job site. New girl needs to deliver the doughnuts."

They shuffled forward a pace as the line moved up, and he stepped off to the side so she could stand next to him. Wayne's comments this morning loomed like a sleet-filled cloud, darkening the brilliance of his attraction. She was innocent until proven guilty as far as he concerned, but a little cautious questioning couldn't hurt. "So, how new is new? How long have you been working for your grandfather?"

"About a week." A corner of her mouth quirked up.

What would it take to make her break out into a full-bore smile? he wondered. It would knock him on his ass if that elegant, classic face ever unleashed a grin.

"That is new," he said. One person stood between him and the order counter. He hadn't thought of Elizabeth once since Camryn's arrival, and found himself reluctant to break the spell. Impulsively, he asked, "Do you have time for a coffee? Or is Mattie expecting your delivery right away?"

Her eyes narrowed. He knew he was considered the competition but didn't think such a simple suggestion merited quite so much deliberation. Just as he was about to make an excuse for her, she answered.

"Why not? As soon as I get the doughnuts, I'll join you."

Pleased, he said, "Let me get yours. What will you have?"

"That's okay, I'll get it." She waggled the bill again. "On Mattie, remember?"

"Right." He placed his order and when it was ready found a free table in a corner. He watched Camryn at the counter. She stood straight and poised, taller than most of the women around her. Her trench coat didn't look heavy enough for the day's icy weather, but she had wrapped an oversized, woolly scarf in a mixed blue plaid around her neck and shoulders. No hat covered her bright hair. It was even closer cropped than his own, and lay in short, feathered layers in front of her ears and at her nape.

He imagined brushing his lips against the exposed

skin of her neck, felt his body tighten, and banished the thought.

Camryn made her way to the table, box of doughnuts balanced in one hand, a heavy white ceramic mug in the other. She sat and sipped her drink, a plain black coffee. He'd thought she'd go for something more frothy and upscale. Come to think of it, this wasn't really the type of coffee shop he pictured her frequenting. A much trendier place was just up the road, one that suited his image of her better.

Searching for something to say, he ended up with, "Are you settling in okay? How was the move from Vancouver?"

She pursed her lips, glossy with a pale pink lipstick. "I'm staying with my sister for a while, but I hope to find a place of my own soon."

"That's Mattie?"

"No, my younger sister, Jo."

"How many of you are there?"

She smiled and he felt that punch in the gut again. "Three."

When Laura had been a toddler, she'd asked why she didn't have a brother or sister. He'd managed to dodge the question but couldn't dodge the regret. He was an only child himself and had always thought he'd like at least three children. But that didn't look like it was in the cards.

Camryn leaned her forearms on the table, cupping her hands around her mug. "So, what brings *you* here?" she asked.

The teasing glint in her eye told him she had noticed his gaucherie earlier. He smiled and nodded, acknowledging the jab. "I needed to get out of the office for a minute."

"One of those days?"

He lifted one shoulder. "Yes, but not because of work."

"Oh. I see." She sipped again, staring into her cup.

She had given him a chance to change the subject, so he was surprised when he found himself continuing. "Got an email from my ex. Needed some air."

Her thin, perfectly curved brows lifted. "Not a good email, I take it." Again, her tone did not ask a question. He appreciated her restraint. Maybe that's why he went on. And maybe he just needed someone to vent to.

"No. She's coming for a visit. Didn't ask if it was okay. Just told me she was arriving in a week and how long she'd be here." He tried not to sound bitter but was pretty sure he didn't succeed.

"You separated before you came to Prince George?"

"Long before."

"It does seem weird she'd come all this way to see you." She traced the lip of her cup with one finger, shell-pink nails neat and clean, not the heavily manicured tips he'd seen on other women. "I'm assuming she's in Vancouver."

"Yes, she is." He'd come this far in the conversation, he might as well go all in. Besides, it wasn't like Laura was a secret. "She's not coming to see me. She wants to see our daughter."

Her brows lifted higher. "You have a daughter?"

"Yes. Laura. She just turned five in September. She's in kindergarten."

"Wow." Camryn leaned back in her chair and tilted her head to the side. "Well, that makes more sense, then. Of course she wants to see her. When was she last here?"

He shook his head. "Never."

"But you've been here how long?"

"A year and a half."

If he ever wondered how to break through her calm, serene facade, he'd done it. Whites showed around her bright blue pupils. "Don't you share custody?"

Again, he shook his head. "No." Elizabeth was a criminal defense lawyer and understood the importance of getting things in writing. She had insisted they formalize the arrangements for Laura's care, but she hadn't requested a specific visitation schedule. Even so, Will would never deny her reasonable access to their daughter.

Was one visit every eighteen months reasonable? Would it be traumatic for Laura? But how could he say no? That's what was eating him now.

"I take it the divorce wasn't friendly," Camryn said slowly.

"I'm not divorced," he said. "We were never married. We'd broken up by the time Elizabeth realized she was pregnant." He was still amazed and thankful she had told him. She could have made other choices. Choices that would have meant he'd never known Laura. His heart raced at the thought, one he'd had often during the first months of his daughter's life.

Her eyes on her coffee cup, Camryn said, "You never thought of getting back together?"

"Briefly. Very briefly." If they hadn't been good together without a child, being together simply *because* of a child would have been a disaster.

Camryn's face had returned to its normal, composed expression, but he thought he could see more questions whirling in her eyes. He waited, but she said no more, only sipped the last of her beverage.

The coffee shop was a cacophony of garrulous voices,

burbling machines and clinking dishes, yet the silence between him and Camryn drowned it out. Realizing he'd probably shared too much, been far too personal with a relative stranger, he abruptly pushed back his chair and stood. "I guess I should be getting back."

"Me, too. Mattie will be wondering if I got lost."

Was that relief he heard?

She rose and they gathered their boxes of doughnuts and made for the door. He held it open for her, one arm outstretched, leaning forward with his feet still inside, and as she brushed past he caught a whiff of her subtle perfume. It was a sunshiny, citrusy scent that overrode the heavier yeasty smells of the baked goods.

They stood on the pavement out front. Camryn hunched her chin into the wool of her scarf. "I hope everything goes well for you and your daughter."

"Thanks." He wanted to say more, maybe apologize for the Dr. Phil session he'd subjected her to, but decided he'd said enough. *More* than enough.

"Goodbye," she said, and without further ceremony headed toward a dark blue sedan. He waited until she'd unlocked the door and got inside before turning in the direction of the office, facing into a wind that felt even colder than before.

CHAPTER FIVE

"Camryn!" Helen called from the front office. "Phone!"

In the break room, Camryn looked up from her laptop, startled. Who could possibly be calling her on the business line?

"Are you sure?" she shouted back, wincing. Such behaviour would not have been tolerated at her ex-firm.

"Yes. I've put him on line one. Come and get it."

As she headed for the front, she allowed herself to imagine, just for an instant, that it was Will. His story the other day had touched her, made her want to comfort him. Couple that with his casual charm and warm eyes and she'd had to grit her teeth to keep from taking his hand.

Now was not the time to show interest in a man. She had much more important things to do—like get out of debt, restore her reputation, and salvage her confidence.

Squeezing in behind Helen, she hitched a hip onto the desk and punched the button to connect the call. "Camryn Bendixon."

"Camryn. Abel Quinson, Charette Architects."

She gripped the phone tighter. She'd sent the bid in two days ago but hadn't expected to hear back so soon. "Hello, Abel. Is there something I can help you with?" *Please, please let it be good news.*

"Thank you for your proposal. I have a couple ideas I'd like to discuss. Would you be available for lunch?"

That must mean they were still in the running. Her heart lifted and she answered with a smile. "Of course. Where should we meet?"

Once she had the details, she hung up, but didn't move from her perch on Helen's desk. "I haven't seen Jason today. Do you know where he is?"

Helen hit print on the invoice she had been adjusting. "Lorraine has a doctor's appointment this morning. He'll be in later."

Camryn chewed her lip. "I just set up a lunch appointment with Abel Quinson from Charette Architects. Do you think he'll have time to come along?" She probably should have checked with Jason first. But she was used to meeting with clients on her own at Rosin Interiors and had agreed out of habit.

Helen patted her knee. "I'm sure he'd appreciate a call to let him know, but you're a part of this company now. You don't need his permission for every little move. Don't make any sweeping promises and you'll be fine."

The restaurant Abel had chosen soothed some of Camryn's homesickness for the sophistication of Vancouver. Its long, narrow space had dramatically dark walls lit with elegant sconces, and tables with artfully curated, mismatched chairs boasted gleaming linen and sparkling silverware. Voices of staff and customers alike where muted and hushed. She was escorted to Abel's table by a woman dressed in a sleek black shift wearing stylish footwear Camryn silently coveted.

"Camryn. Glad you could join me on such short notice." Abel rose to greet her, holding his brightly patterned tie back as he leaned over the table to shake her hand. His blond hair was cut very short, possibly in an attempt to disguise it was thinning, although he looked about her own age.

"Of course." She sat, and at the server's inquiry ordered a soda water with lime wedge. Abel already had a chunky glass holding ice cubes and an amber liquid sitting before him.

"I'm glad you called," she said when the server left. "If there's anything I can clarify about our proposal I'd be happy to do my best. Jason is sorry he couldn't make it, but he had a previous appointment." When she'd talked to him, he'd echoed Helen's words, warning her gruffly not to give away the farm but encouraging her to take the meeting on her own.

Abel smiled, the gleam of admiration in his eyes not completely hiding something sharp and wily that put Camryn on her guard. "Business can wait a little. I'm expecting one more guest." His gaze slipped past her. "Ah, here he is now."

Camryn looked over her shoulder to see Will navigating through the tables. She frowned. Why on earth would Abel have invited them both? A chill of premonition wriggled down her spine.

Abel greeted Will and offered him a chair so that he was sitting at right angles to both Camryn and Abel. As he tucked his long legs underneath, he offered her a quick nod. "Camryn."

She nodded back and waited for Abel to explain what was going on, her fingers clenched in her lap.

"I want to thank both of you for your very prompt response to our call for proposals," Abel said. "I have some notions to share with you both, but let's order first."

Camryn's stomach tightened, nerves dancing. She didn't know if she could wait through the social dance of small talk before finding out what fate had in store for Bendixon and Sons. She chose a simple soup and salad and willed her hands to remain loose and lax on the table.

"I was pleasantly surprised by your proposal, Camryn," Abel said after the server had left. "As a presentation, it held up very well against Will's. I didn't expect a bid from a company like your grandfather's to be so polished."

On one hand, Camryn felt she should defend Jason. On the other, she allowed herself a glow of pride that her hard work had finally been recognized. "Thank you," she said.

"That being said, I still don't believe Bendixon and Sons has all the qualifications for this job." He turned to Will. "The Kohlenburg Group, however, does."

The rollercoaster of hope and despair left Camryn queasy. She gathered her resources, ready to battle for whatever scraps she could get.

"I appreciate your confidence," Will said, his deep, bass voice raising goosebumps over her skin. He was angled toward Abel, in profile to Camryn. The small patch of whiskers he'd missed underneath his jaw and the too long hair curling behind his ear should have made him look sloppy, but her mouth dried and her pulse skipped.

This is ridiculous, she thought. He was off limits for many reasons, not least of which was he was currently stealing away yet another chance for Bendixon and Sons to climb out of their financial difficulties.

"I realize we may not be the obvious choice," she said in the sleek, professional voice she used to soothe nervous clients, "but we bring something special to the table. Decades of experience in this community, a solid reputation, and forward thinking when it comes to accessibility."

"Exactly." Abel smoothed his tie, leaning back as the server placed his linguine alfredo in front of him. "You had some very interesting suggestions in your proposal, ideas that were not included in Will's. So, here's what I'm thinking. The Kohlenburg Group will be awarded the bid, and commit to work with Bendixon and Sons to incorporate your ideas."

Camryn's soup and salad were placed before her, the artistic presentation and delicious scent wasted as she grappled to understand Abel's words. "How exactly do you see this rolling out? How would we be compensated for the use of our ideas?"

"You'd be considered a sub-contractor, or a consultant, and be paid accordingly." Abel waved off the details as he swirled noodles onto his fork. "I'll leave that to you and Will to discuss."

"I'm open to the suggestion," Will said. "I'm sure we could come up with a satisfactory arrangement." He turned to Camryn, his eyes crinkling in a small smile, but with no hint of glee or superiority. It was a small blessing.

She swallowed down a childish response to demand all or nothing. She needed Bendixon and Sons to succeed *now*, not later. The weight of her debts was a constant pressure, and job security was the only thing that would lessen it. But she couldn't risk future rewards because of simple pique.

"I suppose we can talk about it," she said reluctantly. "I'll have to get Jason's permission, of course."

"There are still a few details about the KG proposal we need to go over, as well," Abel said to Will. "Once those are ironed out, we'll be able to move forward." He nodded briskly, his pleasure in his little scheme evident. "Now, let's enjoy our meals and talk of other things."

Camryn dipped her spoon into the pale, creamy broth. Bitterness coated her tongue, but it wasn't the soup's fault. She'd failed in her first assignment. If she couldn't prove her worth to Jason and Mattie, how long would they continue to support her?

It was impossible for Will to miss the disappointment vibrating from Camryn. Her luscious pink mouth was pinched, her eyes shuttered by lowered lashes, and she ate her meal with abrupt, tight movements. Abel seemed unconscious of her leashed emotions and made small talk through the rest of the lunch, while she remained polite but distant.

Just that morning, Samuel had reported to Will what he'd learned about the scandal at Rosin Interior Design.

"There is no evidence that Camryn was involved in the fraud," he stated.

Will's relief at the news had been tempered by Samuel's tone. "I hear a *but* coming."

"Anthony Halford is accused of embezzling hundreds of thousands of dollars over the last four years, and there appears to be little doubt he did it. For two years, Camryn and Halford were a couple, living together for about a year, as far as I can find out."

"You're saying she's guilty by association."

Samuel shrugged. "I talked with someone I know at Rosin Interiors. Consensus among those who worked directly with Camryn is that she had nothing to do with the fraud. But higher-ups decided the optics were bad. It's widely believed she was *encouraged*"—he used finger-quotes for emphasis—"to resign."

"We can drop the subject, then," Will said. Even he could hear the question in his voice.

"I also called the Vancouver Police Department," Samuel continued mercilessly. "They wouldn't give me any details of the investigation, of course, but the file isn't closed. The person I spoke to there implied more arrests might be imminent."

It was a warning Will shouldn't ignore. And not just from a business standpoint. He had to be careful who he brought into Laura's life. A few weeks should clarify the legal situation. He could wait awhile, just to be safe.

Except that sitting this close to Camryn, feeling the brush of her leg in the confined space under the table, smelling her scent, was setting off all sorts of fireworks in his body. The jolt of electricity he'd felt at their first meeting had been muted at their second by his preoccupation with Elizabeth's email, but it was back in full force. Thank heaven Abel had made his suggestion. No one could blame Will for spending time with Camryn if it was required by a client.

Abel picked up the cheque with ostentatious generosity, then the three of them gathered in the small foyer to collect their coats.

"I look forward to working with you both," Abel said

as he shrugged into a dark wool overcoat. "As I said, we have some details to work out yet, Will, but they are minor, I assure you."

In his experience, when a client thought something was minor, it was usually a good sign it was exactly the opposite. But he had also learned to hide his misgivings. "How about I come by your office tomorrow?"

Camryn stood by, stiff and silent, as they coordinated their schedules for the next day. He could tell she didn't want to be there but was too polite to leave before Abel. As soon as he departed, she turned to Will and said, "Congratulations. I'll talk with Jason and let you know his thoughts. Have a good day."

She reached for the door, but he put out his hand to keep it closed. "I can tell you're disappointed," he said, "but you should be pleased. Abel is obviously impressed with your work."

She shrugged. "Not enough to give us the contract."

"That's business." He wouldn't insult her by offering platitudes.

Her shoulders straightened, and she gave him an honest, though controlled, smile. "Yes, it is. And I do appreciate your willingness to work with us."

"No problem. Let me walk you to your car."

"There's no need."

"I know. Let me do it anyway."

With her height, their strides matched neatly as they walked down the sidewalk. Camryn stopped in front of the blue sedan he remembered from their accidental meeting at the coffee shop. "This is me," she said.

He didn't want to let her go, not yet. He simply couldn't believe she had anything to do with Halford's crime. The stress she was under must be intense. Had she loved him? It was a betrayal he couldn't fathom.

And there was no way he could say *any* of that to her.

"I'll call you when I have something solid from Abel," he said before the pause grew too awkward. "We can talk details then."

"All right." She reached out her hand. "I hope I don't sound ungrateful. I am disappointed, of course, but look forward to sharing our ideas."

He took her hand. It was chilled and he automatically cupped it with his other to warm it. "You should get in, out of the cold."

She looked down at their clasped hands, then up at him, her expression unreadable. She had upgraded her light trench coat to a wool jacket that hung just to her hips, and a fluffy scarf in a teal green protected the long, slim line of her throat.

"Would you like to have dinner with me?" The question popped out without conscious volition. *So much for waiting to see how the investigation goes,* he thought ruefully, but without regret. Camryn intrigued and enticed him on so many levels. His subconscious obviously didn't want to wait any longer to get to know her better.

"I don't think that would be a good idea." She eased her hand from his grasp.

"Why not?" He knew why he shouldn't have asked the question, but what were her reasons for refusing?

"We're rivals. I need Bendixon and Sons to be successful, and you're standing in the way."

"Like I said before, that's business. Inviting you to dinner is personal."

Her mouth curved, yet her eyes remained somber. "The two are in conflict, I think."

Instead of taking the out she offered, her objections

only made him more determined to convince her. "I disagree. If there's one thing I've learned since moving to Prince George, it's that it's smaller than it appears. If you refuse to socialize with people in the same industry, you'll have a very limited pool to draw from."

She bit her lip, and the small sign of indecisiveness gave him hope. "What are you doing this weekend?" he said.

"I have a family thing tomorrow night."

"Tell you what. Forget dinner. I'm taking my daughter to the museum Saturday." He hadn't yet told Laura her mother was arriving on Monday. It wasn't that he was expecting Elizabeth to change her mind. She always did what she said. But he was hoping the distraction of the museum might help Laura adjust to the news. "Why don't you join us?"

Her pale blue eyes widened. "You want me to meet your daughter?"

"We come as a set," he said, amusement bubbling in his chest. "I don't hide my friends from her."

"We're not friends."

"Not yet." His own indecision on the wisdom of his invitation kept him from pressing further. "Think about it and call me if you want to come along. Otherwise, I'll see you around." After handing her his business card, which included his cell number, he stretched around her and opened the driver's door. "Have a good day, Camryn."

He headed for his own vehicle, parked a couple of slots away. She was still standing there, staring, when he drove away.

CHAPTER SIX

The cozy living room in Mattie's house was decorated with red streamers and gold balloons. She'd taken down a few pieces of the funky artwork that normally covered the walls and hung a long, narrow banner emblazoned with "Welcome Home!" in their place. The coffee table held an assortment of snack trays, still covered in their protective plastic.

"No one touches anything," she ordered just before she left. "Not one thing until I get back with Marcus."

Camryn laughed at her fierceness and sent her on her way, then settled down to wait on a soft squashy hassock, wine glass in hand.

Next to her, Luke Donwell relaxed on the floor, leaning against the button back chair in which Jo curled. He dangled a beer from his fingertips, elbow resting on his bent knee, and chatted with Lorraine, who was seated on a couch rather violently patterned in brightly coloured flowers. She wore a classically cut pantsuit in pale yellow and looked regal and serene. Only a very slight droop at one corner of her mouth when she smiled gave any indication of the stroke she'd suffered months before. Jason hovered over her from behind the couch, ever protective of his bride.

He had been quietly pleased when Camryn had conveyed Abel's plans for Bendixon and Sons' contribution to the dental office. He had even gone so far as to offer a gruff "well done" which made Camryn feel worse, not better. The company had been subsisting on tiny nibbles for months now. She had wanted to serve up a three-course meal—and ended up offering only an appetizer.

Lorraine reached forward to place her glass on the coffee table, and Jason moved quickly to help her. It was Lorraine's stroke that had brought her son, Marcus, home to Prince George. This in turn had been the catalyst that had rekindled the romance between Marcus and Mattie. Now they were waiting for Mattie to bring Marcus home again. A talented cellist, he'd been on a world tour with an all-star Canadian orchestra for the last three months. Mattie had planned this welcome home party and decreed all family must attend, which had given Camryn the chance to deflect Will when he'd asked her out for dinner.

She still hadn't decided what to do about his invitation to the museum. It had occupied her thoughts constantly. During last night's Skype get-together with her parents, a Thursday tradition since they'd left town on their cross-continent adventure, Mattie had had to elbow her several times to remind her to take part in the conversation.

On the one hand, it certainly seemed safe enough to

spend time with Will and his daughter. It couldn't be termed a date, at least. But on the other, meeting his daughter seemed akin to meeting his parents—a little too intimate for comfort.

So, she dithered. Which was so unlike her pre-Anthony self as to be maddening. She fidgeted with her phone, flipping it end to end on her thigh as her brain tossed and turned.

Idly watching the easy play of conversation between the two couples in front of her, she suddenly realized why she couldn't find the resolve to call and say thanks but no thanks.

She was lonely.

Anthony might have been a cad, but he'd been a charming cad. He'd loved to socialize, enjoyed visiting Vancouver's newest and hottest clubs and restaurants, and she'd been happy to go along. Since his arrest, her life had been nothing but a string of endless, empty nights spent battling her feelings of failure and incompetence. Even coming back to Prince George had only highlighted how isolated she was.

Recognizing why she wanted to go out with Will should have clarified her decision, but it didn't. Was it weak to admit she wanted to spend time with him? Or was it a step toward getting over Anthony, a step toward moving on with her life?

As she continued to waffle, her phone buzzed. Checking the screen, she froze at the name on display. *Elizabeth Harrow.*

Camryn's breath caught in her throat. She'd hated the need to hire a criminal defense lawyer to protect her interests but had hoped the worst of it was over. Why would she be calling on a Friday night? After office hours?

There was no way this was good news.

Swallowing at the thought of how much money her defense had already cost her, she connected the call with a trembling finger.

"Elizabeth?"

"Camryn. Do you have time to talk?"

The ice in Camryn's lungs seeped into her blood, jagged crystals of fear. "Just a minute," she said, amazed her voice sounded so calm.

Jo raised inquiring eyebrows as Camryn stepped over Luke's outstretched leg. She pulled her lips into a smile and waved a hand in a dismissive gesture, mouthing *I'll be right back*, then slipped past Jason and ducked into Mattie's tiny kitchen.

"Okay," she said. "What's going on?"

"I received a call from one of the investigating officers," Elizabeth said, going straight to the point in her brusque manner. "They're no longer satisfied with some of our answers."

Camryn appreciated the *our* but knew it was only a lawyerly ploy to sound part of the team. Elizabeth wouldn't go to jail, after all.

"What do you mean? I thought we were done with the police. I thought they'd cleared me."

"It seems Anthony has given them new information."

Camryn felt her knees dissolving. She staggered to the table tucked up against one wall and sank into a chair. "*What* new information?"

"I don't know exactly, but I'll find out. I only learned of this an hour ago. I'll make some calls and get back to you, but I thought you should know, just in case they get in touch. And if they do, what do you say?"

"That I won't talk to them without my lawyer

present." The last word had her already twisted gut tightening further. "I'm not in Vancouver, Elizabeth. What if they do want to talk to me?"

"You are under no obligation to stay here. No charges have been laid yet."

The *yet* had Camryn fighting back waves of dizziness. She pressed her fingers to the glossy surface of the table and struggled to focus as Elizabeth continued.

"Let's cross that bridge if we come to it," she said. "If they do want to speak to you in person, they'll have to wait until you return. Where are you?"

"I won't be returning. Not to stay, anyway. I'm in Prince George. I have a new job."

"Prince George?" Elizabeth's tone was surprised. "Why there?"

"My family is here. I'm working for my grandfather's construction company." As she spoke, she heard a door open followed by excited cheers. She leaned back in the chair and looked down the hall, which ran in a short, straight line to the front of the house. Marcus stood in the entrance, a beaming Mattie tucked to his side. Neither of them saw her. She rocked forward in her seat, out of sight.

"I see," Elizabeth said. "Well, as I said, let's worry about that only when we need to. I'll call you tomorrow if I have any more news."

"Please, call me no matter what." Camryn closed her eyes and massaged her temple with her fingers. "I'd rather hear that you've learned nothing new than hear nothing at all."

"All right, I will." Elizabeth's usually curt manner softened. "Don't worry about this, Camryn. It's the last desperate gasp of a man who knows he's going down for the third time."

"I'll try." That was all she could promise. Although she was pretty sure she wouldn't be able to follow through.

She disconnected and sat for a moment, staring at the wall in front of her. It was papered in a print with tiny bouquets of forget-me-nots. They blurred before her eyes and she blinked to clear her vision. She was done crying over Anthony and his wickedness. She'd gotten through the initial shock and dismay and treachery. She'd get through this, too.

The joyful sounds of reunion continued from the front room. Taking a deep breath, she let it out slowly, then curved her lips into a smile and went to join the party.

"Daddy!" Laura's scream woke Will from deep sleep.

He was up, out of the room and down the hall before even registering he'd heard it.

Sobs—harsh, gut-wrenching sobs—tore at his heart, already racing from the sudden awakening. He hurried to Laura's bed, flipping the light switch as he passed. She could only dimly distinguish light, but it was something to do, so he did it, every time she had a night terror. There was little else he could offer to comfort her, other than his presence.

"I'm here," he soothed, dropping to his knees beside her bed and smoothing the tangled hair from her flushed, tear-stained face. "I'm here, sweetie."

"Make it stop, Daddy." Her arms flailed, fending off whatever terrible vision her brain had inflicted on her. Although *vision* was the wrong word. It was frightening, horrifying *sounds* that Laura experienced in her dreams.

He cradled her to his chest. She clutched his soft jersey T-shirt, rubbing her face against it, seeking solace.

Her tactile awareness was so acute that he always wore especially cozy clothing to bed, for just such a reason.

He gathered her up, stood, then sat on the edge of her bed. Rocking back and forth, making soft, meaningless noises, he waited for her sobs to ease, the tension in her body to abate. As usual, it didn't take long. She never fully awakened during these episodes, but that didn't make her fear any less frantic.

Her grip on his shirt slackened and her breathing evened out. He continued to rock, letting his eyes drift, taking his own comfort in the simple pleasure of holding her.

The terrors came less frequently now, and he sincerely hoped the reason for this one wasn't because he'd told Laura her mother was planning to visit. She had appeared to be beside herself with joy and excitement at the news, but he wouldn't be surprised if she was also secretly frightened, at least a bit. After all, she had not been in the same room with her mother since she was three years old.

Elizabeth didn't totally ignore her daughter. She scrupulously sent birthday and Christmas presents, and called or Skyped every few months. In his opinion, she did those few things to assuage her guilt, because she felt she should, not because she wanted to.

When he was certain Laura had returned to a peaceful sleep, he laid her on her side, tucked her faithful plush companion, Mr. Rabbit, under her arm, and pulled the covers over her. Turning off the light, he headed for the kitchen, too awake to settle into sleep again himself.

The clock on the microwave showed 5:45AM. Despite the fact it was Saturday, it was no use going back to bed. Laura was an early riser, popping up bright and cheerful at six-thirty most mornings no matter how late she'd gone to bed the night before or how disturbed her sleep.

Dropping onto the upholstered leather couch in the lounge area of the kitchen, he picked up the television remote. Making sure to keep it muted, he flipped desultorily through the channels.

He hadn't heard from Camryn since he'd invited her to join him and Laura at the local museum and could only assume she wasn't joining them. His disappointment was deep, probably deeper than the situation deserved.

Thinking about Camryn helped keep thoughts of Elizabeth at bay, but they snuck back in as he drowsed, waiting for Laura to wake up. Why had she requested to see Laura? What had changed? Why now?

During the first year of Laura's life, Elizabeth had seemed to settle into being a mother. Sure, she'd only taken a couple of months off work, when she was entitled to much more, and had decided not to breastfeed. But that was her prerogative, and Laura was healthy and thriving and happy so there seemed no cause for concern. Elizabeth had had no issues with Will visiting as often as he liked, and even encouraged him to take Laura overnight. They drifted into a flexible routine that worked for all of them.

Until Laura got sick.

She'd been on one of her overnight stays with Will. At first, he'd thought she had a simple cold or flu, but when her symptoms worsened dramatically, he bundled her into her car seat and broke speed limits and ignored stop signs on his way to the hospital. In the Emergency Admittance area, the nurse on duty had taken one look at his listless, flushed daughter and whisked her immediately into a bed. Elizabeth arrived shortly after, responding to the urgent text he'd sent her.

It was days later, after the initial crisis had passed and

Laura was responding to antibiotics, that he first noticed Elizabeth's withdrawal. During the height of Laura's illness, she had taken command, interrogating doctors, demanding second opinions, doing her own research so she could make suggestions on treatment. Once the diagnosis had been confirmed and a protocol established, she seemed lost, as if uncertain what her role was. Will rarely left Laura's side, and while Elizabeth came many times each day, she never stayed longer than a few minutes.

Then came the pronouncement that Laura's blindness, a side effect of the swelling of the membranes in the brain and spinal cord that made meningitis so dangerous, was permanent.

Elizabeth withdrew even further. Still grappling with the news himself, Will understood the pain and fear he could see in her eyes. But what made him fiercely protective of their fragile daughter appeared to shatter whatever confidence Elizabeth had in her ability to be a mother. When Laura was finally released from hospital, she went home with Will, and Elizabeth came to visit her there. Gradually those visits grew further and further apart, until the day Elizabeth suggested they make things official and give him primary custody.

He still felt guilty about it. He hadn't tried very hard to keep Elizabeth in their lives. She'd never been a warm, cozy parent, but he hadn't doubted she loved Laura. It was bewildering how she could cut her off so thoroughly.

Elizabeth's visit was sure to disrupt Laura. But what could he do? He didn't have the right to deny a mother the chance to see her child.

He must have dozed off because the next thing he knew Laura was patting his face. "Morning, Daddy!

Morning! Your phone is making noises." She placed it on his chest then clambered up and tucked herself next to him.

Groggy, he pulled himself up from a deep slouch, grabbing the phone before it slipped away and rotating his neck until it cracked. "Thanks, sweetie. Did it wake you?"

"No, I just woke up. Can we have scrambled eggs for breakfast?"

"You bet. Just give me a second." He was surprised to see it was almost eight o'clock. By some miracle, Laura had slept in.

His phone buzzed again, signalling an unread text. He swiped the screen and his eyes widened.

Camryn's message, sent five minutes before, read: *Sorry, I know it's early. But I wasn't sure when you might be leaving for the museum.*

Quickly he thumbed a message back. *No problem. We'll be there about ten.*

After a short pause, the reply came. *If your invitation is still open, I'll meet you there.*

Of course it's still open, he typed, pleasure erasing the last vestiges of sleep. *See you soon.*

"A friend of mine is going to meet us at the museum," he told Laura. "I hope that's okay."

Laura tilted her head up at him, her gaze just skimming past his ear. "I guess so. Is he a nice friend?"

"It's a she. Her name is Ms. Bendixon and she is very nice." At least, that was what his hormones were saying. Did she even like children? Maybe the museum was a mistake.

Oh, well, he thought, nuzzling the top of Laura's head and breathing in her warm, sleepy, little girl smell. *I guess we'll find out soon enough.*

CHAPTER SEVEN

Camryn parked her mother's car outside of the museum and surveyed the entrance with trepidation.

She still wasn't sure this was a good idea. But after a horrible, restless night turning Elizabeth's news over and over in her mind as often as she turned over and over in her bed, she'd been desperate for a distraction. And maybe it had a little bit—a *very* little bit—to do with loneliness.

Whatever the reason, here she was.

A black SUV pulled into a slot a few vehicles away. Will got out of the driver's side and circled around the back. He opened the rear passenger door and ducked inside, then reappeared, a small child wearing a pink pom-pom hat and purple parka in his arms. When he reached the museum entrance, he placed his daughter on the ground, took her hand, and went inside.

Taking a deep calming breath—in through the nose,

out through the mouth, just like in the yoga classes she could no longer afford—Camryn followed them in.

The foyer was a high-ceilinged space with a souvenir and gift shop on one side and a wide-open area scattered with tables and chairs on the other. Huge floor to ceiling windows offered a view of a park and, in the distance, glimpses of the sandy cutbanks rising above the hidden Fraser River.

She joined Will and Laura at the admission counter. "Hello."

Will's smile was instantaneous and bright, and some of the tension left her shoulders. "Hey, there. I'm glad you decided to come." He looked down at his daughter, who clutched his hand in both of hers, a frown veeing her brows. "Laura, this is Ms. Bendixon."

"You can call me Camryn," she said and put out her hand. "Nice to meet you, Laura."

The little girl ignored her hand. She lifted her chin in Camryn's direction, but didn't make eye contact. "There's a boy in my class. His name is Cameron."

Camryn glanced at Will. He shook his head, as if trying to convey a message, then took Camryn's hand and transferred Laura's tiny one into it. "Laura, can you stay with Camryn while I pay to get in? I'll be right back." He stepped up to the counter.

A little panicked at being left with Laura, who now gripped her tightly, Camryn struggled on. "You're right, it is a boy's name. But it can be a girl's name, too. I spell mine a little differently."

"I can spell my name," Laura said proudly. "I can type it on the computer. And write it in Braille."

Braille? Suddenly it made sense. The ignored hand, the slightly off-kilter gaze.

Will's daughter was blind.

Before she could fully absorb the revelation, Will returned, tickets in hand. "Ready?" He touched Laura's shoulder. She immediately let go of Camryn and reached for him. Together they headed for a heavy glass door. Will held it open and they stepped through.

"What do you want to do first, Laura?" Will asked.

"The water table, the water table!" The little girl bounced up and down on her toes, clad in purple and pink polka-dotted rubber boots.

"Water table it is." Will led her away, leaving Camryn at the door, still trying to reorder her thoughts.

The large room had navy blue walls and a high ceiling. Dramatic lighting accented the suspended skeleton of a huge dinosaur that dominated the upper space. Two pre-school-aged archaeologists played in a sandpit designed like a dig site, more clambered over the two-storey high prow of a boat in the far corner, and another's nose was pressed against the side of an enormous fish tank. A young woman tended to a fretting infant, invisible inside a stroller, and other adults sat on pint-sized benches and watched their charges with varying degrees of wariness. High-pitched voices rang and echoed.

Will returned and stood next to her. She could feel his heat, smell his scent, and wanted to take his hand like his daughter had and anchor herself to the safe harbour of his presence. *How crappy was her life,* she thought, *that a relative stranger made her feel that way?*

"Have you been here before?" he asked.

"Not since I was a kid. It's changed." Laura was on the far side of the room at a low table with deep edges, slotting flat pieces of plastic into place. "Should we be nearer to Laura?"

"She's fine. She'll call me if she needs me."

Camryn wondered whether she should mention her conclusion about Laura's blindness. It was obviously such a natural circumstance for father and daughter that he hadn't thought to mention it ahead of time.

Will interpreted her silence with an eerie correctness. "It's okay. You can ask about her if you want."

Her cheeks heated and she slid him a sideways look. To her relief, his expression was easy and open. "I don't mean to pry."

He shrugged. "You're not being rude. I'd rather you ask so you know what you need to."

Laura played at the table, laughing as the water ran over her hands, her head tilted as if listening intently.

"Was she born—" Camryn stuttered to a stop. *That way* sounded insulting. *Blind* too harsh.

Will rescued her. "She lost her sight at just over a year old. She contracted meningitis."

He spoke so matter-of-factly she relaxed. "How much vision does she have?"

"She can differentiate between light and dark, if the contrast is high enough."

"That's all?" Camryn's throat tightened. "That's so sad."

"Don't." Will's voice was sharp. She looked at him, disconcerted. "It's not sad. It's the way it is."

She stepped in front of him, her back to the play area, and put her hand on his arm. "I'm sorry. I didn't mean—"

He shook his head, a lock of hair falling across his forehead. "Pity is dangerous. Pity means you make excuses for the person with a disability, or worse, try to do things for them. Laura is smart and happy and as independent as a five-year-old should be. She can also be naughty and cranky and annoying. Just like any child."

"You're right. Of course, you're right." The muscles under her hand were tense. Camryn pulled back, drew in a breath.

"Should I have warned you?" Will's gaze was direct, with the tiniest hint of challenge.

"Why didn't you?" Had it been a test? Shock her with the situation and see how she reacted?

His mouth squeezed at the corner in a wry gesture. "I honestly didn't think of it. Not sure if you'll believe that, though."

As that had been her own first thought, she did. "Maybe I should take that as a compliment. You trusted me enough to take it in stride."

A shriek split the air. Camryn jerked around, searching for Laura, finding her, after a wild second, still standing at the water table.

"It's not her," Will said.

"Daddy!" Laura called. Camryn thought she heard a hint of panic.

"That, however, is." He chuckled and casually took her hand, tugging her with him. "She doesn't like unexpected noises. Coming, Laura," he called back.

Will headed for his daughter, Camryn's hand in his. She'd reacted instantly to the unknown child's frightened yell, her gaze seeking, then settling on, Laura, and he'd lost a little bit of his heart to her in that moment. The pulse-pounding, world-rocking attraction he'd felt at his first sight of her was easier to deal with than the tenderness he experienced now.

"I'm here, sweetie," he said, putting his free hand on

Laura's head without releasing Camryn. The connection linking all three of them felt right, felt natural. "Someone just tripped and fell. Everyone's okay. Want to go to the sandpit?"

She nodded and took his hand. Hers was cold and wet.

Camryn said, "We should probably dry off your hands first, right? Otherwise you'll make mud." She slipped her hand from his and stepped to the wall where a paper towel dispenser hung ready. While he appreciated her thoughtfulness, he had the sneaking suspicion she'd used it as an excuse to separate herself from him.

The sandpit had a ledge around it that kept most of the sand in and offered a seat as well. He and Camryn perched on the side while Laura climbed right in.

"Here's a brush," he said, touching the back of Laura's hand with it so she could grasp it. "And here, do you feel that?" He took her other and placed it on a plaster mold of a skeleton partially hidden in the sand.

"Yes." Using both hands, Laura industriously began to reveal the rest of the bones.

"I went through a dinosaur phase," Camryn said. "Probably when I was about your age."

Will said in a low tone, "When you are speaking directly to her, it's best if you use her name often, or touch her to make a connection. That way, she knows you're talking to her, not someone else."

"Sorry." She nibbled on her lower lip, a sign of nerves he found erotic and innocent at the same time.

"Nothing to be sorry for," he said. "Just a tip I've learned over the years." He gave into his low, constant need to touch her and placed his hand lightly on top of hers where it rested on the bench. "What was your favourite dinosaur?"

"Ankylosaurus."

His thumb caressed the silky skin on the back of her hand. "Spiky dude with the clubbed tail?"

She nodded, her eyes lowered, studying their hands but not moving. "He was so ugly and unusual I felt sorry for him."

"I like parasaurolophuses," Laura said. "I like their crowns."

"They're called crests," Will corrected.

"I call them crowns," she replied, unconcerned. Her chin was lifted toward him, but her hands continued to move busily at their work.

"I can see why you would, Laura," Camryn said. "They do look like crowns. I mean—" She stuttered to a halt, an appalled expression on her face.

He squeezed her hand. "Relax," he said quietly. "You didn't say anything wrong."

"I'm not usually so jumpy," she replied. "I don't want to insult you. Or Laura."

"I mean it. Relax. You're not going to do anything unforgivable, I'm sure. Here." He handed her another brush, found one for himself. "Let's get digging."

Will could feel the tension seep out of Camryn as they joined Laura in her excavations. When his daughter grew tired of that, they moved into the Creature Gallery. A teenage docent offered to take the animals out of their habitats so Laura could experience them.

Camryn stood slightly behind Will as the docent carefully lifted a gecko from its enclosure. "Are you sure this is a good idea?" she said, peering past his shoulder.

"It's not dangerous," he said. She stood so close he could see greenish flecks in her blue irises and tell she blackened her pale lashes with mascara.

"It's a lizard," she said testily, as if that explained everything.

"Are you afraid of lizards?" he asked, unable to hide a gleam of amusement.

"Not afraid," she said. "I just don't exactly like them."

Meanwhile, Laura's face glowed with excitement as the docent placed the lizard on her forearm. "Pretend you are a tree," the docent said. "Geckos like trees."

Laura's forehead creased in concentration as she stood as still as she could, arm extended, assisted by the patient docent. "It tickles," she whispered. "His feet are sticky."

"Do you want to touch it?" Will asked Camryn.

"No, thanks." She did, however, take a step closer. "He kind of looks like a miniature dinosaur."

As she leaned in, the gecko made a sudden sharp movement. With a small shriek, she jerked back, tripping over a stool placed so children could see into the habitats. Will's grab was too late to stop her from falling into the wall and banging her head.

"What's happening?" Laura asked anxiously, swivelling toward the noise and letting her arm droop. The docent rescued the gecko.

"Everything's okay," Camryn answered, recovering her balance. "I was just clumsy and tripped and bumped my head."

"Did you hurt yourself?" Will touched her shoulder and turned her to him. "That sounded like a hard bang."

"I'm fine." She lifted a hand to her temple and winced, belying her words.

"I'll go get an icepack," the docent said and hurried away.

"Honestly, I'm fine," Camryn said, frowning.

"Should Daddy kiss it better? That's what he does when I bump my head."

Camryn stilled and stared at Laura. Her faintly horrified expression amused and challenged Will.

"I think that's a great idea, Laura," he said. Camryn's gaze swung to him, narrowing in disapproval. He grinned. "Daddy's kiss makes almost anything better, doesn't it?"

"Yes. It's magic." She nodded vigorously.

He cupped Camryn's chin and her eyes dropped to his mouth, fixing on it as if hypnotized. Leaning in, he brushed his lips softly against the reddish mark on her forehead. She let out a quiet sigh, and he swept his mouth across her skin a second time. Her breath was warm against his neck, sending a shiver direct to his groin.

"Are you kissing it better, Daddy?" Laura's thin, piping voice broke the spell.

"Yes," he said huskily, moving just far enough away so he could see Camryn's eyes. They were heavy-lidded, her expression stunned yet soft. "Do you feel better, Camryn?"

She blinked and shuddered, as if coming back from a dream. "Hmmm?"

"Does your head feel better?" Laura asked.

"Oh." She cleared her throat, lowering her chin and averting her gaze. "Yes, Laura, it does. Thank you."

Will felt like thanking Laura, too. He'd wanted to kiss Camryn from the instant he'd seen her. While their lips hadn't touched, he could still feel the satin of her skin, hear the susurrus of her breathing.

Next time, it would be much more. He couldn't wait.

CHAPTER EIGHT

Obsessing about Anthony and what lies he had told.

Obsessing about Elizabeth and what she was doing to fix things.

Obsessing about Will…and his kiss.

These seemed to be the only thoughts in Camryn's brain during the rest of the weekend.

She couldn't do anything about Anthony, so did her best to shove him out whenever he managed to worm his way in.

On Saturday, Elizabeth had sent a text saying she was still gathering details and would call Sunday evening. Since it was now late Sunday afternoon, Camryn could allow herself to start wondering when that call might come.

And then there was Will…and his kiss.

Camryn gave her phone a baleful glare. If only Elizabeth would call, then Camryn would have a reason to stop reliving that gentle caress. It barely qualified as a kiss, after all. His lips had touched her temple, nowhere more intimate.

Yet it had been more disturbing than any embrace she and Anthony had ever shared.

Which brought her back to the beginning of her "things to obsess over" list. Yet again.

The program she was pretending to watch on HGTV went to commercial, so she flipped to the Food Network. This was what her life had been reduced to. Self-pity and mindless television.

Jo had offered to keep her company. "It's just dinner with Luke's family," she had said. "I don't have to go."

"Of course you do," Camryn had replied. "They are your in-laws. Or will be soon."

"Honest, I don't mind," she'd said wistfully. "Mrs. Donwell doesn't like me. Every meal with them is an exercise in painful diplomacy and tongue-biting tact. On my part at least."

"In that case, you definitely have to go. It will just give her another excuse to dislike you if you don't." Camryn handed her her jacket and pointed at the door. "Go. Charm her as only you can. No one can resist you for long."

Still Jo had hesitated. "She's resisted me for months with no apparent trouble. I don't think one more evening will change her mind. Luke says she's starting to soften but I don't see it."

"Go," Camryn said, infusing her tone with all the command she could muster, and physically ushering Jo out the door. "I don't need a babysitter."

Which might be true, but that didn't mean she wouldn't have enjoyed the company. Mattie was still secluded with Marcus—for which she couldn't blame her—and there was no one else Camryn could call. She hadn't kept in touch with any of her school friends, certainly not to the point where she could call out of the blue and suggest they get together.

While she refused to miss Anthony, she did miss being part of a couple. Missed having someone to simply hang out with, to spend time with. Other than family, she had no one, except maybe—

And there she was again—back to Will. Will and his kiss. Will and his laughing brown eyes and warm, strong hands, and sweet daughter.

Her phone rang, startling her out of her circling thoughts. In her haste to answer she bobbled it from hand to hand. Gaining control, she swiped the screen. "Hello?"

"Elizabeth here. How are you doing?"

"Fine." Elizabeth wasn't the type of lawyer you admitted your fears to. She was strictly business, not a cheerleader. "Any news?"

"I explained to the investigators that you were not available to come in for another interview. They've agreed to ask their questions by video conference from the RCMP detachment in Prince George."

She knew she should be grateful for small mercies but—"Is another interview really necessary? I've told them everything I can. More than once."

"I'm afraid it is." Elizabeth didn't sound afraid. She sounded calm and competent, almost cold. Which was a good trait in a lawyer, Camryn knew. *But right now,* she thought wistfully, *what I really need is a friend.* Someone to hold her hand and tell her it would all work out.

"If you say so," she replied with a sigh. "I assume you'll be on the video call as well. From your office, or will you be with the Vancouver police?"

"Actually, I will be in Prince George for the interview. I'll arrange a time with the local police and we'll go together."

The thought of paying for Elizabeth's travels make Camryn queasy. Airfare was not cheap. And what about accommodations and meals? "How much will that cost me?" she said, trying to keep the panic out of her voice.

"Being with you for the interview falls into our usual agreement. As for the travel, I have other reasons for the trip, and had already made my own arrangements when this came up. It is good timing all round."

There was never anything good about being interviewed by the police, but Camryn could appreciate what Elizabeth meant. Especially since she wasn't footing the lawyer's travel bill. "I suppose it is."

"I'll get in touch when the details are arranged. Probably tomorrow afternoon," Elizabeth said, and disconnected the call.

Her assumption that Camryn would be able to drop everything to accommodate the interview grated, but it was futile to feel that way. To the police and lawyers, nothing was more important than their business. Gripping her phone like a nun would her prayer book, Camryn cautioned herself to be patient. Someday, all this would be behind her.

She hoped that day was soon.

Will had felt obligated to offer to pick up Elizabeth at the airport and had been ridiculously relieved when she'd declined. Yet knowing she was arriving—probably at this very moment—made it difficult to concentrate. He would have been better off collecting her. At least then he'd be gainfully occupied, unlike the last hour he'd spent here in his office.

He dragged his focus away from the grey and gloomy view outside the window to the revisions in the contract for Charette Architects. Since lunch last week he and Abel had been back and forth with the details, but this version should be the final one. Incorporating the accessibility designs put forward by Bendixon and Sons would make the whole project better, and he was glad about that. When Abel had first suggested—well, demanded—the adjustment, he'd been worried the plans wouldn't be up to Kohlenburg's standards. Now that he'd seen them, he was more than willing to work them in. Abel was right—they were good ideas, and it was only appropriate that Camryn and her family's business get a chance to be a part of the process.

Originally, Abel had wanted Will to pay Bendixon and Sons a onetime fee as compensation for using their ideas, and have the Kohlenburg Group handle it from there. Instead, Will had reworked the budget to include the fee and make sure that Bendixon and Sons would be hired to do the onsite work. It seemed the right thing to do.

Besides, it would give him more chances to speak with Camryn. And he really, really wanted to do that, especially since Saturday, and the non-kiss that had just about knocked him to the ground.

Before he had a chance to get distracted with memories from that day, his phone rang.

Taking a deep breath and letting it out slowly, he

connected the call. "Hello, Elizabeth. How was your flight?"

"It was fine, thank you."

He couldn't help a tiny thrill at the sound of her voice. It had been the first thing that had attracted him—low and husky, with a rasp to it that made him think of classic rock, fine whiskey, and good cigars. Shaking off an unexpected feeling of regret, he said, "Laura is in school until 2:15PM. She knows you are coming, of course. Would you like me to bring her to you then?"

"I'm not sure a hotel room is the best place to reconnect with my daughter."

He gritted his teeth at the last two words, wanting to deny the connection. Sending birthday cards didn't make Elizabeth a mother. Not the mother Laura deserved, anyway. "What do you suggest then? Where would you like to meet her?"

"I thought it might be less disruptive if I visited her at your house."

His first reaction was a knee-jerk *hell, no!* He didn't want Elizabeth in the home he and Laura had made so carefully over the last year and a half. It was too intimate, too casual, too *friendly.* But rationally he knew she was right. It *would* be easier for Laura. Pulling up his big-boy pants, he said, "What if you came for dinner? Corinne usually picks up Laura from school and gets it started before I'm home. If you arrived about five-thirty that would work." He would get home a bit earlier and prepare Laura—yet again—for Elizabeth's arrival. He was no longer worried she'd be upset at seeing her mother. He was worried she'd be *too* happy, and would be crushed when Elizabeth inevitably left.

"Corinne?"

"Laura's caregiver."

"Oh, I see."

Was that relief he heard in the simple syllables? He shook his head. What did Elizabeth think—that he was unable to provide for his daughter?

She continued, "I think that sounds appropriate. I'll see you then," and disconnected abruptly, as was her habit.

He sank back in his chair, feeling as if he'd been beaten with a rubber mallet. This week was going to be brutal. But it was vital it went well, for Laura's sake. No matter how difficult it might be for himself.

Mattie popped her head into the doorway of Camryn's makeshift office in the break room. "There's someone at the front to see you. If she's a potential client, make sure to quote full price. She looks like she can afford it. I'm off to the McInnis job. See you later." And she was gone.

Smiling at Mattie's habitual hastiness—it was rare to see her move slowly—Camryn headed to the front office. She wasn't expecting anyone, but hoped it was one of the many people she had contacted last week. Since it appeared Bendixon and Sons might have found a niche as an accessible renovation specialist—given Abel's enthusiasm, at least—she had decided to reach out to organizations who supported seniors and those with special needs. Maybe one of those calls was about to bear fruit.

Her brisk steps slowed when she spotted Elizabeth Harrow in the reception area. The lawyer wore a black wool coat belted tightly at the waist, sleek forest green trousers and elegantly heeled ankle boots. Her black hair hung in a smooth bob just below her chin, with not a strand out of place, and she carried a large leather portfolio with a zipper closure.

"Elizabeth," Camryn said. "I didn't expect to see you here."

"I was hoping we could speak briefly. Am I interrupting?"

Helen appeared to be working at her computer and ignoring the conversation, but Camryn could feel curiosity emanating like sparks from her politely turned back. She didn't want anyone hearing about the police investigation but couldn't bear to take Elizabeth into the dinky, dingy break room. "Do you think Jason would mind if I used his office?" she asked Helen. It wasn't much better, decor-wise, but at least it didn't smell like burnt coffee.

Looking up from her work with a friendly yet inquisitive smile, Helen replied, "Of course not, dear. It will be yours soon enough."

Camryn led Elizabeth down the narrow hallway and into the office, shutting the door behind them. It was a good-sized room, but the beige walls were marked and scuffed, the carpet an ancient and ugly tan and orange tile pattern, and the furniture worn and beaten. Elizabeth's expression remained neutral as she lowered herself gingerly onto a chair.

Camryn winced as Elizabeth's elegantly clad bottom settled onto the torn seat, and blurted out an apology. "I'm sorry for the condition of everything. My grandfather has always concentrated on his clients, not appearances."

"It's fine." Elizabeth opened her portfolio on her knee, revealing a thick file folder, a yellow notepad, and a tablet. Tapping the device, she said without preamble, "I have the meeting set for tomorrow morning at nine-thirty. I trust that will work for you?"

"I'll make it work." For one wild moment she wondered what would happen if she refused to show up. Not that rebellion had ever been part of her personality. The rule follower, that was her.

"I've prepared a list of questions for you to review." Elizabeth handed over a single sheet of paper. "Of course, I'm not entirely sure what they will ask, but based on my conversations with the investigators I think this is a good start. Go over them and prepare your answers. Then we'll meet tomorrow morning to practice your responses prior to the video call."

Her heart beat faster simply thinking of the interview, and panic flushed her cheeks. "Do you think that will be enough time? Can't we get together tonight?"

Elizabeth hesitated just a fraction before answering. "I have personal business to attend to this evening. If you have any major concerns, text me and I will get back to you."

It would have to do, although Camryn couldn't help feeling a little hung out to dry. "All right."

Elizabeth rose. "I'm staying at the Marriott. I'll see you there at eight for our rehearsal, and then we will go to the detachment together."

CHAPTER NINE

Maybe it was cowardly, but as the time for dinner with Elizabeth crept closer, the more Will felt he needed a buffer. He'd thought a family-only evening would be best for Laura, but before leaving the office, and before he could change his mind, he called Camryn.

As he listened to the ringtone, he mused at how odd it was that, though he had been in Prince George for a year and a half now, the person he wanted to support him tonight was a woman he barely knew. Maybe *sad* was a more appropriate word. He had been so focused on Laura that he hadn't developed any adult relationships, other than those through work. It was probably time to change that.

He would start with Camryn.

"Hello?"

The sound of her voice calmed his nerves while

simultaneously exciting his blood. "Camryn, it's Will. How are you?"

"Fine. Do you need something? Is it about the dental clinic?"

She sounded rushed and distracted and his anxiety returned. Maybe he shouldn't have called her. Maybe he was making a fool of himself.

And what was he, fourteen years old, asking a girl out for the first time? Too late to hang up now. "Yes, I do need something," he said, overly cheerful, "and no, it's nothing to do with work."

"What is it, then?"

"Are you busy tonight? I told you my ex was coming this week, right? Well, she's arrived, and is having dinner with Laura and me. I would really like you to come, too."

The pause was telling. Finally, she replied. "Me? Why on earth me?"

He went with honesty. "This is going to sound stupid, but you're the closest I have to a friend in this town. I need someone who will help keep the conversation going. I have no idea how Laura is going to react to seeing her mother again after so long. I thought having you join us might provide a distraction, a cushion."

Another pause, this one not quite as long as the first. "You can't be serious. You must have someone else you'd rather invite."

"I told you it sounded stupid. But nope, you're it. Please, Camryn. Laura needs you."

She snorted. "Oh, that's low."

He heard a quiver of amusement. At least he hoped so. "I do what I need to."

"I have a meeting tomorrow to prepare for. I don't think—"

"An hour. Two hours max." Even to himself he sounded desperate, but he didn't care. "I promise. Dinner's at five-thirty. I start getting Laura ready for bed at seven-thirty on school nights."

A sigh whooshed down the line. "I guess I could use a break. Are you sure—"

He cut her off a second time. "Yes, I'm sure. Thanks, Camryn. I'll text you the address. See you in an hour." He hung up before she had a chance to say anything more.

Camryn had spent most of the afternoon angsting over the list of questions Elizabeth had left. They weren't difficult. All she had to do was stick with the truth. But previous experience had shown her how certain investigators could twist an honest and straightforward answer into something guilty and convoluted.

Even as she drove to Will's home, she couldn't quite believe she'd agreed to go. She really should have stayed home and kept preparing. She didn't accept his statement that she was the closest person to a friend he had. He didn't strike her as the type to have trouble in that area, so he must have had another reason to ask her.

What that was she couldn't possibly imagine.

Will's directions took her to a subdivision that was neither very old nor very new, but friendly and inviting with established gardens and well-maintained houses. She pulled to the curb in front of the address he'd provided, but stayed in her seat, gripping the steering wheel. It wasn't too late. She could still change her mind, drive out of sight and call him with an excuse.

Except that she wanted to see him, wanted to spend a little time not thinking of Anthony and investigations and jail.

She climbed out, shut and locked the door, and made her way up the driveway and along the cement path to the front door. Squaring her shoulders, she drew in a calming breath, let it out slowly, and pushed the bell.

Through the wooden panel she could hear the chime ringing. It had barely faded away when the door opened. She had to adjust her gaze downward to see who had opened it.

"Hello, Laura," she said. "It's Camryn."

The girl's bright smile twisted into a scowl. "I thought you were my mother."

Camryn's heart clenched in compassion. "I'm sure she's on her way. I think I'm a bit early." If anything, she was a couple minutes late, but she needed to ease the disappointment she read on Laura's face.

From a doorway down the hall, Will appeared, wiping his hands on a tea towel. "Laura, let Camryn in. It's chilly outside."

Laura stepped back, pressing against the wall, her gaze following Camryn, just off enough to reveal she was listening, not seeing. Once Camryn passed, she shut the door, then moved confidently down the hall toward Will. "Mommy is still coming, isn't she?"

"She'll be here soon," he said, "I promise. Why don't you finish setting the table while we wait? I've taken the plates and cutlery out for you. You just need to lay them in place."

"Do I have to?" she said plaintively.

The reaction reminded Camryn of herself as a child and she smiled. Will caught it and shared a grin.

"Yes, you do. Camryn and I will be there in a minute."

"Fine," Laura said with a put-upon sigh and trudged

away, pausing at the opening from which Will had emerged, one hand on the corner, then disappearing.

She left a humming silence behind. Will fiddled with the towel absently, his eyes on Camryn. Unsettled and not liking the feeling, she blurted, "I still don't believe you have no one else to invite. How many did you go through before you got to me?"

"None." He stepped closer and she forced herself to hold his gaze. "You were the first person I thought of. I swear."

"Isn't it going to be awkward with me here? Wouldn't it have been better with just you and Laura?"

"It's going to be awkward no matter what. Consider yourself moral support. I'm going to need it."

He reached out and trailed one finger along her jaw, from just under her ear to the point of her chin. She closed her eyes briefly, his touch lighting each and every nerve ending, not just in her jaw but at the tips of her fingers, the depths of her belly, the muscles of her thighs.

His head lowered and she watched his mouth, waiting, wanting. His lips were a hair's breadth away when the doorbell rang again.

"Mommy!" Laura raced into the hall, one hand trailing along the wall.

Camryn jumped away from Will's touch. He caught Laura before she collided with him and stopped her headlong rush. "Hang on there," he said. "Careful."

He appeared to have completely forgotten Camryn. Together, he and Laura stepped to the door and opened it.

Elizabeth Harrow stood on the stoop.

Will clutched Laura's hand tightly. For what seemed

like an endless moment, no one spoke. Elizabeth stood silent just outside the door. She looked exactly as he remembered her—sleek and polished and self-contained. Her hair seemed darker—was she colouring it?—but her face was smooth and unlined.

"Is it Mommy?" Laura asked, her voice high and excited. "Mommy, is that you?"

Elizabeth's face paled at Laura's question and the trance that had fallen over Will broke. He shook himself and answered. "Yes, it is. Elizabeth. Will you come in?"

Her chest rose and fell as she took a deep breath before stepping over the threshold.

Laura held out a hand, searching. "Mommy? It's me, Laura. Do you recognize me?"

Elizabeth didn't reply, her mouth a tight, pinched line. He stared at her. If he didn't know her better, he'd think she was speechless with nervousness. But Elizabeth never let her emotions control her actions.

Finally, she spoke. "Of course I recognize you, Laura. I was just surprised at how much you've grown." Slowly she reached out and took Laura's seeking hand. "It's so good to see you."

His daughter let go of him and stepped toward her mother, talking a mile a minute. Tension eased from Will's shoulders as he watched Elizabeth, still looking stiff and uncomfortable, pay close attention to Laura's convoluted conversation.

Looking past them, he saw Camryn standing where he'd left her. Dismay at his rudeness in not introducing her was quickly overridden by shock at her expression. She was staring at Elizabeth, eyes wide, hands raised to her mouth, as if seeing an apparition.

Two steps took him to her side. "Are you all right?"

he asked. "What's going on?"

She blinked and lowered her hands to her sides in a graceless, jerky gesture, like a puppet whose strings had been cut. Darting a glance at him, she asked, "That's your ex-wife?"

"Never wife. But yes."

"Elizabeth Harrow." Her tone was flat, stating a fact she knew would not be denied.

"Yes." A chill stabbed him in the back of the neck. "How do you know Elizabeth?"

Before she could answer, Laura's voice broke through. "Daddy, I want Mommy to meet Camryn."

Turning back to Elizabeth and Laura, Will's confusion grew. Elizabeth appeared less horrified, but just as surprised. "Camryn? What are you doing here?"

Camryn's mouth opened and closed but no sound came out. More and more concerned, Will said, "I invited her. She's a friend of mine."

"We went to the museum together," Laura piped up. "We dug dinosaur bones."

The two women continued to stare at each other. When no explanation seemed forthcoming, he asked straight out, "How do you know each other?" He didn't think he was going to like the answer.

Camryn finally found her voice. "She's my lawyer," she said breathily, as if she didn't have enough air in her lungs.

Samuel's voice echoed eerily in Will's head. *More arrests might be imminent.*

He couldn't be such a bad judge of character, could he? Had he really read Camryn so wrong? Another thought struck him. She didn't know *he* knew about Halford and the embezzlement. But she had to realize he knew

Elizabeth was a criminal defense lawyer. How would she explain the situation? She would have to somehow, sometime. Her story couldn't be left to hang.

"What's a lawyer?" Laura's sweet, high voice demanded.

Elizabeth looked down at her daughter. "A lawyer is a person who knows the law and helps people."

Laura's brow creased. "What's the law?"

"They're kind of like rules," Will said. "It's complicated, though. Maybe you and your mom can talk about it more later. For now, why don't we go into the kitchen? Dinner will be ready in a few minutes."

Elizabeth looked over her shoulder as Laura tugged her down the hall, puzzlement still clear on her face. Will gestured to Camryn, inviting her to follow.

She didn't move. "Elizabeth Harrow is Laura's mother."

"Yes." He was torn between hearing what she had to say and the urge to stop her, tell her it was none of his business. Not knowing might be easier to live with.

"Did you know she is representing me? Is that why you invited me to dinner tonight?"

He shook his head, hearing the humiliation in her voice, seeing it in her stricken expression. "I had no idea. How could I? Elizabeth and I rarely talk, and only about what concerns Laura."

"I'm not a criminal," she blurted.

"You don't have to say anything more," he said, not as relieved as he thought he'd be to hear her deny his unspoken accusation.

"You invited me into your home. I owe you some sort of explanation. I haven't done anything wrong."

Her chin lifted, but the glint of unshed tears in her

eyes was a truer sign of the misery reflected in her face. He reached out, trailing his fingers through the short, cropped hair at her temple, onto the silkiness of the skin along her jaw. "I believe you."

"How can you? You don't even know what it's all about."

Now was not the time to tell her she was wrong about that. "It doesn't matter. We may have just met, but I know you. I know you'd never do anything intentionally wrong."

Her mouth thinned as she struggled for control. "I should go."

"No," he said.

"Yes," she said, a shade desperately.

"No," he said. "You shouldn't. You should come with me and eat dinner with your lawyer and my daughter. We can talk about it more later."

She resisted briefly when he took her arm, but he smiled and urged her along. With a shaky sigh, she allowed him to lead her to the kitchen.

Camryn wasn't sure how she made it through dinner. Thank goodness for the artlessness of children. Laura was cheerfully oblivious to the tensions weaving a web between the adults, and nattered on about school and friends and dinosaurs and who knew what else. Camryn tried to keep track of the conversation but couldn't help falling back into her own thoughts.

The clues connecting Elizabeth to Will had been right in front of her. She had known Laura's mother was coming to town. Had known Elizabeth was coming to Prince George on personal business. Had even known they were—she was?—arriving the same day. But hundreds of people flew to Prince George every day. The possibility they were one and the same hadn't even crossed her mind.

If it had, though, she wouldn't have been blindsided tonight. Wouldn't be in the situation she was in now, having to explain the whole sordid story to Will.

"The lasagne was delicious," Elizabeth said, crossing her silverware neatly on her empty plate. "Where did you order from?"

Will's eyebrow lifted. "It's homemade. A recipe Corinne introduced to us."

"We got it ready after school," Laura said. "Daddy just had to make the salad when he got home and put the garlic bread in."

Camryn didn't know who Corinne was but didn't have the energy to ask. Every forkful of tender noodles and rich sauce transformed into a tasteless wodge in her mouth, but she persevered to the end. The crisp white wine Will served helped. She was on her second glass, and it would have to be her last, so she'd have her wits about her later.

"Can I show Mommy my bedroom?" Laura asked, bouncing slightly in her chair.

They'd had their meal in the dining area of the open plan kitchen, serving themselves direct from the baking pan, for all the world as if it were a normal, everyday dinner.

Nothing about tonight was normal.

"Of course," Will said. "Take your plate to the dishwasher first."

Camryn watched Laura confidently locate the edge of the counter and move the few steps needed to reach the dishwasher. She fumbled with the latch, and Elizabeth rose as if to help, then sank down when the girl opened the appliance.

"Go with Laura," Will said to Elizabeth. "I'll take care of cleaning up."

"Let me help." Camryn jumped to her feet, reaching across the table to take Elizabeth's plate.

Mother and daughter left the room. Camryn kept her head down, stacking dishes and silverware. Will worked silently beside her. Before long the table was clear and the dishwasher loaded, leaving only a few pieces to be washed by hand.

"Don't worry about those," Will said. "Corinne will do them tomorrow."

"I like to wash," Camryn said, filling the sink with hot water and looking underneath it for detergent. She squirted in a dose and watched the foam rise. Putting off the inevitable for a little longer she asked, "Who's Corinne?"

"Laura's caregiver. She also does some light housekeeping and cooking." Will stood beside her, towel in hand, ready to dry.

"I see. It's tough being a single parent."

"Yes, it can be. Corinne is worth her weight in lasagne."

She appreciated his attempt to lighten the mood, but it didn't really help. She paid careful attention to the wineglass she was washing. He placed a hand over hers, suds and all, and stopped her obsessive wiping. She looked up at him, shying away from the compassion in his warm brown gaze. "Relax. I told you, you don't owe me an explanation."

"Maybe not," Camryn said, rinsing every last speck of soap off the wineglass and trying to match his casual tone, "but telling you is probably better than letting you dream up your own horrible scenario."

"Considering Elizabeth only takes on white-collar crimes, I doubt I'd come up with something too horrific. Unless you were scamming little old ladies."

Camryn snorted. "White-collar crimes. It sounds almost classy, doesn't it? When it's anything but." She put the casserole dish in the hot water, glad it was crusted with baked on cheese and sauce. It gave her an excuse to avoid looking at Will as she told her story.

CHAPTER TEN

"You know I recently moved back to Prince George from Vancouver," she said, scouring vigorously. "I moved there thirteen years ago or so, first going to university to get my degree in Business. I was lucky enough to get a job at Rosin Interior Design right out of school." She scrubbed at a stubborn chunk of food. Will remained silent. He had nothing left to dry but remained at her side. She could feel him watching her but didn't look up.

"I loved it. I didn't do design, of course, but I worked with clients and designers, was part of a team that made homes beautiful. It was rewarding and fun and exciting. Most of our clients were very well-off, able to afford the best materials, the newest trends. It was a multi-million dollar a year business. Still is, I imagine." She rinsed off the dish, checking for grimy spots, and was pleased to see a few so she could keep at it.

"Anthony started working there a year or so after I did. He was brilliant, attractive, sophisticated. The small-town had rubbed off me by then, so I can't blame my naiveté on that. I keep telling myself he fooled everyone, not just me. That it's not my fault. It doesn't help much."

"What did he do?" Will asked quietly.

"He was the Vice-President of Finance." She drew a deep breath and stopped scrubbing, forcing herself to meet his direct gaze. "He stole from the company. Embezzled hundreds of thousands of dollars."

Most people took a minute to assimilate that information. Will barely took a breath before speaking. "I can see why *he* would need a lawyer. But why do *you*?"

"I was his girlfriend. More than that. We lived together for the last year or so."

"Guilt by association? That isn't fair."

"Fair or not, the police interviewed me. When they set up a second interview, I decided not to be stupid and retained professional help." She rinsed the pan once more, and finding it clean, leaned past Will to lay it on the drying rack. "One of our clients was a lawyer, so I asked her for advice. She introduced me to Elizabeth and I hired her."

"How long ago was this?"

"A few months. I thought it was all over, but—" She bit her lip, cutting herself off. Pulling the plug, she watched the water drain out.

"But what?"

In for a penny, in for a pound. "The police want to interview me again. Thankfully, they agreed to do it by video call, so I don't have to go to Vancouver. Elizabeth has set it up for tomorrow morning."

"I see. When did you find out about this new interview?" There was an odd tone in Will's voice.

"Friday," she said. A sudden realization struck her. "I'm not the reason Elizabeth came," she said hurriedly. "She told me she'd already made plans before the police got in touch with her."

"I see," he repeated thoughtfully as he dried the lasagne pan.

She wanted to touch his arm, reassure him, but it seemed too personal, too intimate. Especially after what she'd just confessed. "It's the truth. It's also some sort of awful coincidence. I just about died when I saw her at your door. Things were going to be awkward enough. Adding this to the mix just made it worse. You should have let me leave when I wanted to."

"You have nothing to be ashamed of, if what you're telling me is the truth." He turned away from her to place the pan on the counter.

That had her spine stiffening. "Of course I'm telling the truth!" she protested to his averted back.

Bright, girlish laughter chimed in the hall, signalling Laura and Elizabeth's return. Quickly drying her hands, she brushed past Will and met the two as they came into the kitchen. "Thanks very much for dinner, Laura. I have to get going."

"Camryn," Will said from behind her.

She was exhausted. It had taken all her energy to get through the evening, and to top it off Will didn't believe her. "See you later, Laura. See you tomorrow, Elizabeth."

The lawyer nodded. "Yes."

Will followed her out of the room. She grabbed her coat and purse from the hall tree. "Camryn. Don't leave like this. I didn't mean it that way."

"How did you mean it, then?" Horrified, she felt the catch in her voice. "Never mind. I can't deal with this anymore. Not tonight." She escaped out the door.

Will cursed under his breath, knowing he'd screwed up. He believed Camryn's story—or, at least ninety-nine percent of him did. That one percent had snuck out for an instant, though, and broken her trust in him.

"How did you meet Camryn?"

He turned from glaring at the closed door to see Elizabeth standing in the entrance to the kitchen.

"Where's Laura?" he asked.

"She went to her playroom. She wants to have a tea party with me." She waited, still and calm, for him to answer her question.

"Through work," he said. "Her grandfather owns a local construction company."

"You know I can't talk about her, in any relation to our lawyer/client relationship."

"I had no intention of asking."

She tilted her head. "Did you know I was her lawyer?"

"I didn't know she *had* a lawyer. And certainly not a defense lawyer." Maybe it was his own guilt that made him add, "Why would I have thought she needed one?" He had intended to tell Camryn he knew about the embezzlement once she'd told him her version of events. He saw now he'd been hedging his bets. If she'd admitted to any sort of wrongdoing, would he have come clean? Or would he have quietly drawn back from their friendship, keeping things professional while watching for any further misconduct?

"Why did you invite her tonight?" Elizabeth's voice jarred him from his uncomfortable thoughts. "She can't have been in town more than a few weeks, as I saw her not that long ago in Vancouver." One corner of her mouth lifted in a wry movement, not quite a smile. "Maybe it was credulous of me, but I thought this evening would be just family."

"Family?" He shook his head and kept his voice low in case Laura left her playroom. "We're not a family, not a real one. Which is exactly why I invited Camryn. I thought she'd be a buffer between us, keep us on our best behaviour."

"Of course we're family. We're Laura's parents."

If he'd heard any regret in her tone, he would have been careful to reply gently. He didn't. "You haven't seen Laura in person for two years. You've missed two birthdays, her first lost tooth, her first day of school. You haven't put her to bed and read her stories or comforted her after she has a nightmare. You haven't disciplined her when she's been bad. Worst of all, you chose this path. *You* stepped away from *her*. On purpose."

The skin around Elizabeth's mouth tightened, a reaction so tiny he wasn't even sure it had happened. "That doesn't mean I'm not her mother."

"You gave birth to her, for which I'll be forever grateful." As usual, his heart thudded and skin crawled when he considered the other options Elizabeth could have chosen. "And I would never deny you the chance to take a more active part in her life. But you have to earn her trust, Elizabeth. Earn *my* trust. You can't just take up where you left off."

"Doesn't the fact I've come all the way here mean anything to you?"

"It's no more than you should have done many times since we moved," Will said, holding his anger in check. "You don't get Mommy points for finally fitting your daughter into your schedule."

"It's not like that," she said. "It was never like that."

He had no reply to her protest. For a long moment there was silence between them. Finally, he asked the question he'd been wondering for a week. "Why are you really here, Elizabeth?"

"I told you in my email. I think it's time to be a part of Laura's life again."

"Why now? What's changed?"

"Do I need to have a reason? Isn't it enough that I want to be?"

He studied her closely. Beneath her careful makeup she looked pale, and there were lines around her eyes he hadn't noticed until now. Something was going on. He could feel it. He needed to know what. He needed to protect Laura.

Camryn was done. Done with feeling guilty. Done with letting the world walk over her. Done with men.

It might not be the best attitude to have going into an interview with the police, but she was done with being scared, too.

Just done.

This bravado helped her through the initial awkwardness when she met Elizabeth to prep for the interrogation.

"I had no idea you were Laura's mother," she said as she strode past the other woman into the hotel room. By the window, two club chairs waited next to a round table on which rested an open laptop and several file folders. Gripping the back of one of the chairs, she kept her voice firm. "I was hesitant to go in the first place, but I let Will persuade me. If I'd known, I wouldn't have, no matter what." It was an explanation, not an apology. She owed her that much.

Elizabeth nodded. "I appreciate that. Will told me you met through work. Based on the fact he invited you to dinner, though, I assume your relationship is more than professional." Her tone made it clear she didn't approve.

Camryn refused to be cowed. "That may be. But if so, that is between Will and me. It should not affect how you treat me as a client." She paid Elizabeth good money—*very* good money—to protect her interests when it came to the mess Anthony had tossed her into. The fact they both knew Will should have no bearing on that at all.

Elizabeth gestured to a chair and took the other. "I assure you, it won't. Shall we get started?"

A brain-draining hour later, they set out for the RCMP detachment. Camryn was already exhausted, but nervous energy filled her. All she wanted to do was get it over with—for what she prayed was the last time.

The video conference took place in a small room with beige walls and no windows. There was just enough floor space for a table with four chairs and a narrow bookcase. A webcam perched on top of the bookcase, and above it a monitor mounted on the wall showed a very similar looking room at the Vancouver Police Department. On the screen, two investigators sat at a table. Camryn recognized them both from previous interviews.

Elizabeth and Camryn took their places. The RCMP officer who had escorted them in fiddled with the webcam, making sure they were framed correctly and testing the audio. Once Elizabeth and the Vancouver investigators were satisfied, she left the room, closing the door behind her.

After some initial posturing, which Camryn had come to expect in these situations, Elizabeth let them get down to business.

The investigator on the left said, "Mr. Halford continues to repeat his statement that you were aware of the embezzlement."

Camryn opened her mouth to deny it, yet again, but Elizabeth stopped her with a hand on her arm. "Ms. Bendixon has answered that ridiculous accusation multiple times. I was under the belief new information had come to light. She will answer questions regarding any new lines of inquiry, but nothing else. The rest is a matter of record."

"Then perhaps Ms. Bendixon will answer questions about her financial statements."

"How did you gain access to her statements?" Elizabeth demanded. "I didn't see a request for them."

"The statements in question relate to credit cards owned jointly with Mr. Halford. He volunteered them to us as proof of her involvement."

A chill crept up Camryn's neck, to her cheeks, her scalp. She tried to hold onto the defiance that had carried her so far, but it slipped away.

Elizabeth said, "How long have you known of these statements?"

The investigator ignored the question. Through the cold blue screen, he stared at Camryn. "Mr. Halford says you were in financial difficulties and had been for months. That you learned of his fraud and insisted you get a cut, in exchange for your silence."

"I still haven't heard a question," Elizabeth said.

"Fine. When did you discover the embezzlement?"

"I didn't discover it," Camryn said. "I couldn't

believe it when Anthony was arrested."

The silent investigator flipped through a file resting on the desk in front of her and pointed at something. The first nodded. "How many credit cards do you share with Mr. Halford?"

"Three."

"Are you certain of that?"

"Of course." She knew the exact balance on each of them. The total made her break out in a cold sweat in the middle of most nights.

"There isn't one you might have forgotten about? Or maybe two?"

"No. I remember signing for three cards."

"We are currently in possession of statements for seven cards."

"Seven!" She couldn't help the exclamation. The thought of having to take responsibility for those cards made her so dizzy she had to grip the table to stay upright.

"How do you know Ms. Bendixon signed those cards?" Elizabeth asked. "Who's to say her signature wasn't forged?"

"Mr. Halford assures us she knew very well what she was doing."

"Mr. Halford is grasping at any straw, trying to save his own sorry ass." Elizabeth's tone was crisp and condescending. "Have you had an expert examine the documents?"

"It's in process."

Elizabeth closed her leather folder. "I would suggest we forgo any further discussion until those results are in. My client has taken responsibility for the cards which she knowingly signed. If Mr. Halford forged her signature on others, she cannot be held responsible."

"I didn't sign them," Camryn said, trying to match Elizabeth's composure but hearing the tearing edge of panic in her own voice.

"Was there anything else you wanted to ask?" Elizabeth said. The investigators in Vancouver shook their heads. "Then we'll wait to hear from you. Have a good day." She rose and gestured for Camryn to follow. She closed the door of the interview room behind them and turned immediately to Camryn. "Tell me the truth, now," she said, low and urgent. "Did you sign for those cards?"

"No!" Camryn shook her head vehemently. "I didn't. Just the three you already know about."

"I can't do my job properly if you don't tell me the truth."

"I am telling the truth. I haven't lied to you once during this whole ordeal. Why would I start now?"

Elizabeth's eyes flickered back and forth, searching for something in Camryn's face. "Maybe your trust in me has changed."

For a moment Camryn was at a loss as to what she meant. Then it clicked. "Because of you and Will? Is that what you mean?"

Elizabeth hesitated, then nodded.

"I was upset last night," Camryn said frankly, "but mostly because I didn't want Will to know about this mess. Whatever is between the two of you has nothing to do with me. I can't start over with a new lawyer."

If she'd expected her response to soften the tension in Elizabeth's shoulders, she was wrong. If anything, the other woman seemed even more keyed up. But she didn't question Camryn further, and headed for the main entrance.

"I'll let you know when they get in touch regarding

the possible forgery," she said as they passed the guarded reception desk and exited the building.

"Okay." Camryn pulled her coat tighter and huddled into her scarf. No snow had fallen since she'd arrived in town, but the chill had deepened, and something in the air this morning had given warning it wouldn't be much longer in coming. But the cold in her bones wasn't only from the weather.

CHAPTER ELEVEN

Will wasn't sure exactly when Elizabeth and Camryn were meeting with the police, except that she had said Tuesday morning. Which meant he could put off calling her until after lunch. He needed to talk to her about the dental office project.

And about what had happened last night.

He dropped Laura off at school and into the care of the teacher's assistant assigned to her, then headed to his office.

Samuel was already at his desk. Will sometimes wondered if he ever went home.

"Morning," he called as he strode past Samuel's open doorway. He was barely in his seat before the other man appeared in the entrance.

"The Crossroads Corner proposal is up." Samuel dropped into one of the visitor's chairs on the other side of the desk. "I've been checking the Charette site every day for a week."

"Sweet." Will opened his laptop and navigated to the architectural firm's website. "I'll take a look right away and we'll get started on the proposal this afternoon."

Reviewing Crossroads Corner and taking care of a myriad other emails, phone calls and duties filled his morning. The work stopped him from thinking about Camryn more than once or twice every few minutes. He couldn't imagine how terrifying it must be to be interrogated by the police. His conscience gave a guilty twang at the sight of a patrol car, even when he knew he'd done nothing wrong. Camryn was innocent, he was sure of it, but her association with Halford inevitably looked suspicious to police.

He ate a sandwich at his desk while studying the Crossroads Corner request for proposals. It would be the biggest project he'd ever handled on his own—residential blocks, a retail strip, and a restaurant, all in its own complex. It would be a real feather in his cap if he could secure it for the Kohlenburg Group and bring it to a successful, profitable conclusion. He knew Wayne had gone out on a limb, giving him the opportunity in Prince George. Others with just as good, possibly even better, qualifications had applied to manage the new location. Maybe he hadn't been the obvious choice. But he was determined to be the *right* one. He owed it to Wayne.

In the early afternoon he called Camryn. She answered after the second ring. It was obvious from her guarded tone she already knew it was him. He hadn't thought of it before—she couldn't ignore his calls just in case they were business related. He might have a hard time getting her to answer except for that.

He wanted to ask how the interview had gone but figured that wasn't the best way to start the conversation. "I have the final contract for the dentist's office," he said. "I'll email it to you, but we should meet to go over it and discuss the schedule."

"All right," she said. "I'll connect with Mattie and Jason and get back to you. They need to be in on this, too."

"Sounds good." He paused. He'd had all morning to figure out how to broach last night with her, and still hadn't made up his mind.

Camryn broke the silence. "Is that all?"

"No." He took a deep breath. "About last night—"

"I don't want to talk about it."

"I want to apologize. I didn't mean to sound as if I didn't believe you. I do."

"Don't worry. I'm used to it."

"Please, Camryn. I mean it."

A gusty sigh sounded in his ear. "Fine. I accept your apology."

"Thank you." It didn't sound like she did, but he'd take what he could get.

"I've got to go. Bye."

The call disconnected. He held the phone away from his ear and stared at the screen. He wasn't sure what he expected to see on it. Maybe the answer to his Camryn conundrum.

It wasn't helpful.

Camryn had known all along that having any sort of personal relationship with Will was bound to backfire. But it was cold comfort to tell herself *I told you so*. After ending the call with Will, she tossed her phone on the faded laminate tabletop and leaned back in her chair.

Bendixon and Sons needed the dental job. Ergo, Camryn would have to work with Will, at least until she could hand everything over to Mattie. And the quickest way to do that was to get this meeting over with.

She rose from her makeshift workstation and strode into Jason's office. He was seated at his desk, his cheaters perched on the end of his long, dignified nose as he studied a colourful pamphlet.

"Hey," she said, drawing his attention.

He looked at her over the frame of his glasses. "Hey."

She took a couple steps further into the room. "Will is emailing the contract for the dental office. He wants to meet to discuss the schedule. Mattie's out all afternoon, but I think she's free tomorrow morning. I figured we should get together first and then set up a time with him."

He tossed the booklet aside. It was a seed catalogue, Camryn saw in surprise. Given the cold bite of winter had only started nipping through the breeze block walls it seemed an odd choice of reading material. Besides, she had never known Jason to be interested in gardening.

"Yes, the three of us can go over it tomorrow," he said, "but then you should meet with him on your own. Or you and Mattie, if you like."

A thrill of panic rippled to Camryn's fingertips. "I'm not ready for that."

His steady gaze held hers. "That's why we'll meet first, so I can help you prepare. It's a relatively simple project, our portion of it, anyway. It's a good one for you to sharpen your teeth on. The quicker you get up to speed, the better off we'll be."

Two more steps put Camryn near the visitor's chair. She sank into it, her knees wobbly. "You're serious about retiring, aren't you?" It was a question she had wanted to ask ever since he'd made his announcement. "I didn't quite believe you at first. This business is your life."

Her grandfather leaned his head against the seat back and swivelled gently. "It was. And I loved every minute of it. Love most of it, still. But it's time to let go. You and Mattie will make changes, I understand that. You need to do what you think is right, both to get us through this patch and to be successful in the future. That won't happen if I'm constantly hovering."

"You're still sticking around for a few months, though, aren't you?" She pointed at the bright red and purple blooms splashed across the cover of the discarded catalogue. "It'll be awhile before you're able to take up gardening, after all. Spring is a long way away."

"I've decided I'll be here until Christmas. After that, you can call me whenever you need something, for advice or help or whatever. And Helen will stay on a little longer than that, to smooth out the transition. But as of January, this office will be yours."

It was the ugliest office Camryn had ever seen. Yet he swept a hand through the air as if bequeathing a castle to her, and she couldn't help but be touched. She understood it wasn't just the physical space he was offering, it was the chance to build a new life, one that had treated him well, one he was proud of.

"Thank you," she said. Pressure built behind her eyes and she swallowed. "I'll try not to call too often."

"You'll be just fine. Mattie knows this business inside and out. You'll see."

"If you say so." She smiled at him. "So, tomorrow morning? As long as Mattie can make it."

He nodded, and she headed back to the break room.

She sent a quick text to Mattie to set up the meeting, then got back online. She wanted to review Charette Architects' website, make sure she really understood who they were, what they were looking for, so she'd have a firm grasp on their approach to the dental project.

As she clicked through the beautifully designed site, she saw a new menu item. A request for proposal for something called Crossroads Corner. Curious, she opened the PDF.

By the time she'd finished reading it, her heart was racing, her palms sweating. It would be a risk. A *huge* risk. If they were successful at securing the contract, they'd have to call back employees who'd been gone for months—if they were still available—and possibly even hire more. But the need to prove to Jason that he was right in trusting his valued company to his granddaughters was overpowering. She'd been close on the dental project, so close. She was going to study this one word for word before she mentioned it to Mattie or Jason. There'd be pushback, but she was ready to fight for what she thought was right.

She hit print on the PDF and headed to the front office to retrieve it from the printer. On her way back down the hall she heard her cell ringing, and hurried into the break room, snatching the phone off the table and connecting the call without bothering to read the display.

"Hello?"

"Camryn? It's Sandie."

Sandie Larsen was one of the only people at Rosin Interiors to stand by Camryn after the news of Anthony's crimes had surfaced. She was also the friend who had agreed to store the possessions she had left in Vancouver.

"What's up?" Camryn replied. "I'm sorry I haven't

been in touch about getting my stuff out of your storage, but I'm not quite settled yet."

"That's not why I'm calling." The other woman sounded hesitant and unsure, and Camryn's heart rate kicked up a notch.

"What is it then?"

"I had a phone call from a Samuel Antoski. He says he works for the Kohlenburg Group in Prince George."

Camryn didn't recognize the name, but that didn't mean anything. Her grip on her phone grew slippery. "What did he want?"

"He'd heard about the embezzlement. He didn't ask outright, just kind of slid around the point, but he was pumping me for information about you, whether you had a role in it. He asked why you'd left the company."

"When?" Camryn licked her lips, her mouth dry as dust. "When did he call you?"

"Last week." A sigh travelled through the speaker. "I wasn't sure whether to tell you or not. I said you had nothing to do with the embezzlement, that you were a wonderful colleague, that I missed working with you, and I hoped that would be enough. The more I thought about it, though, the more I realized I should probably let you know." *Warn you* was implied by her tone.

Will had known.

Last night, when she'd humiliated herself in front of him, he had already known about the scandal. He must have. She couldn't accept that someone in his office would have investigated her without his knowledge.

Yet he had made her say it. Had made her confess the whole sorry tale. No wonder he hadn't believed her.

A tiny voice in the back of her mind whispered, *If he thinks you're a criminal, why did he invite you to dinner?*

but she was enjoying the surge of righteous indignation too much to listen. It glowed bright and fierce and powerful.

Will had toyed with her, and he wasn't going to get away with it.

Will had given Corinne the afternoon off, as Elizabeth has said she would pick up Laura from school. He had wanted to protest, to tell Elizabeth she was disrupting Laura's schedule, one he'd worked very hard to build. It soothed her anxiety when she had a routine she could depend on. But she'd been so excited when Elizabeth had suggested the plan that his worry seemed petty and unnecessary, so he'd gone along with it.

"If it's all right with you, I'll bring her to my hotel," Elizabeth had said the night before, after they'd put Laura to bed. "We'll do her homework, if she has any, and go for dinner at the hotel restaurant. Then I'd like to take her to that museum she was telling me about for an hour or so. I'll have her home well before bedtime."

"She's only in Kindergarten, so she doesn't often get homework," he said, knowing he was being testy but not caring. "She is supposed to do occupational therapy every day. It isn't good for her to miss that."

"Surely one day wouldn't hurt."

Of course it wouldn't, not one day. Besides, some of the exercises were simple enough that he could easily explain them to Elizabeth and she could do them with Laura. But he wasn't ready to have her become that much a part of Laura's day, not yet. Trying to hide his bad grace, he'd given in. His own behavior irritated him. He had thought he was a more accepting and forgiving person.

Brenda Margriet

Obviously not.

The upshot of it all was that Will had an evening free. He couldn't remember when he'd last had this much time completely to himself, away from work, away from Laura. Arriving home in the early dark, he moved restlessly from room to room, tidying what was already tidy, missing Laura's constant chatter. He warmed up leftover lasagne for his dinner and had it with a beer while he watched the evening news.

And still had two hours to fill.

When the doorbell rang, he jumped from the couch, hoping Elizabeth had decided to bring Laura home early. Finding Camryn on his front step was almost as welcome a sight. Except for—

"Did you have me investigated?" she demanded, eyes narrowed.

"Did I—what?" He stepped back automatically, inviting her in, his brain scrambling.

She closed the door behind her with a decisive slam. "One of the few friends I still have at Rosin Interiors called me. Apparently, she received a phone call last week from someone at the Kohlenburg Group asking probing questions."

Samuel. "Oh," Will said.

"I'll take that as a yes." She poked him in the chest. "You knew about Anthony, didn't you? Yesterday, when I told you the whole stupid story, you already knew, and yet you made me tell you anyway. What were you hoping for? To catch me in a lie?"

He was unsuccessful in keeping the guilt off his face. This time her poke was going to leave a bruise.

"You were, you jerk. I can't believe it." She spun around and grabbed for the door handle, obviously intending to storm out.

"No, wait." He reached for her wrist. She jerked out of his loose grip, but stopped, her back toward him. "I can explain."

"Really?" She shot him a withering look over her shoulder, disbelief dripping icily from the word.

"It wasn't me. I didn't call." It was a pathetic denial, and she gave it the scorn it deserved.

"I know that." Twisting to face him, she planted her hands on her hips. "You had a flunky do it, instead."

He winced. "Samuel's not a flunky. It was his idea, not mine. I didn't want him to do it. My boss in Vancouver told us he'd heard rumours about Rosin Interiors, and Samuel thought we should check it out."

"Fine, I get that. But why didn't you tell me? Why hide that you knew?"

"It wasn't exactly easy to work into a conversation."

"You had the perfect opportunity yesterday," she retorted, "once you knew Elizabeth was my lawyer. You could have brought it up then."

"I was just as surprised as you were. The last thing I expected when I invited you over was that you'd be my ex's client." He could still feel the echo of that shocking punch. It was tough enough having Elizabeth back in his life, but to know she was also a part of Camryn's had been—disorienting. To say the least.

"Maybe, but you could have stopped me. When I started to explain, all you had to do was tell me you knew." Her eyes sparked fiercely blue, daring him to deny it.

"All I knew was hearsay through Samuel. I wanted— *needed*—to hear your side of the story."

"What if he'd talked to someone other than my friend? What if he'd talked to one of the many, many people who believe I *did* know what was going on? Would you have believed me then? Or do you only believe me now because my story matched what you've been told?" She paused, eyes widening. "Wait a minute. You *don't* believe me. How could I be so stupid? You said it last night—*if. If* I was telling the truth."

"I do believe you." He reached out to touch her shoulder. She jerked away from his hand. He dropped it to his side, clenching his fingers. "I do. You didn't have anything to do with the embezzlement, I'm sure of it."

"Why? Why should you believe me?" she challenged. "We barely know each other."

"I don't know why. I just do." It was something he felt in his bones, something he couldn't put into words. "I just do," he repeated, helpless to define it further.

She stared at him. As he watched, the anger seeped from her expression, leaving her face pale, dark circles under tired eyes. "I want to believe you," she said. "It seems like forever since someone other than my family has trusted me. But I don't know if I can."

"Elizabeth believes you," he said. The last word wasn't out of his mouth before she was shaking her head.

"Elizabeth's a defense lawyer. Defense lawyers are paid to believe their clients are innocent. Or, at least, not as guilty as they could be. She doesn't count."

What she said was the truth. He searched for a way to prove he believed her. She waited quietly and his heart ached to comfort her.

Slowly he reached out. He lifted her chin. For a moment her eyes remained downcast, then her lids fluttered upward.

He leaned in and kissed her.

Her lips, at first firm and closed, softened, opened.

Her breath trembled out, swirling from her mouth to his, warm and sweet. He tasted her sadness, her need, and gathered her in, his arms surrounding her, hoping the press of his body would express what his words hadn't.

Her hips arched into his as her arms wound around his neck and he felt the pull of desire strike deep. She fit him like water in a glass, filling an emptiness he hadn't realized consumed him. Their tongues met, darted, teased, their lips separating only long enough to gasp in a breath before connecting once more.

He'd thought to offer comfort, reassurance. Instead he found himself drowning in sensations that had nothing to do with those tepid emotions. He was fire and ice, she was challenge and surrender.

He was lost.

He pressed her to the door, his hands on her hips, her breasts soft against his chest. As much as he wanted to continue his exploration, a hazy sense of reality managed to break through. He gentled his kiss, forced down the pulsing need. Drawing back, he opened his eyes. Her face, scant inches away, was flushed a rosy pink, her lips full and heavy. Her eyelids lifted, revealing a blue so cloudy with passion he groaned. Keeping her clasped to him, he rolled so their positions were reversed. He leaned against the door, her head tucked under his chin. Lazily he trailed his hands up and down her back, coming down from the high her kisses had rocketed him to. She rested against him, her hands at his waist. He could feel her ribs rise and fall as her breathing slowed.

He knew the exact moment she started thinking again. Her fingers curled, no longer resting on the waistband of his jeans but balled into fists. The muscles in her back tightened, no longer soft and supple but hard and tense.

She pushed herself off him, took two slow, staggering steps back. He immediately felt her loss. Cool air swept away the wonderful warmth she'd brought him. But he didn't reach for her.

"Don't believe me because you want me," she said, her expression stark. "Attraction is no judge of character, as I've learned from bitter experience."

"I don't," he said. "I believe you because I watched you when you told me your story. You were ashamed and humiliated. You also felt guilty." Her eyes never left his face as he spoke. "You felt guilty you hadn't known what he was up to. If you were trying to deceive me, you wouldn't have let that guilt show."

"Maybe I'm a good actress." She poked at it like it was a scab she couldn't leave alone.

"Now who isn't believing who?" he asked. "I don't know how else to tell you."

She sighed, as if putting down a heavy load. "You know what the worst thing is?" she asked, her words a whisper. "I don't know what I would have done if I *had* discovered what he was doing. Would I have turned him in? I loved him. At least, I *thought* I loved him. Maybe I would have kept quiet. I hope I would have tried to convince him to give back the money. But what if I hadn't? I would have been as bad as he."

"It's no use borrowing trouble. It didn't happen that way, and you have enough going on without wondering about would haves and could haves. Let it go."

CHAPTER TWELVE

Camryn tried to do what Will had said.

Let it go.

She'd been fighting the current of despair for so long that giving herself permission to float made her feel as if she was taking her first full breath in months.

Pushing Anthony, the police interviews, her debt into the farthest corner of her mind, she locked it all away and let herself look forward. When she'd tried to distance herself from the scandal, she had only dragged it along with her. After that evening at Will's, she did her best to cut the rope, leave it truly behind.

She met with Jason and Mattie and went over the dentist's office project. Together they worked out how they'd fit into the Kohlenburg Group's bigger plan. Then the following day, she and Mattie met with Will.

They hadn't spoken since the kiss, dealing only

through email, and Camryn found herself unaccountably shy as a man in tight yellow pants ushered them into Will's office. It was in a new building which had recently replaced a ramshackle hotel on one of the most historic streets in downtown Prince George, and was as different from the dingy, beat up offices of Bendixon and Sons as it could get. The lovely, large space boasted wide windows looking onto the treed lawn—right now, sere and brown after recent hard frosts—in front of City Hall, and it was appointed with sleek, efficient furniture that hadn't been around in the previous century.

Mattie and Will had never formally met, so Camryn performed the introductions.

"It's a pleasure to meet you," Will said.

Mattie shook his hand in her usual brisk fashion and nodded. Camryn sighed and silently thanked the powers that be that Mattie had refrained from making any of the comments she had shared on the drive over, mostly muttered threats about what she'd really like to do to the man she blamed for her beloved company's financial woes.

"Will's a good guy," Camryn had cautioned. "He's just doing his job. We should be grateful he is willing to work with us on the project."

Mattie eyed her with disgust, but the warning seemed to have done its job, as she was scrupulously polite throughout the meeting. At the end, as they rose to take their leave, she even unbent enough to make small talk.

"I understand you've only been in town a year or so," she said. "How are you enjoying it so far?"

"My daughter and I like it," Will said as he walked them to the front reception area. "It was a big change, but we like that it's small enough to get everywhere quickly yet has all of the amenities we need."

Mattie cocked her head. "You have a daughter?"

"Laura," he said. "She just started kindergarten this fall. Oh, by the way, Camryn"—he turned to her—"Laura's class is doing a performance tomorrow. She wants you to come if you can make it."

He smiled, and Camryn instinctively returned it, then wiped it from her face, all too aware of Mattie's raised eyebrows.

"As it's Halloween," he continued, "they'll be reciting poems—very spooky ones, Laura assures me—and showing off their costumes."

Camryn wanted to ask about Elizabeth, whether she'd be there as well, but it was going to be tricky enough explaining Will's daughter's invitation to Mattie without mentioning Will's daughter's mother, too. Her convoluted thoughts had pain spiking behind her eyes. She gave a noncommittal answer, and it was Will's turn to raise an inquiring eyebrow, but before he could say more, she hurried out of the office, Mattie on her heels.

"Okay, spill," her sister said even before they'd hit the sidewalk. "What's going on?"

"It's no big deal." Camryn kept her head down, ostensibly searching for her keys in her tote. She took a couple more steps before realizing Mattie was no longer at her side. She stopped and looked back. Her sister was standing stock-still in the middle of the sidewalk, eyes narrowed.

"Why on earth would Will's daughter want you to come to her school performance? When did you even meet her?"

Camryn shrugged, as if her answer was supremely unimportant. "We went to the museum together and dug up dinosaur bones."

Mattie's mouth dropped open. "You went to the museum with her? Wait a minute. Was Will there, too?"

Camryn swallowed and lifted her chin. "Yes."

"You went on a date with Will?" Mattie's voice was a trifle shrill, and Camryn winced.

"It was *not* a date. His daughter was there."

Mattie held up her hands and approached slowly. "I don't care. Start from the beginning. Tell me how you and the head honcho at our biggest competitor ended up so friendly."

Today was the sunniest it had been since Camryn had arrived home, but there was little heat in the weak rays. She tucked her gloveless hands into her armpits to keep them warm. "He asked me out to dinner after we had lunch with Abel from Charette Architects. I said no. I had the same concerns about our professional connection. Then he asked if I would go to the museum with him and Laura. It seemed like the polite thing to do. He's not our enemy."

"He's stealing work from under our noses!"

"No, he's beating our bids, which is what he's paid to do. As well, he's open to giving us opportunities." Camryn could understand Mattie's protectiveness, but she didn't have to be so militant about it. Not wanting to delve into why she felt the need to defend Will, she said, "He's a nice guy, not the devil. Maybe building a relationship with him would be good for Bendixon and Sons."

Even if Mattie fell for that line, Camryn was pretty sure her sister wouldn't include kissing Will as part of a good business plan.

Camryn had been trying to let go of that kiss, as well, but couldn't. For the first time in months she'd felt cherished, safe, desired. Looking back, she realized

Anthony had been ignoring her for weeks before the fallout. When Will looked at her, she knew he *saw* her.

She didn't want to lose that.

Mattie was staring at her like she'd spoken in a foreign tongue. "I'm cold," Camryn said, tilting her head toward the sedan parked a few metres up the street. "We can talk more in the car."

Despite her invitation, Mattie remained silent on the ride back to the office.

Maybe Camryn's words had gotten through to her.

Maybe she was plotting ways to get back at Camryn for her treason.

Camryn wasn't sure which one she hoped for.

It struck Will the instant Camryn and Mattie left his office.

Camryn's family didn't know she'd been seeing him. At least, Mattie didn't. That was why Camryn had looked so discombobulated when he'd invited her to Laura's performance. He didn't have time to examine how this revelation made him feel, however, as Samuel joined him moments later.

He'd carefully instructed Samuel not to introduce himself, and banned him from the meeting, afraid of Camryn's reaction if she learned who he was. He wasn't sure if her friend at Rosin Interiors had mentioned Samuel's name, but he'd blurted it out when she'd confronted him, and wasn't willing to take the chance she'd put two-and-two together. Starting the meeting by having to deal with that minefield would have been awkward—at the very least.

Samuel lounged with his usual casual elegance in the

seat Mattie had just vacated. "Satisfied?" he asked, just enough snark in his tone to remind Will he wasn't happy to have been kept out of the loop.

Refusing to take the bait, he simply said, "Yes. Thank you."

"I'm not sure who you thought you were protecting. Me from her anger or her from possible embarrassment."

"You didn't see how pissed she was," Will said, absently rubbing his sternum where a fingertip shaped bruise had blossomed, "or you wouldn't be wondering."

Samuel waved that off. "And you still don't see her reaction as suspicious? She sounds very defensive."

He didn't want to tell Samuel that Camryn's real issue had been with Will for hiding what he had learned. "She was upset," he said mildly. "Anyone would be, especially an innocent anyone."

Samuel ran his hands through his hair, somehow not disturbing his stylishly rakish look. Will knew it was stylish because Samuel had told him so. Otherwise he would have thought it was just messy. "I can see I'm not going to convince you. I just hope I never have a chance to say *I told you so*."

"On that, we are in agreement." A ping sounded from his phone and he checked the time. "I told you I was leaving early, right? Elizabeth and I are taking Laura out of class for the afternoon."

"How is *that* going," Samuel asked as he moved toward the door. "Elizabeth and Laura?"

Will slid a couple file folders into his briefcase, planning to work this evening to make up for the missed hours now. "Better than I expected," he said. "Elizabeth is on her best behaviour. The biggest issue we've had so far was when she wanted to take Laura out of school so she could spend more time with her."

"It is only kindergarten. I can see why she didn't think it would be a big deal."

"She should have asked about it before she arrived." If nothing else, it would have given him time to let Corinne know about the changes. As it was, he felt obligated to pay her as if she was working her usual hours. "To be honest, I didn't have a problem with it. It was Laura who caused the turmoil," he said as he and Samuel headed down the hallway. "She didn't want to miss any of the Halloween activities going on at school. But she also wanted to spend time with her mother. So, she did what most kindergarteners would do and had a meltdown."

Samuel pursed his lips. "How did Elizabeth handle that?"

"She didn't. She let me do it." To give her credit, though, that had been the right decision. Laura had been so over the top there was no way Elizabeth could have dealt with it. "Upshot was we compromised with half days." Yesterday Elizabeth had taken Laura to a local hobby farm that doubled as a petting zoo. Laura had enjoyed it, from her excited chatter last night. Elizabeth, however, had looked a little frazzled, so when she'd asked him to join them this afternoon he'd agreed. He wanted this week to be a success, for Laura's sake. It would be better in the long run if she and her mother had a good relationship. Besides, he was feeling a little compassion for Elizabeth. Diving full bore into motherhood like she was attempting must be exhausting.

"Well, have fun with your family." Samuel ducked into his office and Will made his way down the stairs to his vehicle.

Samuel's words echoed in his head as he drove to

Elizabeth's hotel to pick her up before getting Laura from school. Elizabeth was making an effort to connect to Laura. The fact it was still an effort was bothersome. She was trying too hard, and there was no way she could keep up that intensity much longer. He hoped if she did break, it wouldn't be in front of Laura.

She was waiting for him at the entrance, a beach-themed tote slung over her shoulder, an amusing contrast to her black wool coat and knee-high leather boots. He pulled to the curb and she slid in, shivering.

"I can't remember the last time I was at a public pool," she said, "but I have to admit I'm looking forward to the heat and humidity. I don't know how you stand this cold."

"It's not even true winter yet." He shoulder-checked and pulled back into the flow of traffic.

"I'll grant you this. The city isn't as bad as I thought it would be. But the weather—" She shuddered, apparently at a loss for words.

The backhanded compliment raised Will's hackles, and he bit back a sharp retort. He'd had his own reservations moving to Prince George, although those doubts had been overcome quickly. He supposed she was entitled to her own opinions.

When they arrived at Laura's school, Elizabeth went to fetch her. A couple minutes later they appeared, the pink pompom on Laura's hat bouncing with every step. They held hands across the parking lot and he could see Laura talking, face upturned to Elizabeth. The expression on Elizabeth's was one he'd seen on it more than once in the last few days—a soft yearning.

If he was a better man, maybe he would interpret Elizabeth's behavior as a sign that they should reconcile, try to put their family back together.

He obviously wasn't a better man. Because the person he truly wished was spending the afternoon with him and his daughter was Camryn. His imagination replaced Elizabeth with *her* image. It was Camryn opening the door for Laura, Camryn smiling as she strapped his daughter into her safety seat.

Given her lacklustre response when he'd invited her to Laura's school tomorrow, and the fact she didn't appear to have told her family they'd been seeing each other socially, he figured he was the only one having such daydreams.

"Let's go, Daddy!" Laura squealed. "Let's go swimming!"

He waited for Elizabeth to secure her own seatbelt and then put the car in gear. He would do his best to keep thoughts of Camryn at bay. This afternoon was for Laura. He wouldn't do anything to ruin it.

On the television shows Camryn had grown up watching, distraught women ate ice cream right out of the carton. Somehow it had always looked cosmopolitan and sophisticated. Eating out of an ordinary bowl didn't have the same sense of drama.

Right now, all she wanted was the sweet, sticky comfort ice cream slathered in chocolate sauce could give. Who cared what it was held in.

She slouched on her parents' couch, feet up on the coffee table, flicking through the billion offerings on Netflix in between spooning globs of ice cream into her mouth. She wore soft, faded yoga pants and an oversized T-shirt.

The front door opened and closed, and Jo's quick

footsteps approached. She hadn't seen much of her sister lately, as her studies involved a lot of time at the university, and when she wasn't there she was usually with Luke. Their wedding was only six weeks away.

"Are you wearing my clothes?" The question came from behind her.

"I don't have anything casual to wear," Camryn said.

"And is that ice cream?" Jo rounded the end of the couch and stared down at Camryn. She wore a thin knit turtleneck in a vibrant orange and slim-legged jeans and carried her vintage, fur-lined leather bomber jacket over one arm, her backpack slung on one shoulder.

"You can't have any." Camryn cuddled the bowl to her chest.

"Okay, now you're scaring me." Jo dropped onto the cushion, bouncing Camryn up and down, and laid her jacket and backpack on the floor beside her feet. "Why do you need comfy clothes? And why are you bingeing on junk food?"

Camryn scowled. "I'm not bingeing, it's one bowl. I just wanted to relax for the evening. Is that so odd?"

Jo nodded vigorously. "Yes, it is."

Just to prove she could, Camryn put the bowl on the coffee table even though there was still a spoonful of ice cream left. "Don't worry, I won't make a habit of it. I just needed a treat this evening."

"Are things getting worse at work?" Jo curled up sideways so she could lean one elbow on the back of the couch. "I wish there was more I could do to help."

"The website you're designing looks amazing." Camryn had seen a draft a few days ago, and her earlier doubts had disappeared. "Anyway, it's not work. Not really."

"Then what is it?"

The age-old instinct to shield her younger sisters wouldn't let Camryn give a straightforward answer. "It's been a long couple of months, what with Anthony and all," she said truthfully.

"I can only imagine." Jo cocked her head to one side. "What is it about time? Sometimes it flies by, and sometimes it drags its heels. The wedding seemed so close when we decided back in July to get married in December. But it is taking forever to get here."

Glad for a chance to deflect the conversation from herself, Camryn asked something she'd been dying to know. "You said Luke doesn't believe in sex outside marriage. But you're engaged. Are you guys really not"— she waved her hand around vaguely—"you know."

Jo flushed. "Yes, we're really not *you know*," she said tartly. "I'm finding it rather—liberating. And frustrating. Which is probably why the time is going so slow."

"So you've never had sex with Luke?"

The rosy tint on Jo's cheeks deepened. "That's none of your business," she said, in way that completely confirmed Camryn's suspicions that the two had been together at least once.

Just as she was about to indulge in some big sister ribbing, the phone tucked under her thigh vibrated. She checked the screen, and all lightheartedness drained away. "I've got to get this," she said, standing. "I'll be right back."

As she headed down the hall, she connected the call from Elizabeth. Another evening phone call. Her stomach rolled, queasily churning the ice cream lodged there.

"Camryn here." She shut the door to her bedroom quietly and sat on the bed. "What's going on, Elizabeth?

Have the police been in touch?"

"No, nothing from them. Don't worry about that for now."

"All right." If she'd said *any longer* instead of *for now* Camryn would have been much happier. "You needed me for something else, then?"

"I don't think you should come to Laura's performance tomorrow."

The statement was so far outside the realm of what Camryn had been expecting that she needed a moment to absorb it. "Excuse me?"

"You seem to have formed a relationship with Will and Laura," Elizabeth said in her usual brisk fashion. "I don't think it's a good idea, and you should put an end to it."

Completely puzzled, Camryn stumbled over a response. "Why? Do you think it looks bad? To the police, I mean?"

"It has nothing to do with the embezzlement." After a slight pause, Elizabeth continued. "How much has Will told you about what happened to Laura?"

"You mean how she lost her sight? He told me she got sick. Meningitis." Camryn was now thoroughly at sea.

A rough sound came through the speaker, a sound of nervousness she'd never heard from Elizabeth before—that of Elizabeth clearing her throat. "I don't know what he said about me. About my reaction to—well, to her disability. Knowing Will, he probably made it sound better than it was."

To Camryn, Elizabeth's desertion of Laura had sounded terrible, so if Will hadn't told her the full truth she couldn't imagine what it had really been like. "It was a very difficult time for everyone," she said cautiously.

"I was a bitch," Elizabeth said. "I hadn't meant to get pregnant in the first place. But once I was"—she paused, and when she spoke again her voice was low, tender—"I wanted that baby, so much. I was going to be the perfect mother. She was going to be the perfect child."

Camryn switched her phone to the other ear and wiped her palm along her thigh. "No one's perfect." What a burden to put on a tiny baby. To put on herself.

"I didn't cut myself off from Laura because of her blindness," Elizabeth said. "I couldn't bear to be reminded every day of how I had failed her. There had to have been some sign, some way to prevent…" She trailed off, a sigh breathing through the speaker. "Anyway, I've worked my way through that now. I know it wasn't anyone's fault. And I want to make it up to her."

"That's good." But what did that have to do with Camryn?

"So that's why I've decided to get back together with Will."

Camryn's breath caught in her throat. *Oh.*

"Laura deserves a complete family. Will and I will be reconciling."

CHAPTER THIRTEEN

Laura was asleep before Will had read the last page of *Goodnight Moon.* Swimming was an exhausting sensory experience for her, and that, along with the exercise it provided, always knocked her out.

Elizabeth hadn't stayed to take part in the bedtime ritual, even though she had the last few evenings. She'd gone back to her hotel shortly after dinner, perhaps reading the signs that Laura was reaching the end of her endurance and making the polite choice.

He tucked the comforter snugly around Laura's delicate shoulders and brushed a kiss on her forehead. She released a soft sigh but didn't wake. He headed for the family room, intending to catch up on work. He'd brought the Crossroads Corner file home. It was a complex project, with many layers and multiple possibilities, and he was taking great care with it. Deadline for submission was still a couple weeks away. He had time to make it perfect.

Just before Laura had drifted off, she'd asked drowsily, "Is Camryn coming tomorrow? I want her to see me do my poem."

"I don't know yet, sweetie," he'd replied. "I'm sure she'll call tonight. I'll let you know in the morning."

Laura had gone down even earlier than usual, and it wasn't yet seven-thirty. There was still plenty of time for Camryn to get in touch, but he was as anxious as Laura to find out her decision. Maybe it would be best if he reached out to her.

His eagerness to talk to her had nothing to do with the kiss they'd shared. Just as his anxiety had nothing to do with the fact she was hiding him from her family.

Nope, nothing at all.

Her cell rang multiple times, long enough for him to assume he'd be sent to voicemail. As he debated whether to leave a message, she answered.

"Hello, Will," she said. "Sorry, I was on another call."

"I can call back if you like."

"No, it's good. I was done, anyway."

The sound of her voice soaked into his bones, seeped into his veins. It loosened tensed muscles and tightened others. He wanted to stretch out the conversation, so opened with the banal. "How's your evening?"

"Fine, I suppose."

"You sound tired."

"I said I'm fine."

Except now he was paying closer attention, she didn't. She sounded strung up and wired, unlike herself. But she obviously didn't want to admit it, so he let it go. "I'm calling about tomorrow. Laura wants to know if you're coming."

"Of course I'm coming." Her tone was vehement. "Laura invited me and I'm going to be there."

"Okay, then," he replied, slightly taken aback at her intensity. Was her family giving her grief? "I couldn't help but notice Mattie seemed a little surprised when I invited you. I got the feeling you hadn't told her we've been seeing each other."

"Is that what we're doing, Will? Seeing each other? And if so, what are we? Rivals? Professional colleagues? Friends?"

He couldn't suppress a twinge of something akin to dread at her tone. "I'd like to think we're friends."

"We barely know each other."

"Well, then, I'd like to think we *could* be friends. Good friends, once we get to know each other better. And to do that we need to see each other. So, yes, I guess you could say we are seeing each other."

"I wish it were that simple."

Now he was certain Mattie had taken her to task for the invitation he had so casually made. "It *is* that simple. If someone is telling you that we can't be friends—or anything else we want to be to each other—then tell them to get their nose out of your business."

A tired chuckle rolled out of the speaker. "Don't worry, I did. That's why I'm coming tomorrow. I won't let anyone dictate how I live my life. It's just that—" She broke off.

When she didn't resume a few seconds later, he prodded gently. "What, Camryn? What's bothering you?"

"I don't want to be selfish. I don't want to mess things up for you or Laura."

"I'm not sure how you could."

"There's something I need to know. You told me once

you'd briefly considered getting back together with Elizabeth. Has that changed, especially after this week?"

His answer was firm. "No." He couldn't tell her he wanted *her* in Elizabeth's place, not yet, but maybe it was time to clarify his feelings. "Why would you even ask that, especially after last night?"

Another slight pause, then a hesitant question. "You mean because we kissed?"

"I would never kiss one woman if I was thinking of being with another. I'm not that kind of guy, and I thought you knew that."

"I suppose I do. But we were in the middle of an argument."

"We weren't arguing," he said. "I was trying to convince you I believe in you."

"I probably didn't say so before, but I appreciate it." Her tone was stronger now, without the soft wistfulness that had permeated it after her first fierceness. "And for what it's worth, I'm sorry I doubted you."

"All right, then. We've got that cleared up." He wished she was here, beside him on the couch. He wanted to put his arm around her shoulders and tuck her head under his chin and hold her. But he'd have to wait. She wasn't ready for that. "Goodnight, Camryn."

"Goodnight."

In the humming silence that followed, he allowed himself a few moments to daydream about what a future with Camryn might look like. He knew it was early days yet, and there were obstacles in his path.

But he also knew it was what he wanted.

She was what he wanted.

Laura's performance was scheduled for ten-thirty the next morning. To make up for all the time he'd been out of the office lately, Will had worked until he saw double the night before, then dropped onto his mattress and slept solidly for the few hours left in the night. Laura woke bright and cheerful like the morning person she was while he had to mainline a second cup of coffee to jump-start his brain.

He dropped her off at school and put in a couple hours with Samuel before returning. As he pulled up, he saw Elizabeth and Camryn standing in the playground. It still gave him an odd shock to see them together—a sense of disconnect and discomfort that he wasn't sure he'd ever get over.

Maybe it was the lack of sleep, but it took him a couple moments to realize they were having a rather intense discussion. Elizabeth, a few inches shorter than Camryn, was standing close and looking up at her, a pointed finger jabbing the air between them with short, vigorous movements. Camryn held herself stiff and straight, her face blank as she listened.

He climbed out of his SUV. The door closed with a loud clunk, but neither woman turned. He was too far away to decipher specific words, but Elizabeth's tone was strident. A few steps brought him near enough to understand, though, and what he heard had him stopping in his tracks.

"You need to focus on yourself right now," Elizabeth was saying, somehow sounding both reasonable and irritated. "Starting a relationship at this stage would be ill-advised. Especially with Will."

Camryn didn't back down. "You have no right to tell me who I can and can't be friends with. You're my lawyer, not my jailer."

The wrath bubbling in his chest came to a full boil when he heard Elizabeth's next statements. "As I told you yesterday, I fully intend to be a part of his life, and the life of my daughter. You have no place in that situation."

Well, *that* explained his conversation with Camryn last night. Three quick strides brought him between the two women. "Elizabeth." He snapped out her name, low but forceful. They were already drawing interested looks from the other parents arriving for the presentation and he didn't want to cause more of a scene.

They spun toward him, surprise in both their expressions. He thought he also saw relief cross Camryn's face before she recovered. But he was only peripherally aware of her reaction, as he hadn't taken his eyes from Elizabeth.

"What is going on?" he demanded.

"I was just giving Camryn some advice." She lifted her chin and met his gaze calmly.

"Telling her to stay away from me and Laura? How on earth is that your business?"

"Of course it's my business who is spending time with my daughter."

"You gave up that right years ago, when you walked away from her. The last few days have done nothing to change that." The high, hectic brands of colour staining her cheeks faded abruptly.

"It's you she's worried about," Camryn said. She cleared her throat, delicate tendons flexing, a flush rising up the slender column. "She doesn't want me spending time with *you*. Laura's just a—a bonus, I guess you could say."

Will swung his gaze back to Elizabeth. "You

definitely don't get a say in who I spend time with."

All the colour that had drained from her face came rushing back. She bit her lip and couldn't meet his eyes—all signs of nerves he'd never seen in her before.

"I don't think this is the time or the place to discuss this," she said.

"And I think you're hedging instead of answering."

Her tone lacked its usual confidence, threaded instead with a quiet desperation. "Laura's performance is about to begin. We don't want to disappoint her."

Will checked his wristwatch and bit back an oath. "No, we don't. We should get inside. But don't think this discussion is over."

Without another word, Elizabeth strode past Camryn, keeping her chin up and eyes averted. She joined two other last-minute parents at the main door of the school.

"Maybe I should go." Camryn stepped back.

He took her hand quickly. "No. Laura specifically asked you. You have to come."

She tugged at his grip, looking over her shoulder to where Elizabeth had disappeared inside. "I hate causing trouble for you."

"Trust me," he said grimly, leading her toward the school and giving her no chance to escape, "Elizabeth is the one causing trouble. If she thinks there is any chance of us getting back together, she's crazy."

"Maybe, for Laura's sake—"

He shook his head, cutting her off. "No. Not even for Laura would I get back together with her."

Inside the school, the tinny echo of many voices filled the hallway and they followed the sound down the stairs into a small assembly area in the basement.

Elizabeth had taken a seat on the far side of the room.

Will led Camryn to a pair of chairs nowhere near her. As they sat on the slippery metal seats, he leaned in and whispered in her ear, "Leave Elizabeth to me. Ignore whatever nonsense she told you." She stared at him, blue eyes huge in her still pale face. He dropped a quick kiss on her rose-pink lips, not caring if Elizabeth saw the gesture. "But don't even think about cutting me out of your life."

The touch of Will's mouth set panicked butterflies loose in Camryn's stomach. Her fingers were icy despite the heat in the closely packed room, and she was vividly aware of Elizabeth sitting a few rows away. She was regretting her defiance of Elizabeth's decree. Conflict made her queasy, and she really shouldn't be antagonizing the woman hired to keep her out of jail.

Laura's class filed in. Children attired in their Halloween best waved excitedly when they spotted family and friends in the audience. Will's daughter, dressed in a bulky dinosaur costume, her little face barely visible inside the toothy jaws, walked hand in hand with a woman with grey hair swinging in a chin-length bob. The woman scanned the audience, and when she saw Will, leaned down to speak with Laura. The little girl's face brightened, and she waved, too. Camryn's hand automatically rose to return the gesture, but she quickly dropped it into her lap when she remembered Laura couldn't see her.

Will, sitting so close she could feel the heat of his body from shoulder to hip, had no such hesitation, and waved back. The woman with Laura, whom Camryn assumed was her aide, said something to the child, who waved even harder before she joined the rest of her class, sitting cross-legged on the floor.

As the principal introduced herself and welcomed the crowd, Will leaned toward Camryn again. He whispered, "I mean it. Don't let Elizabeth influence you. She has no claim on me."

His warm breath tickled her ear and she shivered, not certain whether it was from delight or fear. She replied as quietly, "Maybe not. But she sounded sincere about making things work with you, for Laura's sake."

Camryn snuck a quick glance past his shoulder. Elizabeth was surrounded by other parents yet seemed isolated, and she couldn't help a small pang of pity.

Will noticed the direction of her gaze. "I would never keep her from Laura," he said, slightly louder as the first class was getting up to perform with an excited clattering. "But we will never be a couple again." Ducking his head so close she could feel his lips on the shell of her ear, he continued, "Because I want *you* more every time I see you."

Camryn closed her eyes, as if the darkness behind her lids would block out what she'd just heard. She was a planner, an organizer. She didn't believe in love at first sight—or even second, third, or fourth sight—so he had to be talking about nothing deeper than attraction. Also, she was barely out of a disastrous relationship that may not have broken her heart but had certainly bruised her pride and cracked her self-esteem. She wasn't ready for anything serious.

The first class finished, and Laura's group made their way to the stage. Camryn did her best to focus on the performance—a sweet and lisping presentation of a five-stanza poem—and clapped enthusiastically when it was over. For a moment she let herself imagine what it might be like if she did become a part of Will's life. Laura was a bright, intelligent child she'd be proud to call her daughter. And Camryn was only thirty-one. There was still time for her and Will to have more children, give Laura a sister or brother, maybe more than one.

Her drifting thoughts came to a crashing crescendo, much like the piano accompanying the third group of children.

What was she thinking? She was caught in the middle of a police investigation, had a dying business to resurrect, and had never seriously considered having children. Now she was planning a family with a man she'd just met?

Her face prickled with clamminess. She must have made a movement or sound, as Will looked over sharply, concern creasing his forehead. "Are you okay?"

She shook her head. "I don't feel well. It came on all of a sudden." Which wasn't a lie, even if her discomfort was emotional, not physical.

"Should I drive you home?" He half rose from his seat.

"No, you stay." She pulled him back down. "I probably just need some fresh air. I'll sneak out." She reached down to pick up her tote and the metal chair leg shrieked against the vinyl flooring. A woman in front of them shot a disapproving look over her shoulder. Camryn nodded a weak apology at the disruption and fled.

The brisk October air did help quell her rising nausea. She dropped onto a bench in the playground, welcoming the iciness of the wooden slats under her thighs. The heated dread that had suffused her body abated. Afraid Will might follow her out, she only gave herself a couple minutes to settle before escaping to her car. It was time to get back to Bendixon and Sons. She needed to work on the proposal for Crossroads Corner. It would be a good way to remind herself of all the reasons she'd come home, none of which involved a certain handsome brown-haired man who made her want things she shouldn't.

Who said he wanted her.

CHAPTER FOURTEEN

"I still think this is a ridiculous idea." Jason's baritone was gruffer than usual. "Bendixon and Sons has never done something of this scale, ever. I was open to bidding on the dentist's building since I was the one who brought it up in the first place. Look how that turned out."

"We've lost bids before," Mattie replied firmly. "That doesn't mean we never bid again. A project like Crossroads Corner could keep us solvent for years, give us a chance for the future."

"I think I side with Jason on this," Helen said. "It is awfully ambitious."

Jason was definite. "We'll never get it. It's a waste of energy."

Camryn rubbed her forehead, trying to smooth away the tension gathered behind her eyes. A tension she couldn't completely blame on the current argument. "It's mostly my energy being wasted. So I think that makes it mostly my decision."

As soon as she had returned from Laura's performance, she had gathered everyone together, determined to forget the turmoil of the morning. The four of them were now crammed around the corner of Jason's desk, studying the screen of her laptop. He had a computer, a throwback from the early 2000s that chugged like a steam locomotive when asked to do anything, which is why Camryn refused to use it. And since there was no room in *her* office—still the break room—this would have to do.

Earlier in the week she'd taken her sister and grandfather through the request for proposal for Crossroads Corner in detail, getting as much feedback as possible—Mattie enthusiastic, Jason reluctant. Over the last few days she'd spent most of her time preparing the proposal, adding her own touches and ideas, always keeping Mattie's focus on accessibility in mind. There were minimum guidelines, of course, but that didn't mean certain subtle touches couldn't be added, like they'd done with the dental office. The work had kept her up late into the night more than once, for which she'd been thankful. At least when she was concentrating on Crossroads Corner she wasn't thinking about Will. Or Elizabeth.

Or Will with Elizabeth.

She dragged her attention back to Mattie, Jason, and Helen. The latter had been so much a part of Jason's success that she couldn't be left out, although she had protested that, since she was seriously making plans to retire as well, it wasn't necessary to include her.

"Is the Kohlenburg Group bidding on this?" she asked.

"I don't know," Camryn said. "But I would assume so."

Mattie eyed her. "Will hasn't told you anything?"

"Why would he?" Jason's brows drew together into a single, bushy fringe.

Camryn glared at Mattie, who smiled innocently.

"Camryn?" Jason's gaze flicked between the sisters. Helen's face also displayed keen interest, although she remained silent. "Why would Will Danson be talking to you about Crossroads Corner?"

She drew in a deep breath. "I've seen him socially a couple of times. We have never discussed work, though."

"You're dating Will Danson?" Jason looked puzzled more than pissed off.

"No," she replied, her denial miserably weak. "Not really." *Right, like that's better.*

Jason ignored her words and correctly read her tone. "I'm not sure how I feel about that. Not that I've got anything bad to say about the young man, but he is—"

Mattie cut him off. "Our competitor. And I am sure he wouldn't let an opportunity like Crossroads Corner pass by. So what can we do to beat him to it?" Her narrowed eyes turned sly. "Are you sure you haven't talked about it?"

Now that Camryn thought about it, it was odd that she and Will *hadn't* ever talked shop. After all, that's what had brought them together. But the week had been so rife with personal issues that the fact he was a rival had almost slipped her mind.

The phone on Jason's desk rang. Helen, standing behind his chair as they clustered around the computer, hustled for the door. "I'll take it in the front office. Don't wait for me to come back. I think the three of you need to hash it out on your own." Camryn detected an air of relief in the woman's departure and couldn't blame her. She wasn't much looking forward to the next couple of minutes either and would have escaped if she could. The pounding in her temples amped up a notch.

"If we knew what *he* was planning," Mattie continued, "we would have a better idea of what to put in our proposal."

"I am *not*, repeat, *not*, going to ask Will anything about anything," Camryn said. "That wouldn't be right, even if we weren't—" She choked herself off.

"Weren't 'not dating?'" Mattie put finger quotes around the last two words.

The double negative didn't hide her meaning, and Camryn found herself confronted with the need to decide exactly what Will was to her. To figure out, right then and there, what their relationship truly meant.

"Will says we're learning about each other," she said, lifting her chin. "We're discovering if we want to know each other better. He has a little girl who seems to like me, and I don't want to hurt her by toying with her dad and then falling out of her life." *Like her mother did.* "Right now, Will is a friend. He could turn into a really good friend, or even something more. I refuse to let our professional lives poison that possibility."

The room was quiet when she stopped speaking. Jason studied his fingers, picking at the cuticle on his thumb with his index finger, his expression blank. Mattie stared openly at Camryn, wry speculation in her green eyes.

"Well," Camryn said, huffing out a breath. "I guess that's that. Can we get back to work now?" She ran her finger in a zigzag pattern on the laptop touchpad to bring the screen back to life. "I wish Jo was here, so she could give input into the computerization I've mentioned, but I'll go over that with her tonight. I began the proposal with a biography of Bendixon and Sons, emphasizing our long-standing support of Prince George and highlighting some of our bigger projects, even those going back four decades…"

Jason and Mattie remained quiet throughout the rest of the review. When she wrapped up a few minutes later, she sat back—carefully, as the chair she was using had a loose seat and a wonky wheel—and asked with trepidation, "What do you think?"

After a slight pause, during which Jason and Mattie exchanged a glance Camryn couldn't interpret, her grandfather said, "I haven't seen many such things to compare yours to, but it certainly looks impressive."

"I'm not worried about the aesthetics," Camryn said. "I can make anything *look* good. What about the numbers? Have I estimated how many workers we'd need to hire correctly? What about timelines for all the sub-contractors? Did I miss anything vital that would make us look stupid?"

"No, I think you have all that right." Jason's tone was gentle. Too gentle. It was the tone a doctor would take when announcing a fatal diagnosis.

"You still don't believe we can do this," she said flatly. More disappointed than she cared to admit, she turned to her sister. "What about you, Mattie? You want this, too. Now that you've seen the proposal, do you think it's doable? Or is it a pipe-dream and we should just lock the doors and call it a day?"

"It's a long shot. I always knew that. I also think it's the last chance we have. If we don't want to keep clinging to life with smaller individual renovations, this is the way we have to go."

"You see it has a Hail Mary pass, too." Camryn had almost forgotten about her headache, lost in the details of the presentation, but now it returned full force. "Fine. Maybe it is. But I believe we can win this."

"I'm just worried you're pinning all your hopes onto something unrealistic," Jason said. "Wouldn't it be better to try for smaller, more manageable projects?"

"I'm not ignoring those, either, but think about it. That's what you and Mattie have been doing for years now. You wanted me to come on board and I assume that's because you thought I had something new to bring to the company. We can't keep doing the same things over and over." She drew in a deep breath. "I think this is the way to go. I think you need to trust me on this."

Jason sighed. "I won't stop you from sending it in. We can worry about the details if we win it."

But we won't was blatantly implied in his tone.

"Okay then," she said, drawing a deep breath. "Abel Quinson is doing a walk-through of the site on Monday. Although the deadline to submit is end of that week, I want it in by Wednesday at the latest. I'll fine-tune it after the site visit, but unless you have any further concerns, this is the framework we'll be presenting."

Jason and Mattie nodded.

Will couldn't forget—or ignore—the scene at the schoolyard. Camryn seemed convinced that Elizabeth had plans to reunite their family, and while he was dubiously pleased she wanted to spend more time with Laura, he had absolutely no desire to return to any form of intimacy with Elizabeth himself.

They'd arranged to take Laura out of school as soon as the Halloween performance was done. Will had convinced Elizabeth to spend the afternoon quietly at home, and insisted she get Laura to nap. He was worried that she was reaching her social saturation point after her busy week, and they still had plans to go trick-or-treating that evening. So as soon as Laura was excused by her teacher, he drove them both to the house and left them there while he went back to work.

He returned around five o'clock, skipping out slightly early despite Samuel's raised eyebrow. Elizabeth, never one to do much cooking when they'd been together, had made a simple meal of pasta and sauce. With Camryn's comments hovering in the forefront of his mind, he watched her throughout the meal. She didn't seem overly affectionate to himself, and treated Laura with calm casualness, much more relaxed than earlier in the week. Yet he still detected a certain stiffness and a lack of warmth. It was subtle, though, and he was sure their daughter didn't notice.

Of course, that could also have been because she was vibrating with excitement for trick-or-treating.

"Can I go get my costume, Daddy?" she asked, after fidgeting with the noodles on her plate but eating few of them.

"You haven't finished your meal," Elizabeth said.

"I'm too excited to eat," Laura said. "Last year, Nadine got a pillowcase full of candy, and I want to get lots, too."

Knowing it was no use battling over a few strands of spaghetti, Will piled Laura's plate onto his own. "Remember the rules—no eating anything until I go through it, and you can choose a few of your favourites but the rest goes into the candy stash."

"Daddy, I know." She dragged out the last word, rolling her eyes.

His heart clutched. What would she be like ten years from now? A fifteen-year old Laura couldn't be imagined. He answered through the tightness in his chest. "Okay, go get your costume."

She slid off the chair and made her way rapidly to her room.

As Elizabeth began to clear the table, she glanced over at him.

"So, have I passed?" Her tone was light, yet he detected a hint of vulnerability. "She napped just like you instructed. And I didn't think you'd mind if I made dinner."

"I haven't been testing you," he said.

"Are you sure?" One elegantly shaped eyebrow quirked in silent disagreement.

When he'd uttered the words, he'd thought he was telling the truth. But then again—hadn't he been watching her all week, waiting for her to fail?

"I've been in enough courtrooms to know when my performance is being critiqued," Elizabeth said.

Any guilt he might have felt was wiped out by that statement. "Is that what this week has been? A performance? You've only been playing at being a mother?"

She blinked, and he saw the moment she realized what she'd said. "I didn't mean it like that. It was a poor choice of words."

Will had never seen Elizabeth in a courtroom, but he knew her reputation for scalpel-like arguments. If she was struggling with her word choices maybe she was more sensitive to the situation than he'd thought.

"It's just that"—she paused, her gaze flicking over his shoulder then determinedly back to him—"I don't think I've done what I set out to do yet."

Before Will could ask her exactly what she meant, Laura's quick steps pattered down the hall toward them. "I need help," she announced, her dinosaur costume dragging behind her. "Can you help me, Mommy?"

"Of course," Elizabeth answered quickly. "It's cold outside, though. Let's put your jacket and snowpants on first."

As she helped Laura into her costume, Will tidied the kitchen. He could tell Elizabeth was trying, but if Camryn was right and she wanted to get back together with Will, it didn't matter what she did. It wasn't going to happen.

The cloudy sky made the evening dark as midnight. Jack-o-lanterns glowed bright orange on doorsteps, and huge inflatable witches and goblins bobbed on their tethers. Groups of children giggled and chattered, running from house to house with their spoils.

At the first door, Will had to encourage Laura to knock, to give the traditional greeting, to say thank you. By the third house she was more comfortable, but it wasn't long before he could see her getting overwhelmed.

"Do you think you've gone far enough?" he asked as they reached the end of the street. "We can do a few more houses on the way home, if you like, but your bag is pretty full."

"I want to get more candy," Laura said, a mulish frown creasing her brow.

"Your dad is right," Elizabeth said. "It's getting late, so we should go home. I have to go back to my hotel and pack before I leave tomorrow."

Laura's frown deepened. "Do you have to go, Mommy?" she asked. "I want you to stay."

Recognizing the signs of an incipient meltdown, and unwilling to have this conversation on the street, Will opened his mouth to soothe, but Elizabeth spoke first.

"I wish I could, but I live in Vancouver. I have to go."

Laura came to a full stop. "I don't want you to live in Vancouver. I want you to live with us." Her glare blazed from under the floppy dinosaur head that was the hood of the costume.

"I have to go back tomorrow," Elizabeth said, "but I'll come for another visit, I promise."

"I don't want you to go!" Laura's voice rose. A passing adult gave Will a sympathetic glance. "I want you to live here!"

"Let's go home, and we'll talk there," Will said.

"I want Mommy to stay! I don't want her to go!" Laura shrieked.

Will picked her up, her little body stiff with fury and frustration. She drummed her fists on his chest, sobbing loudly. Once they were in the house, it was many minutes before she calmed down.

Throughout the tantrum, Elizabeth sat silent at the far end of the couch. Whenever his attention lifted from their daughter, he saw her, calm and remote. But now he wondered if that smooth exterior was a façade, hiding emotions she was embarrassed to share.

Once Laura had quieted down, Elizabeth moved closer. She gently brushed her hand on Laura's head, smoothing the tousled brown strands.

"I'm sorry you're sad that I'm leaving. But I'd really like to come back, if you want me."

"Soon? Will you come back soon?" Laura's voice

hitched, her breathing still uneven after her crying jag. "I really want you to." She reached out and Elizabeth caught her small hand and held it. "Could you come next week?"

Elizabeth's laugh held a sober edge. She didn't look at Will, but he could sense her tension. "I think that might be a little too soon. Maybe in December. That's only a few weeks away."

Joy and anticipation glowed in Laura's red-rimmed eyes. "What about Christmas? Could you come for Christmas?" She cocked her head. "Daddy? Could Mommy come for Christmas? We could all open presents together."

He wouldn't deny Laura anything if he could help it. But he couldn't bring himself to commit to something so fraught with potential turmoil. "We'll see," he hedged. "Your mom and I will talk about it." He didn't miss Elizabeth's wry, sidelong glance. "For now, why don't you let your mom give you a bath and put you to bed."

It was a sign of how much energy the tantrum had used up that Laura agreed to this without demur. Almost as exhausted as his daughter, Will slouched down on the couch and waited for Elizabeth to return. The day already seemed excruciatingly long, and he still had the unpleasant task of disabusing Elizabeth of any fanciful notions about their relationship. He couldn't let her leave without making sure she understood his feelings.

He started when the couch cushions dipped, his arms and legs jerking reflexively.

"Sorry," Elizabeth said. "I didn't mean to scare you. I didn't realize you were asleep."

"Just dozed off, I guess." Will rubbed his hands briskly over his face. "Is she out?"

Elizabeth nodded. "She didn't make it through one

story." She paused, then said, "I want to thank you for this week. You could have made things difficult for me, and you didn't."

"I did it for Laura, not for you," he said frankly.

"I know." An expression crossed her face that on a less forceful personality Will would have described as wistful.

"We need to talk about this morning," he said, diving right in. "About what you said to Camryn. You realize that was completely out of line."

"Do you think so?" She shifted so she could face him directly. "At dinner on Monday, it was pretty obvious she hadn't told you about her situation."

"There was no reason she should have." He defended Camryn automatically, although he couldn't deny a small kernel of frustration. He knew it was unrealistic of him to wish she *had* shared voluntarily, instead of being forced into it. But still, he wished.

"When I first met her, directly after the accusations were levelled at her ex, it seemed to me she was upset more on a personal level than because of the embezzlement. No one gets over that kind of treachery quickly. She's on the rebound, and you shouldn't be bringing that toxicity into Laura's life."

His fingers spasmed, flexing and releasing. How had he ended up on the defensive? He'd meant to tell her, firmly and decisively, to mind her own business, and now he was flailing to keep his mental balance. "Don't you think you're exaggerating just a bit? Camryn is not toxic."

She leaned forward and he caught a waft of her musky perfume. "I know you don't think highly of me for taking this long to come back into Laura's life."

He opened his mouth to reply, then snapped it shut.

There was no way he could respond with kindness and understanding. It wasn't the coming back that bothered him. It was that she'd left in the first place. Maybe Elizabeth had been in a bad emotional state at the time. Maybe she had thought she was doing the right thing.

But she had been wrong. She should have stuck it out, put Laura's needs ahead of her own.

"I must have underestimated your disapproval," Elizabeth said, "since you can't even talk about it."

"It doesn't matter if I disapprove or not," he said. "You made your decision. It's too late to fix it now."

"Is it?"

Out of the corner of his eye he could see her long, elegant fingers clenching as her hand rested on her thigh.

"Is there nothing I can do to heal what I did?" Despite the appeal in the words, her tone carried only curiosity. "To be given a second chance to have a family?"

"Just how do you see this playing out, Elizabeth? Your work is in Vancouver. Laura and I live here. We're not moving back, not for the foreseeable future. Are you going to parachute in every couple of months?" He tried to match her calm, but found himself gritting his teeth.

"I'm thinking of making some changes," she said quietly.

He stared at her. "Don't tell me you're thinking of moving to Prince George. I won't believe you."

"It doesn't matter what you believe. If moving here is what it takes to make it up to Laura, to you, then I'd seriously consider it."

He was growing to love the town, but he couldn't see Elizabeth fitting in. Perhaps he was doing both her—and the town—an injustice, but he simply couldn't see it.

The silence between them hung for long moments.

After a minute, she sighed.

"I guess I'll get going," she said, rising gracefully to her feet. "I didn't expect you to kill the fatted calf, but I had hoped for some sign of encouragement."

"Elizabeth…" His mind was blank, unable to grapple with the bombshell she had dropped. "We'll talk," he finally said. "We'll talk later."

Because no matter what, she was Laura's mother. And he would always be grateful that she had given him his daughter to love.

CHAPTER FIFTEEN

Camryn dressed with defiant care for the walk-through of the Crossroads Corner site. Some women might not approve, but remembering Abel's quiet yet obvious appreciation of her looks during their previous meetings, she had no compunction using them to her advantage. And if it made her think of how Anthony had used his charm to hide his criminality, she pushed it aside. The two strategies were completely different.

It wasn't the motivation behind her fashion choices that betrayed her, though. It was the fact she completely underestimated the fall-by-the-calendar-but-might-as-well-be-winter weather.

Goosebumps rippled from knee to thigh as the wind whipped under her skirt. She wrapped her trench coat tighter around her body in a vain search for warmth. Icy feathers brushed the nape of her neck and she wished she'd worn a woolen scarf instead of the light silk one she'd chosen. Wished she'd worn a hat, and gloves, and a parka.

The stiletto heels of her boots sank into the gravel and she staggered. "Oopsy," Abel said playfully, grabbing her elbow to steady her. "Careful there."

"Thanks," she said, smiling through teeth clenched from both cold and embarrassment. "Please, go on."

Abel released her cautiously, as if expecting her to topple over again. She straightened her shoulders and nodded.

He turned back to the group and continued his orientation, opening the razor thin laptop he carried and flipping the keyboard out of the way so he could use the touch screen easier. Bringing up an architectural rendering, he said, "Crossroads Corner will be an upscale community, with two blocks of apartments featuring high-end finishings and modern design, as well as services such as a restaurant, spa, gym, and daycare."

As he spoke, he moved slowly across the huge, empty lot, followed by his small entourage. Camryn had been disconcerted by how many people had shown up for the tour. She'd developed tunnel vision, thinking it would only be the Kohlenburg Group and Bendixon and Sons competing for the contract. A number of other companies also appeared to be interested, and why shouldn't they be? It would be a major coup for anyone.

The knowledge made the frozen fist in her stomach tighten.

The one person who wasn't there, the one she had expected to see, was Will.

I want you more every time I see you, he had said last Friday. Today would have been the first time they had seen each other since then.

Did she want him to want her more? Is that why she had hoped to see him today? Did she want him?

Thank god no one could hear her thoughts. They'd think she was a dithering idiot.

Not that there was no representative of the Kohlenburg Group here. On the opposite side of the circle stood Samuel Antoski. She had seen him at the Kohlenburg office the day she and Mattie had met Will there but had only learned who he was today when he'd introduce himself to Abel.

His name had struck her like a bolt. *This* was the person who had snooped around, looking for ways to discredit her.

Like Camryn, he was dressed with cosmopolitan flair, looking no more suited for a construction site than she did. But his shoes, while trendy, were designed for warmth, and his stylish coat a heavy wool that she deeply envied at the moment.

The tour wound its way to the far side of the lot. "Residents will have priority access to all services as part of their strata fees," Abel said. "It will be the first complex of its kind in Prince George. Others have been constructed for retirees and seniors, but none for our target demographic of twenty-five to forty-five years old."

The lot was on the corner of two busy streets, next to a small shopping centre with a popular grocery store and backing onto a heavily treed green space. It was easy to see the potential, and she knew Charette Architects had chosen the site wisely. An elementary school was just down the road, with a high school close by. On the way here, she had passed a retail area where new stores were being built. It seemed obvious the city was growing in this direction. Crossroads Corner was a prime location.

She felt a frisson of excitement. Right now, she stood in a gravel pit, surrounded by flimsy orange plastic fencing, yet she could see exactly how it would be. If she could secure it for Bendixon and Sons, it wouldn't just be a financial success. It would be a creative challenge, one where she could really prove her worth.

"Does anyone have any questions?" Abel swung his laptop shut and surveyed the group with a bright smile.

Camryn had dozens, but was afraid her inexperience would show, so she kept quiet and let the other attendees take the lead. She was smugly pleased when Samuel asked one of the questions she had wanted answered. Maybe she wasn't as far out of her depth as she felt.

The tour broke up, and people scattered to their waiting vehicles. Abel escorted Camryn to her car. Samuel walked with them, and she noticed an SUV with the Kohlenburg Group logo on the side parked just behind her mother's sedan.

"I look forward to reading your proposal," Abel said, ignoring Samuel to focus on Camryn. "I'm especially interested in any accessibility ideas you may have, like you did with the dental office."

"I think you'll be very pleased with what we've put together for you," she said. Conscious of Samuel standing just behind Abel's shoulder, she said, "I know we may not be the biggest firm bidding on this project, but we have a long-standing reputation for excellent work, and have been in this community for four decades. We understand what this town needs, and Crossroads Corner would definitely fill a void. We would love to be a part of it."

Wind whipped around them. A skiff of snow had fallen overnight, dry, and powdery, and it blew like dust, curling around Camryn's knees, snaking under the hem of her thin skirt.

She wasn't the only one to feel the cold. Abel shuddered and rubbed his hands together. "Well, enough of this," he said. "Time to get back to my office. I'll speak to you later, I'm sure." He smiled at Camryn and turned away, acknowledging Samuel as he headed for his own car parked further down the road.

His departure left Camryn facing Samuel with no buffer. He studied her with his head tipped to one side, and she raised an eyebrow, going for lofty but afraid she only pulled off pained. Her face was so chilled she was surprised she *could* change her expression.

"You look uncomfortable," Samuel said, breaking the silence between them. "A little bit frozen, in fact."

It was no use denying it. "Yes." With determined unconcern she lowered her head and searched in her tote for her keys. "Definitely time for me to get going as well."

He held up one hand, stopping her move toward the car. "Will tells me you were upset when you found out I'd been asking questions about you."

She was really cold. And she really didn't want to get into this now. "It's fine," she said. "I understand why you did."

"It's my job to look out for the Kohlenburg Group. Anything that could give us an advantage over a competitor—" He shrugged.

She answered with a shrug of her own. "I get it. You were just doing what you thought you needed to." She still hadn't quite forgiven Will for not telling her, but that was a different issue.

Samuel tucked his hands into his pockets, looking prepared to stand and talk all afternoon. "The woman I talked to told me quite firmly you had nothing to do with the embezzlement."

Camryn suppressed a shiver and resisted the urge to hunch over in a futile effort to conserve her body heat. If he could stand the chill, so could she. "Sandie told you the truth."

"I'm sure she believed what she was saying. I'm still not convinced."

Maybe it was the cold, but it took a minute for his skepticism to sink in. When it did, she glared at him. "I don't care if you're not convinced. It's the truth, and what you think does not matter to me at all."

"I just don't see how you couldn't have known," he mused. "You were living with the guy. How could you *not* have?"

"Easy," she snapped, righteous heat flooding her cheeks, warming her chest. "I trusted him. He didn't spend extravagantly. We shared expenses on everything. There were no signs."

"If you want to run a business," he said, "any business, you have to be a good judge of character. You might want to work on that."

She gaped at him. His expression was noncommittal, despite his sharply worded advice.

"I know you're trying to keep your grandfather's business going," he continued. "Your loyalty is admirable. But Crossroads Corner is not a project for a novice. You'd be taking on more than either your company or yourself is able to handle. You've already lost one venture to us. Don't waste your time again. Look for deals that are better suited to your abilities."

Before she could collect her thoughts and deliver the retort such an insult deserved, he spun on his heel and strode away. Moments later she was standing alone in the bitter breeze. Shaking with cold and anger and nerves, she dropped into the driver's seat of her mother's sedan and turned on the ignition. Setting the heater as high as it would go and blasting the fan, she waited for the interior to warm up.

Samuel had basically reiterated what Jason had already told her. But instead of depressing her, Samuel's words had fired her hope.

Why would Samuel care if Bendixon and Sons was bidding, unless he thought they had a chance to win? If he truly thought there was no possibility of their success, he would have ignored her. Instead, he'd gone out of his way to dissuade her from presenting her proposal.

Maybe she was being delusional. But thinking that Samuel saw her as a threat was better for her morale than thinking he pitied her.

She put the car in gear and pulled into traffic.

That was her story and she was sticking to it. No matter what.

Will came out of the break room with a fresh cup of coffee as Samuel swept into the office. "How was the walk-through?" he said.

Cold clung to the other man's coat. The tips of his ears and nose were red. "Other than frigid and dirty? Fine." He shook out of his coat and hung it neatly in the closet. No tossing it over the back of his chair like Will usually did. "Sorry I'm running a bit late. I'll be right in. Go ahead and call Wayne."

Will left Samuel making a reviving cup of tea and carried his own mug to his office.

Normally, Will would have been the one to attend the

tour. But he'd lost a lot of time in the office last week due to Elizabeth's visit, and used that as an excuse to send Samuel, who was perfectly competent to handle it, but regarded fresh air as unnatural to man. Especially cold fresh air.

Missing the tour had nothing to do with the fact that Camryn would be there, he told himself. He hadn't seen or talked to her since Friday, when he'd been blatant about his intentions regarding her. Looking back, he thought he might have been a tad too direct. He had decided to give her a little space before bringing it up again.

He wasn't changing his mind. Just his tactics.

At his desk, he chose speaker on his phone and pushed memory dial. Normally they would have already had their Monday conference call with head office, but Wayne had sent an email Friday postponing it to the afternoon.

Just as their boss answered, Samuel came in, clutching his teacup in both hands with his tablet tucked under his arm, and arranged himself in the visitor's chair.

"Thanks for being able to reschedule." Wayne's voice crackled through the speaker.

"No problem," Will said. "I hope things went well with Conrad."

Conrad Kohlenburg, Wayne's uncle, had started the company decades ago, and while he had stepped back from day-to-day operations, he still owned a sizable chunk of the business and carried a lot of influence. When he asked for a meeting, it happened, no matter what.

"When he called me on Friday," Wayne said, a smile in his voice, "he left me hanging, the old rascal. Wouldn't tell me what it was about. My imagination ran rampant over the weekend."

"Sounds like it wasn't all bad news." Will swivelled

gently in his chair. Samuel appeared to have recovered from his outdoor adventure and was frowning at his tablet, tapping rapidly with one finger. He wouldn't be missing any of the conversation, however. Whoever said men couldn't multitask had never met Samuel.

"It's not. In fact, it's very good news, and especially for the Prince George branch."

That pulled Samuel's attention away from his screen. "Do we get details?"

"Conrad was having lunch with cronies last week. One of them has a connection with the mining industry. Rumours are that several new mines will be launched over the next few years in Northern British Columbia, and Prince George is smack dab in the middle of them. New jobs bring new people, and new people want places to live. He already likes what you're doing up there, and he wants you to expand."

Will's heart beat so heavily it blocked his lungs with every thump. "That's great news," he said, although his excitement was tempered by panic. He'd barely gotten comfortable with what they were doing now. And if they won the Crossroads Corner bid... His thoughts whirled.

"We don't need to recreate the wheel, though," Wayne added. "Conrad wants you to look at existing businesses, suss out which ones would be the best to approach regarding acquisition. We get their existing client base, increase our influence, and position ourselves for upcoming growth."

Will was still having trouble absorbing the news, but Samuel stared at the phone as if he could read Wayne's expressions through the line.

"I know the perfect place to start," he said with satisfaction. "An established firm is having some financial difficulties, but nothing good management and a better business plan won't solve. They have a solid reputation but haven't kept up with the times."

It took Will a moment to see where Samuel was going. Before he could say anything—whether in accord or dissent, he wasn't sure—Samuel continued.

"Bendixon and Sons."

CHAPTER SIXTEEN

Camryn shifted, her back and butt aching. The ancient dinette chair and table in the break room was anything but ergonomically designed. If she asked Jason for a better place to work he'd probably accommodate her somehow—there was room in his office if they squeezed together. But she wanted to be *invited* into his office, not force herself on him. If he didn't think of it, she wasn't going to mention it.

She still had *some* pride, after all.

Propping her elbow on the table and her chin in her palm, she scrolled desultorily through various websites, searching—for the second time that day—for other requests for proposal. The Crossroads Corner bid had been sent in today, two days before the deadline, just as planned, polished up as bright and shiny as a new penny, and now all she could do was wait for the decision. In the meantime, however, she'd keep searching for other ways to put money in Bendixon and Sons' coffers.

Her eyes drifted to the bookmark bar on her web browser. Specifically, to the heading *Kohlenburg Group.*

Since Monday, Will had texted her a couple of times. Breezy, casual messages asking how she'd survived the tour (*Samuel said it was frigid out*) and saying Laura was asking about her *(She wants to know when you can come to dig for dinosaurs with us again).*

Nothing about wanting her. Nothing about seeing her.

She'd replied to his texts, trying to match his tone, but hadn't initiated any contact. She still needed time. Time to think about what *she* wanted.

"Helen!" Jason's shout, a few degrees politer than a bellow, sounded from the next room. Camryn winced, not yet reconciled to this gruffly casual way of communicating. His phone was right there. Why couldn't he just *call* her?

He shouted again. "Helen!"

"Hold your horses, I'm coming." The tap-tap of Helen's heels grew louder then faded away, but Camryn didn't look away from her screen.

A few minutes later she realized she could no longer hear the murmur of Jason and Helen's voices. She listened closely. Other than the low hum of air blowing from the furnace vent over her head she could hear—nothing. She couldn't have missed Helen returning to the front office. Pushing her chair back, not caring about the screech it made, she took the few steps necessary to reach the door to Jason's office.

It was like a tableau in a stage comedy. Jason sat at his desk, Helen at his shoulder. They'd obviously been studying something on the computer screen, and just as obviously hadn't wanted to be disturbed. Their expressions were matching images of surprise and dismay—wide eyes, rounded mouths, pale cheeks.

"You two look like I've caught you planning to rob a bank." Camryn tried to keep her tone cheerful, but something in their furtiveness had the hair rising on the back of her neck. "That might be just what we need. Can I help?"

Jason and Helen broke from their trances. They shared a wordless glance that spoke of their many years together, years spent almost as close as a married couple. Helen nodded, and Jason's shoulders slumped.

"I was hoping we wouldn't have to tell you about this," he said, "but I guess it's only fair."

Her hands grew damp and icy, as if she'd dipped them in a fresh mountain stream. "What's going on?"

Jason drew in a deep breath, let it out on a huff. "We've reached a crisis point," he said bluntly. "Helen and I agree that we're only a couple weeks away from a serious cash flow issue. We're going to have to apply for a loan to get us through the next little while. It's either that or go without salaries."

Camryn shook her head. She couldn't have heard correctly. "I'm sorry, what?"

"Don't make me say it again, girl." Jason's bushy grey brows lowered.

Keeping her back straight, as if balancing a book on her head, she advanced further into the room. It was very odd, walking when you couldn't feel your feet. She placed herself gently into the chair on the near side of Jason's desk.

"I went through the books," she said. "I know things are tight, but I thought we'd have several months before it became dire." Long enough for her to jump-start new work. "What about the dental office contract?"

Jason shook his head. "It won't come soon enough."

Grasping for any lifeline, she asked, "What about your line of credit? You must have one."

"I've been dipping into that already. It's not a big one, only meant to tide us over if someone's slow to pay or we have extra supplies to buy."

If only they'd won the *whole* contract for the dentist office, not just the sop that Abel had thrown them. Guilt settled on her shoulders.

"Will the bank even give you a loan?" she asked, proud her voice was calm. Her heart thudded so heavily it vibrated through her like the deep bass of a stereo.

In jerky movements, Helen pulled down the hem of her emerald green cardigan, smoothed the sleeves. "Of course they will," she said. "We've been good customers for years. It's not the first time we've had to take out a short-term loan. They know we're good for it."

Some of the anxiety pulsing through Camryn's veins eased. "That's good then," she said. "Will you call them now?"

Jason nodded. "Right away. I suppose I should tell Mattie, too."

"I can do that." She didn't want him to put off calling the bank. Her credit card minimum payments—*which aren't too minimum,* she thought in despair—were due soon. Not getting a pay cheque was not an option for her.

Will never intended to let nearly a week go by without seeing Camryn. But after Wayne's announcement of the expansion plans on Monday, and Samuel's enthusiastic suggestion of Bendixon and Sons, he'd delayed, and delayed again. He'd erased more texts than he'd sent, worried he'd somehow give away the fact her company might soon be under siege.

While calling himself a two-time traitor for not being able to protect Camryn *and* do his job.

He waited until he was on his way home from work on Wednesday to call her. Before leaving the parking lot, he used his hands-free system to connect to her cell, restlessly tapping the steering wheel as he drove.

"Hi, Will."

The sound of his name spoken in her warm, elegant tones had his toes curling in anticipation.

Trying not to sound like a drooling idiot, he said, "I was hoping you'd have time for a late dinner tonight." He had decided his best plan was a straightforward attack.

"It's a work night."

He chuckled at the primness of her voice. "It's just dinner, Camryn, not a night of carousing and drinking. Corinne can come back after I give Laura her meal and put her to bed. That's usually done by eight o'clock. I thought we could meet at Borealis around eight-thirty." For once, he hadn't brought any work home with him.

"I don't know if that's a good idea."

"Why not?" he challenged, even though he could think of numerous reasons why without breaking a sweat. Especially if Samuel had his way regarding the buyout. But he couldn't let that stop his pursuit. That was business. This was personal.

A sigh sounded through the speakers and he pictured her nibbling on her lip.

"Time's up," he said, pulling to a stop at a traffic light. "If you can't answer quicker than that, I'm not going to believe your excuse anyway."

"I was trying to decide which *excuse"*—her sarcasm was clear—"to use first. The one where I shouldn't get between you and Elizabeth, or the one where I feel like I'm betraying my family."

"Camryn—"

"Or what about the one where we're competing for the same contract?"

"Stop." His voice was sharper than he intended, but she'd started to sound panicky. "We've been through this before."

Her reply was quiet, subdued. "What about the one where I really, really want to have dinner with you. But I really, really don't want to want that?"

A horn sounded angrily behind him, and he realized the light had turned green. "It's just dinner," he coaxed, pulling into a service station, and parking next to the air hose. Her confession gave him badly needed hope and furthered his resolve. "Two friends who might turn into something more, sharing a meal and conversation. No strings, no expectations." "No drama?"

"No drama. We'll only talk about safe subjects like the weather. And music. What's your favourite season? Do you like jazz?"

"Summer. And no."

"Well, I guess those topics are out then," he teased. "Don't worry, I'll think of something."

He was fairly certain he heard a snort, and when she next spoke she sounded lighter, less burdened. "Fine," she said. "You win. I'll meet you there."

"Excellent," he said, satisfaction warming his chest. "Until later, Camryn."

Camryn had come to the very sad conclusion that she had no friends. Despite what he had said, she didn't count Will.

She rarely thought about kissing her friends—when she had any—and she couldn't seem to stop thinking about kissing Will. Ergo, he was not her friend.

She had no one to talk to about all the screwed-up things in her life. No one to pat her shoulder and tell her it would all work out. No one to listen to her bitch and moan, all while agreeing that life really sucked sometimes.

Jo and Mattie had fed her wine and chocolate when she'd first arrived. But now all Mattie wanted to discuss was the business, which only depressed Camryn further, and Jo was so involved in wedding plans Camryn didn't want to bother her. Her friendship with Sandie Larsen had mainly been during working hours, and there was no one else in Vancouver she could call or Skype or text. Not since the Anthony fiasco, anyway. She had learned that nasty little fact within hours of his arrest.

These thoughts circled in her head as she showered, shaved her legs, styled her hair, and put on her makeup. They distracted her so much that it was only when she spritzed her "sexy-night" perfume into her cleavage that she surfaced enough to stare at her reflection in horror.

She was preparing for this dinner as if it were a date. A real, honest-to-goodness-maybe-we'll-end-up-in-bed date. Her own mind had played her false. Had taken advantage of her inattention to proclaim, "Hey, Will, get a load of this!"

With a groan, she closed the lid of the toilet, sank onto its cool, smooth surface and dropped her head in her hands.

No matter how much she denied it, no matter how the

timing could not be worse, she was attracted to Will. Deeply. Viscerally. Sexually.

She was honest enough to recognize loneliness was part of that attraction. Ever since Marcus had returned, she'd seen little of Mattie outside of work, and Jo was a will-of-the-wisp, leaving the house before Camryn and returning late in the evening, if at all. But Will—

Will sought her out. He wanted to be with her, even when she tried to shove him away. He had welcomed her into his home, invited her to spend time with his daughter, had defended her against Elizabeth.

He made her feel—she couldn't settle on a word. Instead, she stood and leaned over the vanity, peering into the mirror to check her makeup closely. With a defiant nod, she told her reflection, "He likes me. I like him. I'm going to stop feeling guilty about this, damn it."

At eight-twenty she pulled into the parking lot of Borealis. She'd never been to the restaurant before, but the location confirmed her hopes—and fears.

She was on a real date with Will.

Set on the banks of the Nechako River, the restaurant celebrated the dichotomy of Prince George—casual elegance found on the same road leading to two pulp and paper mills. Even as she sat there, a huge tractor-trailer loaded with wood chips rumbled briskly past. But the cedar-sided building was nestled romantically among autumn-denuded apple trees, planted in precise lines next to the silvery water, and it was easy to forget the multibillion-dollar industry going on out of sight around the corner. As she approached the arched doorway, discreet lighting cast dreamy pools onto the red brick of the path, and she could hear the rippling rush of the river's shallow depths.

The hostess took her coat and escorted her to a table for two near the window. As she waited for Will, she read the menu with interest. It was exhausting, being frugal all the time. With a recklessness reminiscent of her time with Anthony pre-embezzlement, she debated between arrabbiata with prawns or the dry-aged sirloin. She was driving, so could save some money by not ordering wine.

The soft swoosh of the outer door opening was followed by the quiet greeting of the hostess. The hair on Camryn's arms rose and her stomach squirmed in anticipation.

Will wore tan trousers, a white dress shirt, and had kept his worn leather jacket on. His eyes glowed when he saw her, their friendly brown darkening with something she hoped was appreciation.

She smiled at him and that something deepened, heated.

"Hi, Camryn," he said. His voice, bass and gravelly as always, wrapped around her, stropping like raw silk against her skin.

"Hey," she replied, breathless.

He took the seat across from her, his long legs brushing against hers as he tucked them under the table. She'd worn knee-high black boots with a red skirt that stopped a few inches above where they ended, and the fabric of his trousers rubbed softly against her bare skin. Suddenly she felt shy. She dropped her gaze to the cutlery on the table, smoothing its lustrous surface with unsteady fingers.

The hostess assured Will their server would be right with them as Camryn opened the menu blindly. A broad fingertip appeared at the top edge and pulled the heavy leather folder down. Forced to look at him, her mouth dried at his wide grin and laughing eyes.

"Don't go all girlie on me now," he said.

Firming her chin, she said, "I don't know what you mean."

"Forget all the reasons you *think* you shouldn't be here. You're here now, so let's enjoy ourselves."

She sighed, deliberately releasing the tension in her neck and shoulders. Allowing the menu to lay on the table, she relaxed in her chair and said what she'd been thinking ever since she'd first met him.

"Do you try for that messy but handsome look, or does it just come naturally?"

"Handsome, hey?" He raised an eyebrow.

She waved a hand. "Don't let it go to your head. I honestly want to know, though. How long did it take you to get ready tonight?"

"I don't know, ten minutes? I showered, combed my hair, got dressed. How long should it take?"

She smiled and shook her head. "That's what I would have guessed. It's not fair." Anthony had often taken longer than herself to prepare for an evening out. She'd teased him about it once, and he'd sulked for the whole night. She had a feeling that sulking was not something Will did.

"What do you mean, it's not fair?"

She was not going to tell him she'd primped for more than an hour. "That you can look so good in so little time."

"I'm going to take that as a compliment." His smile was a little smug, but she could cut him a break on that. After all, she was the one doing the flattering. "I suppose you're used to swankier guys. I understand from Samuel that the interior design firm you worked for was pretty high-class."

She stiffened at the mention of Samuel. "Yes, it was," she replied, telling herself not to feel defensive. Will knew almost everything about the scandal, and yet here they were. "A man who cares about his looks isn't automatically a jerk, you know."

"That's not what I meant." He was about to go on when the server appeared.

"My name's Patti and I'll be your server tonight," she said, smiling perkily at Will. "Can I get you something to drink? We're featuring a number of lovely wines from our own vineyard, as well others from around British Columbia."

"Camryn?" Will asked.

"I'll have club soda with a wedge of lime," she said. "I'm driving and even one glass is too much for me."

"All right then." Will closed the wine list and handed it back to the server. "I'll have water as well. Just flat is fine."

With an air of disappointment Patti nodded and left them alone again.

"She's seeing a big tip vanish into thin air," Camryn said. "We don't exactly look like big spenders, ordering soft drinks."

"I don't feel right ordering alcohol if you're not. But to get back to what I was saying before—" He crossed his arms on the table and leaned in.

He wasn't an extraordinarily large man, but for some reason he seemed to take up more than his fair share of the oxygen around Camryn. She breathed deeply through her nose.

"I didn't mean people who care what they look like are jerks," he said. "I just never got caught up in that whole style thing. I was raised on a small farm on Gabriola

Island. Not exactly urbanite material."

"You were? I assumed you were Vancouver born and raised. Or at least the Lower Mainland area."

"My parents still live on the island. They weren't that happy when we moved here, as it makes it tougher to visit Laura."

Patti was back with their drinks. "Would you like to order any appetizers?" she asked hopefully.

Feeling she owed the young woman something for the cheapness of her drink, Camryn replied, "I'll have the bruschetta."

"Excellent!" The bounce was back in her posture. "And you, sir?"

"I'm sorry, I haven't even looked at the menu. What was your second choice?" he asked Camryn.

"Probably the calamari."

"I'll take that." He smiled at Patti.

She beamed. "I'll be back in a few minutes to take your entrée order." She zoomed off.

"She makes me feel old," Camryn said. "All that energy and enthusiasm."

"Now, there's a trap if I ever heard one." His eyes crinkled at the corners. "Almost the same danger level as *does my butt look good in these pants*."

Camryn laughed, her heart feeling lighter than it had in weeks. "Sorry. Not trying to scare you off."

He reached across the table and stroked one finger up and down the knuckles of her hand as she held her glass. "I don't scare that easily."

Giving into temptation, she released her hold on her drink and turned her hand over. Will accepted her wordless invitation and linked his fingers with hers. His hand was warm and comforting. She couldn't remember the last time she'd held hands on a date.

She said abruptly, "I'll be thirty-two on my next birthday." It suddenly seemed important to tell him.

It didn't appear to shock him. "Hey, me, too. When?"

"February."

"September for me. I guess I'm dating an older woman."

She laughed at the silly gleam in his eyes. Why such a simple exchange made her feel as if she was teetering on the edge of a precipice she didn't know. Grabbing her courage, she took a tiny step forward. "Tell me about your family, about growing up on an island."

CHAPTER SEVENTEEN

Across the table, Camryn glowed. As the meal progressed, her eyes lost the haunted look he'd grown accustomed to seeing and sparkled like the sunrise on a sapphire ocean. She was telling a story from her childhood involving her sisters, a tea party, and a mud puddle, but he was having trouble keeping track. He kept getting distracted by her mouth, and his need to kiss her again. Thank goodness they were at the coffee stage. In a few minutes he could reasonably ask for the cheque, settle the bill, walk her to her car...and kiss her goodnight.

She paused in her storytelling and he nodded encouragement, hoping she wasn't waiting for him to answer a question. With a grin, she continued, and he relaxed.

He wanted to get her into bed. *Not tonight,* he thought with no little regret. Having a daughter meant he couldn't simply invite Camryn over, no matter how much he wanted to. But soon.

"I don't think Jo has forgiven me yet," Camryn said, laughing, the flush of nostalgia warming her cool, pale skin.

"You should do that more often," he said.

"What? Talk about myself for an hour?" She pulled her lips down into a lighthearted frown.

"I don't have a problem with that at all. I meant laugh." He tilted his head to one side in thought. "You know, I don't think I ever heard you laugh until today."

Her glow dimmed a little. "Am I really that much of a sourpuss? I used to laugh all the time."

"You've had a tough few months, and you're just getting back to the person you really are." He waved at Patti, hovering near the bar, and realized they were the only people left in the restaurant. "I think we're holding up closing."

"Oh!" Camryn reached for her purse. "Two bills, please," she said as Patti trotted up to the table.

"No." Will shook his head. "This one's mine."

"I can't let you do that."

Patti's head swivelled back and forth like she was watching table tennis.

He levelled a direct stare at Camryn. "I invited you out on this date. I pay the bill."

She frowned. "Do you realize how chauvinistic you sound? You said this was two friends having dinner, nothing about it being a date. I'll pay my own way."

"You can get the next one, if you want," he said. "But I'm paying tonight." He nodded at Patti and she scurried off before Camryn could protest any further.

"The next one?" Camryn said, managing to sound

affronted and intrigued at the same time.

"If you insist. And one more thing." He leaned in. Her eyes widened. "This *was* a date. And it won't be our last."

After he settled the bill, they rose from the table. Camryn walked ahead of him and he had his first sight of what she was wearing below her white silk blouse—a red skirt that outlined her hips, high-heeled leather boots that rose to just above her knees. He bit back a groan at the flashes of milky skin between the two as she strode along.

She retrieved her coat from Patti and he helped her into it, casually but deliberately brushing her nape with his fingers as he did, gaining satisfaction from the shiver she couldn't hide. He suspected she was still exasperated over the cheque, but ignored it, taking her hand and tucking it into the crook of his elbow as soon as they were outside. He could feel her tension and guessed she wanted to pull away. It was easy to spot her car, just a few steps past his own, as they were the only two vehicles remaining in the lot. He directed her toward it.

"I can walk on my own," she said, nose in the air.

"And you do it very well, as I just had full evidence of," he replied with mischief. "Your legs are endless in those boots."

"What is it with men and long legs?" she asked.

He bent down slightly—not much, she was almost as tall as he was in those amazing boots—so he could whisper in her ear. "We dream about them wrapped around us."

Her breath hissed and she came to an abrupt halt. Of course, the latter was probably because they'd reached her car. "Goodnight, Will," she said, a note of finality in her voice.

"Not quite yet." There was no wind tonight, but the

air was crystalline with cold. He placed his hands on her hips. She held herself stiff, then suddenly softened, relaxing into him, bringing her arms up between them so she could grasp the lapels of his jacket.

It was after ten, and the intense darkness of the near-winter night draped the orchard, painted shadows in the air. Over the chattering of the invisible river he could hear distant traffic, but otherwise they were in their own little world.

The soft blue of her eyes faded to grey in the dimness. He couldn't look away. An invisible strand stretched between them, like an ancient ley line connecting two mystical points. He breathed shallowly, unwilling to break whatever spell the night was weaving.

"Are you going to kiss me again?" she whispered, giving a little wriggle that jolted a bolt of lightning to his already alert groin.

"Yes," he whispered back.

"Good."

She tasted of coffee and dark chocolate. He sipped at her lips, exploring, discovering, determined not to miss one sensation, one impression. Her hands, chilled by the cold, cupped his jaw, a welcome, sensuous contrast to the heat pouring into him from her lips. He pressed her against the car, realizing in some faint and far off corner of his mind that the metal must be icy even through her clothing, but she didn't seem to care, giving a little breathy moan low in her throat and hooking one booted foot behind his knee to bring him closer.

Rucking up her coat and skirt with one hand, he touched the silky softness of her thigh. Goosebumps raised under his fingers, whether from his touch or the chill air he didn't know. Her hips tilted toward him, pulsing in invitation. He spread his palm on her lean flank, the tips of his fingers brushing the lacy edge of her panties.

The roar of a diesel engine rushing by on the road only metres away burst his cocoon of passion. Camryn jerked in his arms. Panting, heart racing from the shock of surprise and all that had preceded it, he lowered his chin to the crown of her head. Her breath puffed in uneven gasps against his neck.

Oh, my god, Camryn thought dazedly. *More. I want more.*

Ever since Anthony's arrest, she'd been careful. Careful to keep her distance with people, careful about what she said, careful about money, careful about everything. She'd been feeling the lure of letting go all evening, and Will's kiss had broken any remaining boundaries.

She sighed deeply, her nose nuzzled close to his throat, breathing in warm male skin and crisp, icy air. "How long can Corinne stay with Laura?"

He stilled, his chin on her head, his arms wrapped around her. He was quiet, and it finally dawned on her arousal-fuddled brain that no answer was *not* the answer she had expected. Or wanted.

She pushed against his chest, but he barely moved, and she couldn't go far, sandwiched as she was between his warm body and her cold car. "That long, huh?" she said, going for lighthearted but failing miserably even to her own ears. "I guess I should get home, then."

Still silent, he rested his weight on her, pinning her tighter to the doorframe. She held back a moan, crushing the urge to wrap her legs around his hips, just as he'd so recently—and erotically—suggested.

"I told Corinne I'd be home no later than eleven," he finally said.

She had been prepared for a gentle let down. Will would never be anything but kind. But her acute disappointment and embarrassment was tempered by the look in his eyes. He watched her with longing and regret, and then placed a tiny kiss on the crease of her mouth, trailed his lips up her cheekbone, dropped kisses on each eyelid.

When his touch vanished, she dragged her eyes open. "What time is it now?" she replied, horrified at the hopeful lilt of her question.

He chuckled softly. "There's not nearly enough time to do all the things I want to do with you. To you."

His hands linked at the nape of her neck, his thumbs brushing her jaw. Her knees drained of any strength his kiss had left her and she sagged.

Gathering in the tattered remains of rational thought, she said, "I guess that means goodnight."

He dug in the pocket of his jacket and then rested his forearm on her shoulder. Out of the corner of her eye she could see his thumb moving rapidly on the screen of his phone. His eyes left hers only for brief instances. When ringing sounded tinnily through the speaker, he held the phone to his ear.

"Corinne? I'm going to be a little late. Is that okay?" He paused. "Everything's fine. Excellent in fact." Another short pause. "Great. See you around midnight."

He tucked the phone back in his pocket and took a step away. Glacial air immediately swooped in to replace his body heat. Camryn shivered.

"I have enough time now."

She nodded, mouth too dry with anticipation to speak. "Drive safe, Camryn. I'll follow you home."

Thank god the streets were deserted. She was mesmerized by his headlights in her rear-view mirror, and drove slowly, making sure he didn't get left at stop lights or miss a turn. She pulled into the driveway of her parents' home, thankful that Jo's little yellow convertible—which she drove any season, all seasons—wasn't there. Not that she was ashamed of Will, ashamed of what they were going to do. But she'd have to introduce him, and given who he was, Jo might have questions, and Camryn wasn't in the mood to deal with them. Also, it would take longer to get to her room. She was about to jump out of her skin, and any further delay would be...well, torturous might be too strong a word, but definitely unwanted.

He stayed behind her as they walked the path to the front door. She was so aware of his presence she fumbled with the lock, taking three attempts to insert the key. Her spine prickled, her breasts felt full and tight. As soon as they were inside, she shrugged out of her coat, eager and restless.

Will paused in the entrance hall, thumbs tucked into the front pockets of his trousers, his gaze taking in the living room to their right and the kitchen and dining area toward the back.

"Are you renting?" he asked. "This is a really nice place."

"It's my parents'," she said. "They're on the last leg of a cross-continent tour, and Jo and I are living here until they come back in a few weeks." Not wanting to appear any more of a loser than that made her sound, she added, "I might move out sooner, of course, if I find my own place before then."

"Of course." He studied the room. "Did you live here before you went to Vancouver?"

"We moved in when I was ten."

"Really?" He smiled, eyes lighting with a teasing gleam. "This is where you had birthday parties and played dress up and fought with your sisters?"

"Well, yes, I guess."

"No wonder if feels lived in. I like its personality." He took a few steps past her and surveyed the kitchen and dining space with a professional expression. "Looks like it's been recently renovated."

"Yes." She was losing the heated glow his kisses had generated. The next thing she knew, he'd be asking for a beer and talking about laminate versus hardwood, marble versus granite.

Not that she wouldn't find that discussion fascinating at any other time. But that was the operative phrase—*any other time*.

"What about the bedrooms?"

"They've been painted recently," she said, disappointment building, "but no other renovations."

He stepped toward her, unzipping his jacket and tossing it on the back of the couch. "That's not what I meant. How quickly can we get to one?"

His lopsided grin made her heart kick. "This way," she said, breathless yet again.

He took her hand. They couldn't walk side-by-side in the hallway, so she bent her arm and rested their clasped palms at the small of her back. She drew him into her bedroom and shut the door.

The next instant she was pressed against the wall, his long, firm body ranged against hers from head to toe. He lifted her hands over her head, making her breasts strain upward. She could have tugged out of his loose grip, but let him take the lead, let him direct her.

It was all part of letting go.

God, did she want to let go.

"Where were we before we were interrupted?" he muttered, his lips brushing against the skin just under her ear. One hand kept her arms raised, the other dropped to her thigh, lifting her skirt out of the way. "Was it here?"

"Almost," she whispered.

"Here?" His fingertip traced the edge of her panties at her hip bone.

She shuddered. "Yes, somewhere near there," she said. At least, she meant to say that. What came out was a low moan.

"If...we hadn't been...disturbed," he said, sucking her earlobe between words, "I would have done this, next."

He stroked her, slicking the damp lace of her panties, touching her where she wanted to be touched but not close enough, not with the fabric between her flesh and his fingers. She wriggled, tilting her hips, her body tense with a rising need to be skin-to-skin. His mouth was hard and hot on hers, his tongue exploring, discovering, but even that wasn't enough to take her mind from his teasing touch.

In frustration she tugged one hand free from his hold over her head and pulled her panties aside, showing him exactly what she wanted. His chuckle vibrated from his chest to hers, and she resisted the urge to kick him. How could he *laugh* at a time like this? She was about to go up in flames if he didn't give her more and he was *laughing*?

Her legs gave way when he lightly pinched her heated, throbbing core. The touch shocked her, not from pain but an intense, unexpected pleasure. Instead of repeating the touch, though, he spun her around, away from the wall, and walked her backward a few steps until her calves touched the bed.

"Sit down," he murmured against her mouth, "and lay back."

She did what he said, welcoming the support of the mattress, her muscles trembling.

He found the zipper at the side of her skirt and slid it down, then worked the material over her hips. His eyes, hot and heavy-lidded, heated even further when she lay stretched out before him wearing nothing but her thin white blouse, lacy rose-toned underwear, and knee-high black boots.

He crooked a finger and she raised herself up on her elbows. She watched him undo each button on her blouse, his fingers lean and elegant as they worked the tiny, tortoiseshell fasteners.

"All the way up," he said, his deep voice rough and hoarse, and she thrilled with power. *She* made him speak that way, made him demand and take. He slipped the blouse from her shoulders, down her arms and tossed it aside.

"I love these boots." He crouched in front of her and ran his hands up and down her calves, the heat of his touch permeating the leather. His head lowered until his lips brushed her skin where the boot ended, and the sight of him—brown hair even more tousled than usual and even more attractive because of it—between her thighs made her bite her lip.

Desperate to gain a little control, she said, keeping her voice as casual as possible, "While you're down there…" She tilted one leg to the side and gestured with her chin to the zipper on the inside of the boot.

He gave her a cocky grin. Instead of reaching for it with his fingers, his breath swept her kneecap and she felt the moistness of his lips as he nibbled the tab with his teeth and pulled it down.

Oh, god, she thought as his hair tickled the inside of her thighs, causing her legs to drop open even further. He kept the tension on the leather with one hand and supported her ankle with the other. Every couple of inches he dropped open-mouthed kisses on the skin he revealed.

By the time he'd removed both boots she was limp and quivering, lying flat on her back with one arm over her eyes and trying not to hyperventilate. She'd known he was a patient man. She just hadn't known that patience could be put to such excruciatingly erotic use.

"If you don't hurry up," she said, eyes still hidden, "you'll have to go home and miss all the good stuff."

"Oh, I'll get to the good stuff, don't you worry." He sounded intent and purposeful and she licked her lips. "Keep your eyes closed."

"Your wish is my command," she said, going for snark, but judging by his soft exhalation of laughter, only serving to amuse him.

Her hearing, enhanced by her lack of sight, identified the sounds of unbuttoning and unzipping, the soft susurrus of clothing sliding from skin and dropping to the floor. A weight dipped the mattress and she rocked slightly toward it. Her eyelids flickered, lashes tickling the crook of her elbow. Warm fingers slid over her ribcage, encouraging her to arch her back so they could deftly unfasten her bra. She had to lower her arm so he could slip the strap off, but she kept her eyes closed. The lace scratched softly over her taut nipples, down her stomach, and then disappeared, along with the matching panties, all in a single smooth swoop.

Some more movement next to her, then all was still. Her breath tore at her throat as she panted, aching, waiting. Unable to bear it any longer, she opened her eyes.

Will lay stretched out on the bed, naked. He smiled down at her, a smile so sweet and sexy it made her dizzy. She reached out to cup his cheek, tenderness and lust and joy and want so tangled up inside her she didn't think she'd ever figure out exactly how she felt.

She rolled so they lay front to front, the light scattering of dark hairs on his chest rubbing against her nipples when he breathed, the hot heaviness of his cock bumping her stomach. She couldn't look away from his eyes, caught in his intenseness, the irises flecked with chocolate and amber and chestnut and gold. His hand rested on her hip, thumb circling lazily.

When his lips touched hers once more she fell, lost, tumbling deep. Into what, she didn't know. She only knew she didn't want to think about it, not now. Shifting, she pushed him to his back and stretched out on top of him. They were lying crosswise on her narrow bed, his legs bent over the edge, and she pulled her knees up so she crouched on top of him, his cock between them.

She couldn't get enough of his mouth. Their lips and tongues played and jousted, and she could have kissed him all night. But they didn't have all night.

She levered herself up. Reaching between them, she positioned him so she could take him into her body. He gripped her hips to help her, just as a thud reverberated, followed by someone calling her name.

Lost in a fog of need, it took another shout before Camryn realized it was Jo. She froze.

"We are *not* stopping now," Will muttered against her mouth, and pistoned his hips upward, driving himself deep inside. She contracted around him, unable to stop a moan from escaping.

Footsteps sounded down the hall. "Camryn? You home?" Jo called.

"Yes," Camryn said, loudly enough to be heard. "But if you love me, do *not* open my door."

CHAPTER EIGHTEEN

"Who is that?" Will whispered. Without conscious thought, his hips tilted upward, rotating, revelling in Camryn's wet heat. Her fingernails dug into his chest as she swayed above him.

"My sister." She sounded understandably distracted, and her expression had lost the soft, dreamy look she'd had only moments before.

He thrust again, determined to bring her focus back to him. "Did you lock the door?" Right now, buried in her warm, welcoming body, it would take more than a nosy sister to get him to stop. He clamped his hands to her hips and kept her seated on him.

"There is no lock," she hissed back.

"Are you okay?" the voice on the other side of the door asked, but thankfully obeyed Camryn's request as the door remained closed. "Whose car is parked in the driveway?"

Will lifted his hips—once, twice, three times—and the springs on the mattress squeaked in an unmistakable pattern. Camryn's head dropped back and her mouth opened on a silent moan before she settled firmly down and picked up his rhythm.

"Oh," the voice said. "Right. Leaving now."

Will quickened his pace and he forgot all about inquiring sisters. A deep, inner trembling began to build in Camryn's body as he moved inside her. She was slick and smooth and almost unbearably hot. She collapsed on top of him, her breasts squishing delightfully against his chest and he whispered in her ear, "Let go, Camryn. Come for me," and she did, her body clenching around him, shaking, and her release set him free to pound into her as he needed, holding her tight to him as he shuddered and emptied himself.

She lay curled on top of him, her face tucked in the hollow between his shoulder and neck. Her heart, which he could feel thudding in frantic beats, gradually calmed.

It was then he thought of the mistake he'd made.

"We didn't use a condom," he said, his satisfaction evaporating in dismay.

Camryn tensed, then relaxed. "That's okay," she said. "I'm on the pill." Her breath puffed against his neck.

"It doesn't matter," he said, "I should have thought of it."

She pushed herself up, hands resting on either side of his head, and looked down at him. "You don't have anything to worry about. After Anthony proved himself to be the lying, cheating scum he was, I had myself tested, just in case he'd screwed me in more than one way. I'm clean."

"That's not the point. The pill isn't one-hundred percent effective."

"It's close enough. You have nothing to worry—"

She cut herself off, and he knew she'd just connected the dots.

"Did Elizabeth say the same thing to you?" she said.

He swept one finger down the bridge of her nose, over her lips, and gave her chin a tap. "Yes. We used condoms the first few times, but she didn't like them, so she convinced me we didn't have to bother. And while I do not regret Laura, not for one instant, you'd think I would have learned." *Why didn't I think of it?* he wondered silently. It hadn't even crossed his mind.

"Well, you don't have to worry this time. I'm very careful about taking my pills, and I'm right at the end of the twenty-one days, so I'm sure everything is fine."

The sound of a movie explosion made itself heard from the living room. Camryn yelped and twisted off him, causing him to wince and bring his knees up to protect his most sensitive bits. "Oh my god, I forgot. Jo's home. What am I going to tell her?"

He sat up slowly, his feelings a convoluted mess. Anxiety simmered, even though he knew the chances were astronomical that Camryn might be pregnant. And now she needed to explain his presence to her sister? Coolly, he said, "How about nothing? I think she figured out what was going on." He gathered his scattered clothes and began to dress.

Camryn grabbed her robe off a hook on the back of the door and yanked it on. "Yes, I'm sure she did. It's not what I was doing. It's who I was doing it with."

He stilled the act of pulling on a sock. "Your sister has a problem with me?"

Camryn waved a hand as she paced the small room. "She might not have as much to do with Bendixon and Sons as Mattie, but she's one of the most loyal people I know. It could be tricky to explain what's going on between us."

The mention of Bendixon and Sons reminded Will of the possible buyout looming between the companies. The buyout Camryn didn't know about, the one he'd conveniently forgotten about all evening while he'd enjoyed her company.

"Am I really such an ogre?" he asked, trying to feel amused that he was seen as the bad guy, although his own sense of guilt couldn't be denied. He was *nice*, damn it, everyone knew that. If Camryn's family couldn't see that he was just doing his job, that it wasn't personal, then to hell with them.

"Of course not," she said absently, as if she really hadn't heard what he'd said.

He buttoned his shirt. "I should go."

She focused on him then. "Yes. You don't want to be any later for Corinne than you already are."

It was as if they'd just finished a business meeting. Despite the fact she was only dressed in a robe, Camryn looked poised and elegant, not the ravished and replete woman he'd hope to leave wanting more.

He opened the door and stepped into the hall, careful not to touch her as he passed. A pulsing base beat punctuated with screeching tires and growling engines grew louder as he approached the living room. Jo sat on the couch, her back to him, a movie car chase scene flashing on the TV. He would have preferred to avoid her, but his jacket was right next to her.

"Pardon me," he said politely. "I'll just take this."

She twisted her neck so she could see him. "Hi," she said brightly. "I'm Jo."

Unsure whether she knew who he was, he simply replied, "Yes, Camryn told me. Nice to meet you," and headed for the front door.

"I'm glad she's making friends," Jo called after him, amusement and affection in her voice. "She's been lonely since she moved home."

He paused, hand on the doorknob, her words adding to his mixed emotions. Had he taken advantage of Camryn's loneliness tonight? Just one more thing to wonder about. To worry about.

"Goodnight," he said, and stepped out into the dark.

She had known something bad would happen if she allowed herself to let go. Camryn belted her robe tightly and took a deep breath before leaving her room.

Not only had she had unprotected sex—and despite her nonchalance, she couldn't believe she'd been so careless—she'd been caught having that sex by her sister, and then managed to insult Will in her panicked response to that discovery. He might have hidden it behind a calm exterior, but she'd seen the hurt flicker in his eyes. She hadn't meant to do it, but that didn't make it better.

Right now, though, she had to talk with Jo. She'd figure out how to apologize to Will—for so many things—tomorrow.

After a quick trip to the bathroom, she headed to the living room and lowered herself to the sofa.

"Hey," she said, watching a submarine burst impressively but improbably out of a sheet of ice while various vehicles raced before the shattering surface.

"Sorry about that," Jo said, muting the TV and shifting her position so she leaned against the armrest facing Camryn. "Didn't mean to ruin the mood."

"It's not your fault." No way was Camryn going to admit that the interruption hadn't ruined anything, that in fact she'd been able to shrug off their near discovery and enjoy some of the best sex of her life. *TMI*.

"So, who is he?"

For a moment hope welled. Could she just shrug him off as a random stranger? Could she get away with not mentioning his name?

They were only the thoughts of an instant, though. Jo would never believe she'd brought a random man home, and she couldn't be that cruel to Will. Even if he never found out, she'd always feel guilty that she'd refused to acknowledge him.

"His name is Will Danson," she said, and then paused, waiting to see if the name would ring a bell.

Instead, her sister made an encouraging noise in her throat, waiting for more.

"He's the manager of the Kohlenburg Group here in Prince George."

That got a reaction. Jo's eyes, outlined in the black liner she favoured, widened until white showed all around her blue irises. "*That's* who he was?" She let out a long, slow whistle. "If I wasn't madly in love with Luke, I'd be jealous. He's hot."

Disconcerted, Camryn asked, "That's all you've got to say? You aren't mad at me?"

"What? For sleeping with the enemy?" Jo shrugged. "That seems a bit Shakespearean, don't you think? You're a little too old to be Juliet, so I assume you know what you're doing."

Camryn deflated against the cushions. "Don't tell Mattie, okay? I don't think she'd take this as coolly as you."

"Mattie's always been a bit crazy when it comes to Bendixon and Sons. But you have my word." She mimed zipping her lips and throwing away the key, just like they had when they were kids, but Camryn wasn't reassured.

"You have a history of letting your mouth get away from you," she said. "Remember the birthday present I bought for Dad?"

"I was ten," Jo retorted, indignant. "Are you never going to forget that? When have I let you down since?"

Camryn opened her mouth to enumerate the times Jo had left projects unfinished, or switched jobs on a whim, or generally lived up to her flighty reputation. But when she thought about it, she realized none of those things had injured anyone, except possibly Jo herself. "You haven't," she said.

Jo snorted. "Don't sound so surprised. You'll ruin the moment, and I've been waiting for you to admit that for years."

One more person she'd hurt without meaning to. "I'm sorry." She patted Jo's knee. "Have I really been that mean?"

"Not *mean*," Jo said, lips pursed in consideration. "I just always seemed to disappoint you. It was like you didn't trust me enough to let me live my life my way. You were always correcting me, under the guise of telling me what was best for me, of course."

Camryn winced. "I sound awful, when you put it that way." She searched for something to say that could make up for it, and didn't have to think long. "Now you're the one that has it all together. Luke's a great guy, and you're going to be the first of us to get married. Mom and Dad are so proud they could bust. Me, on the other hand…" She trailed off, knowing Jo would understand what she didn't say.

"That's all behind you now," she said. "It's time to forget about Anthony, move past the whole stupid thing. I think Will is just what you need—a smokin' hot guy that will distract you from it all."

CHAPTER NINETEEN

She woke up the next morning knowing she had to clear things up with Will. She had treated him shabbily and owed him an apology.

Calling before work wasn't an option—he'd be getting Laura ready for school. While she didn't want to have the conversation when she was at the office—Jason and Mattie might overhear—she figured she could at least arrange a time to meet.

The moment she walked in the door, she was met by Jason. "I've set up the bank appointment for eleven this morning," he said.

"Do you want me to come along?" she asked hopefully. It wasn't that she didn't trust Jason, but she wasn't certain he felt the same urgency she did. He would be embarrassed and upset if the company he loved had to close, but he and Lorraine would still be financially secure.

Helen was retiring soon. Mattie would probably be able to find another construction job, or go out on her own on a smaller scale. But Camryn needed the company to succeed. She couldn't be part of another financial disaster, even though neither had been of her own making. Her career couldn't afford it. Her bank account couldn't, either.

"Yes, you should definitely be a part of this," he said. "Showing we have a secure succession plan might help them decide in our favour."

Relieved he'd agreed so readily, she made her way to the break room. Determined to call Will before anything else, she was searching her tote for her cell phone when it started ringing. Her groan of frustration choked off when she saw Elizabeth's name on the screen.

She hadn't spoken with the other woman since Laura's performance, although they had exchanged a couple of brief text messages regarding the possible fraud charges. Camryn *knew* she hadn't signed those papers. If the truth would out, then this should be good news.

Nevertheless, her hand trembled as she connected the call.

"Good news," Elizabeth said in her no-nonsense manner the instant Camryn answered. "The handwriting results are back. You're in the clear."

She realized she was sitting in her chair with no knowledge of how she'd gotten there.

"Camryn? Did you hear me?"

She licked her lips. "Yes. That's great."

"I've been told, unofficially but from a reliable source, that you are no longer of interest in this investigation."

She wanted to lie her head down on the table and weep

tears of relief, but didn't. "Thank you for everything you've done."

"It's my job." After a short pause, she continued, "There is one more thing I need to mention."

She'd *known* it wasn't over. With trepidation she asked, "What now?"

"Anthony has requested to speak with you."

"No." Her response was immediate and firm. She never wanted to see or talk with him again. "Why on earth would I?"

"His lawyer says he wants to apologize. I think they are planning to plea bargain, and showing remorse is a good strategy."

"It won't be sincere. Even if he says the words, I won't believe he means them. And why would I want to do anything to make his sentence lighter?"

"It is entirely your prerogative, of course. He is under an injunction not to contact you, so asking through me is his only legal option."

She couldn't speak with Anthony. What good would it do? Her wounds were just starting to scab over.

"I will text you the number," Elizabeth said. "Ignore it or use it, it's up to you. Regardless, it is finally finished. Congratulations."

She ended the call, and for several minutes all Camryn could do was sit and stare at the wall opposite. Her thoughts swung from elation that the ordeal was finally over to fury that Anthony had ruined what should have been a day of celebration with his selfish request.

How could he ask that of her? If Elizabeth was right and he wanted to say sorry simply to make himself look better, it was just one more way he was using Camryn for his own ends.

For a moment, she wished she'd had the courage to tell Will the whole story about Anthony. Then she could have called him for sympathy and support. Or maybe not, given how she'd treated him last night. As it was, she'd have to deal with it on her own. As usual.

Seeking comfort in routine, she opened her laptop and began her usual troll through websites looking for new projects to bid on. She might be pinning her biggest hopes on Crossroads Corner, but she couldn't ignore other possibilities. After all, Jason and Mattie had struggled along for months on piecemeal work.

This morning, despite her distractions, she found two new opportunities, and using the template she'd created, customized it for each and submitted them by email. By then it was close enough to eleven that she badgered Jason into her car and headed for the bank, arriving a quarter hour early. Her grandfather groused the whole time they sat in the waiting room.

"Doesn't do to look desperate," he said.

"We don't look desperate," she replied, although that was exactly how she felt. "We are politely punctual."

Jason huffed a breath out his nose.

At exactly eleven o'clock a young man appeared in the waiting room. "Mr. Bendixon? Ms. Bendixon?" he said, offering his hand to each of them in turn. "I'm Roger Roswell."

"Where's Brian?" Jason asked. "I usually deal with Brian Alder."

"Mr. Alder only works part-time these days." Roger grinned, perfectly straight white teeth gleaming. His whole appearance was bright and shiny, from his neatly trimmed blond hair to his polished-like-a-mirror, bronze-coloured leather shoes. "He was going to retire a few months ago, but decided he couldn't go cold turkey, so we made arrangements for him to stay on a few hours a week."

The words and tone were polite, but Camryn heard condescension as well. Roger might not admit it even if directly asked, but she was pretty sure he saw this compromise as eccentric and unnecessary, a sop to an older generation who should just get out of the way.

She was gladder than ever that she had come along.

Roger's office had a large window looking onto the sidewalk. People rushed by, wasting no time in the numbing November cold. Camryn had walked by this very window on their way into the bank and hadn't realized it was one-way glass.

After he'd offered coffee, tea, and water, all of which were declined, Roger linked his hands and rested his forearms on his desk, a pose so intent and earnest it had to be by design. "So, I understand you're looking for a short-term loan."

"Yes." Jason's frown had grown steadily since learning they wouldn't be meeting with his long-time banker. "But before we get into that, maybe you could tell us a little about yourself. How long have you been with the bank?"

Roger smiled, and Camryn had the feeling once again that he was humouring an elderly gentleman. "I've been with this branch for just under a year. Prior to that I worked in Edmonton, where I was hired directly out of university. I have a Bachelor of Commerce with a double major in business economics and finance. I can assure you, I am fully qualified."

Jason seemed even more truculent after this resumé. "Experience trumps education in my book."

Before he could alienate the man further, Camryn jumped in. "I have a B. Comm as well. Studied in Vancouver, though."

Roger switched his slightly strained smile from Jason to her. "Excellent. Then you'll understand why I'm hesitant to grant your request."

"I'm sorry?" Camryn clenched her hands, palms suddenly moist.

"I've studied your account closely. While the company has had a long and profitable past, it is obvious that it has been bleeding money for some time. A short-term loan is only a band-aid solution."

"You don't think we know that?" Jason demanded. "But if we don't get it, there will be no time to find another."

Roger leaned back in his chair and swivelled gently. Neat stacks of paper lined the edges of his desk, rather like the battlements of a castle. Camryn waited, heart thudding but prepared to go on the offensive.

"You've already maxed out your line of credit, which is actually very modest for your kind of business," Roger said.

"Then increase that," Camryn suggested. "If you are not comfortable with a straight-out loan, would that be an option?"

Roger ignored her question. "I'm also aware that you've been having difficulty paying your expenses, over the last few months especially. I understand in one instance that an employee used her personal credit card in order to release an order from a local supplier."

"That employee is my other granddaughter," Jason said. "She's been compensated for that purchase, which she did without my permission. The only reason our account was in arrears was because the new owners changed the repayment schedule we were accustomed to."

Camryn wasn't sure what Jason was talking about but made a mental note to ask Mattie about it later.

"My understanding was they simply held you to the normal time limit. If the previous owner was willing to let you take longer to pay"—Roger shrugged, conveying his disdain at that practice—"then you were just lucky." He held up a hand, forestalling Jason's vehement reply. "The account was badly enough behind to be flagged, and it is a black mark against your credit score. Another area of concern is your cash flow. You're not bringing in enough to cover expenses and make payments on an additional loan."

"If we didn't have a cash flow issue we wouldn't be here." A wash of red flooded Jason's cheeks. Camryn had never seen him so agitated. "I've been a good customer of this bank for more than forty years, both personally and professionally. All I'm asking for is a little help until I'm no longer running the company."

That statement had Roger perking up his ears. "You're selling the business?"

"I'm passing it on to my granddaughters. The details are still being worked out."

Roger swung his gaze to Camryn. "If you're open to the idea, selling might be the best option."

"What do you mean? How could that be?" Camryn's stomach twisted greasily. A new owner would bring in new people, and she'd be the first out the door. She didn't have the longevity Mattie did, and while her sister had skills necessary on a construction site, a new owner would want to control the sales side. Which meant Camryn would be let go for sure.

"Bendixon and Sons is not without value," Roger said. "It has a good reputation in the city, and has been profitable in the past. Construction has been slow in the last couple of years, but it is bound to turn around. I heard that you are pushing accessibility as a new market. All that falls on the positive side. It makes you attractive to a buyer, especially as your recent troubles will lower the price."

Camryn waited for Jason to scoff at Roger's idea. She glanced at him, and was shocked to see his choler fading, his head nodding thoughtfully.

"You can't possibly be considering the idea," she said, gripping his wrist where it lay on the armrest of the chair.

"It's not what I want to do," he said, turning to her. His blue eyes, framed by silver brows, regarded her seriously. "But I also don't want to saddle you and your sisters with a dying business."

"It appears I've given you something to think about," Roger said, rising from his seat, obviously considering the meeting over. "Please let me know any further thoughts you have on the matter. In the meantime, I'll have a firm decision for you on the loan by early next week."

"Jason Bendixon will never sell his company," Will said decisively.

"How can you know that?" Samuel protested. His eyes narrowed. "Wait. You haven't discussed this with the granddaughter, have you?"

Will wasn't sure which granddaughter he meant, but the answer was the same in any case. "Of course not." He would never overstep the boundaries that far. But his guilt gnawed at him. A double whammy of guilt, torn between supporting Camryn and his allegiance to his company.

He and Samuel were in Will's office going over the list of businesses the Kohlenburg Group might want to purchase. It was a short list, and Bendixon and Sons topped it.

"Tell me," Samuel said. "If you hadn't met Camryn, would you still be hesitant to commit to this choice?"

Will scowled. "That's not the point. I'm loyal to the Kohlenburg family, you know that. They gave me chances no one else would. But maybe that's what Camryn and Mattie need, too. The chance to prove themselves, the opportunity to make the family business work."

"You're being sentimental." Samuel tapped the edge of his tablet with a fingernail. "Bendixon and Sons is in trouble. They're the most vulnerable to an offer, because it's that or lose any equity they might have in the company. What would you rather do—save them by buying them out, or watch them fail and lose everything?"

Will stood and strode to the window overlooking the lawns of City Hall, covered in a skiff of snow.

If the Kohlenburg Group took over Bendixon and Sons, Will couldn't see Camryn fitting into the new structure. After all, *he* would be doing the job she was doing now. But her skills would be valued in other businesses, not just construction. If she did find a job in another industry, it might ease some of her fears about their relationship. On the other hand, if the Kohlenburg group *didn't* buy Jason's company, and she was connected to another financial disaster when it went under, wouldn't that make it more difficult for her to find work?

Why he was worrying so much about a woman who wouldn't even acknowledge him as part of her life was beyond him. Yet he couldn't seem to help himself. He'd been so certain he could keep personal and business separate. Wasn't that a laugh.

He scrubbed his hands through his hair and turned back to Samuel. "You're right. I hate it when you're right. Call Wayne. Tell him we recommend Bendixon and Sons. He can tell us what price he's comfortable offering and we'll go from there."

Samuel was tactful enough not to gloat but did have one last stab to deliver. "Wayne might decide the amount, but he will want you to make the offer. He's always preferred having the person nearest the situation handle these deals."

"I know." That was *not* going to endear him to Camryn. Not at all. Shaking off his foreboding, he offered a small grin. "That's why I get paid the big bucks, remember?"

It was a standing joke between them. While they were both paid a good salary, Will made just a hair more, which Samuel often used to justify making Will do the tougher jobs. Today, he simply snorted and shook his head.

Alone in his office, Will stared blindly at the computer screen, where Samuel had displayed what he knew or could reasonably surmise about the three companies that had made his shortlist. He was right. Bendixon and Sons was in trouble. But it wasn't insurmountable. Camryn just needed to get some wins under her belt, build her confidence. She might not get the choice, though, now that Will had agreed to Samuel's plan.

After leaving her house last night, he'd been determined to put some distance between them. She obviously wasn't looking for a deeper relationship, given her concerns about Jo meeting him.

The thought burned his gut. He should put her out of his mind. Yet here he was, stressing out over her company, when she wasn't even prepared to admit they had something between them.

He tried to hold onto the anger, because it was better than the hurt. Since Elizabeth, he'd been very careful about exposing Laura to any of his dates, especially in the earlier stages. He'd broken that rule with Camryn, which had him wondering. Was it just the fact he hadn't dated since moving to Prince George, and was obviously ready to fix that problem? Or did it have more to do with that instant connection the day he'd met her?

His cell vibrated with an incoming call. As if his thoughts had connected with hers, he saw Camryn's name on the screen.

He let it ring. He wouldn't be able to avoid her forever, though, and concluding he'd have to answer, he sighed and reached for the phone. "Hello, Camryn," he said, keeping his tone neutral.

"I owe you an apology."

That set him back a mental step. "Why?" he asked.

"I didn't mean to hurt your feelings last night."

It was more than a little lowering that she'd noticed. He thought he'd hid his reaction better. "You didn't do anything wrong," he said, and he meant it. Maybe he wished she'd introduced him to Jo, but he got it. He wasn't exactly *persona grata* with her family.

"I was horrified that my sister just about walked in on us. I would have been horrified no matter who I was with. It wasn't because it was you, specifically."

He fiddled with a pen, tapping it on the table, sliding his fingers down its length, flipping it over and repeating.

"Are you sure?" he said. "That might have been one reason, but was it the only one?"

There was a short pause, then a sigh travelled through the speaker. "You're right. It was more than that. But I was wrong. I should have manned up and introduced you to Jo."

"I know you were hesitant to go out with me at first, because of who I was, where I work." The buyout proposal Samuel was this moment preparing weighed on his shoulders like a pallet of bricks. "I guess I was hoping we'd moved past that."

"We have. I promise, next time I won't be a coward."

It took him a moment to absorb what she'd said. "Next time?" His heart lightened.

"I owe you dinner, remember?" She had shaken the sombreness from her voice. "What about tomorrow night? You, me, and Laura."

The last of his resentment melted away. "That would be great. Thank you."

"Besides, I've finally got something to celebrate." He could hear the joy vibrating in her voice. "Elizabeth called today. I've been cleared of any collusion with Anthony. I'm off the hook for good."

"That's awesome news!" The investigation had droned like an eerie minor chord throughout his time with Camryn. Knowing it was over and done with for good was like the sweet ringing of a bell. "Dinner should be my treat."

"Nope, I refuse to let you. We'll go somewhere casual and fun. Other than celebrating, it will also provide a good diversion." Her happy tone faltered slightly.

"A diversion? From what?"

"Jason is thinking of selling the business."

CHAPTER TWENTY

Not only did Camryn take Will and Laura out for dinner to a kid-friendly place the next day, they made a return trip to the museum on Saturday, and then spent a blustery, first-real-snowfall-of-the-season Sunday afternoon baking cookies and watching Laura's favourite animated movie.

The program did have some special adaptations, such as descriptive video, but after a little while, Camryn was certain Laura would have loved it even without that assistance. She knew all the dialogue, sang along to all the songs, and spent quite a bit of time telling Camryn what was going to happen before it did.

By the end of it, however, she was curled in a ball in the corner of the couch, snoring softly. Will tucked a soft pink throw around her shoulders and she sighed, snuggling deeper.

"She doesn't nap often anymore," he said, gathering up the popcorn bowls while Camryn collected the glasses. "But every once in a while it just seems to catch up with her. She'll probably only doze for half an hour or so."

His tone had Camryn glancing at him as she loaded the dishes in the dishwasher. "You sound disappointed."

"I am. If she was really out, we might have time for ourselves." He leaned his hips against the counter and took her hand, pulling her gently toward him. She stepped into his hold, resting full-length against him, basking in his heat, his scent.

"I've missed you," he murmured into her hair.

She snorted. "We've seen each other more in the last few days than ever before."

"But we haven't been naked."

Just as she'd predicted, Camryn's cycle had continued as normal. When she'd told Will, the combined look of relief and embarrassment on his face had amused her. *You're the single dad of a girl,* she'd thought. *Get used to it.*

"I know what you mean." She snuck her hands under his sweater but was thwarted from touching his skin by the shirt he wore underneath. With small movements she began to pull the hem out of the waistband of his jeans.

"What's going on now?" he said, mock-threateningly.

"Nothing," she said. She freed the fabric and spread her hands against the smooth planes of his abdomen, slid them round to his lower back.

He groaned softly. "Fair's fair," he said, and worked his way under her T-shirt, circling his fingers at the base of her spine.

For long moments they stood quietly. Camryn savoured the silence, the sensations. She felt safe in his arms, quietly aroused, yet too relaxed to take it further.

Maybe it was that sense of safety, of connection, that made her bring up the subject she'd been avoiding all weekend.

"Thanks for not asking me."

"About what?"

"About Jason selling the company."

Since their meeting at the bank, she'd done her best to talk him out of even considering the option. But he'd been firm in his resolve to give it fair deliberation.

"I probably shouldn't have said anything to you about it," she added. "It just kind of slipped out. I appreciate you haven't pushed me on it."

He rubbed his chin on the top of her head. It was oddly comforting. "You know I wouldn't use our friendship against you. We've been walking a thin line this whole time. I won't be the one to step over it."

She burrowed in closer. "Well, thanks."

His hand continued to rub her back. "As a friend, I want what's best for you. So tell me. Would selling out be such a bad thing? Couldn't it be a fresh start, for everyone?"

She reared her head back to look him in the eye. "It would be awful," she said. "I can't let Jason do it."

He ducked his chin, his expression serious. "Why? Why would it be so awful?"

She pushed at his chest with both hands and he let her go. She backed up until she bumped into the counter opposite. "I need Bendixon and Sons to succeed," she said. "I need to save it."

"I know it's the family business. I know you're loyal to your grandfather, your sisters. But you've only been with the company a few weeks. Why do you feel so strongly about it?"

She pushed off the counter and paced the length of the kitchen, putting the large island between them. "Do you understand—*can* you understand—how Anthony stole my confidence? I thought I knew him, and all the time he was a lying, cheating thief. I think that hurt worse than the fact he stole my money."

Will straightened off the counter, his arms dropping to his sides, hands balling into fists. "He stole from you?" he said, his already bass voice deepening to a growl.

She licked her lips, fascinated by the fury blazing in his normally soft brown eyes. "I haven't told anyone. Not Mattie, not Jason, not Jo."

"Tell me," he demanded. "Tell me everything, and then trust me to help you, Camryn."

She approached him slowly. An arms-length away she stopped. He waited, the only sign of his impatience the clenching and unclenching of his fists. The lure to lean into him, to lean *on* him was strong, but she didn't.

"I co-signed credit cards with Anthony. More than one." She vibrated with humiliation. With the clearer vision of hindsight, it was easy to see what a naive, stupid mistake that had been. She swallowed hard and continued. "After he was arrested, I discovered he'd maxed them all out, to the tune of tens of thousands of dollars. He also hadn't paid the rent on our condo for months. A very expensive rent, I might add. Since the lease was in my name, I am on the hook for that, too. That's on top of the bits and pieces he borrowed from me over the years we were together, bits and pieces that add up to an awfully large amount. He bought things for the condo—furniture, decor, expensive kitchen appliances—and I paid half of everything, without asking to see receipts. There's a good chance he inflated those prices, too. If he could get away with it, he took it."

"He stole from you," Will repeated flatly.

"He conned me," she said with a snap. "I took him at his word, and he conned me out of one hundred thousand dollars. More, probably. I quit adding it up after a while. It made me nauseous." That was the literal truth. When she'd realized the extent of Anthony's deceit, she'd vomited until her stomach had nothing left.

"You need Bendixon and Sons to profit so you can profit. So you can pay off those debts."

"If Jason sells, I won't get anything. It's not like I've invested in the company. Mattie and I are going to take over, but we're just going to run it for him, not buy in. If he sells, I'll be out of a job. Since the only people willing to give me a chance after the way I left my last job were family…" She shrugged. "I think you can see why I think it's a bad, bad idea."

As Camryn told her story, Will became conscious of an overwhelming urge to find her no-good bastard of an ex-boyfriend and beat the living crap out of him. The blood pounded through his veins, rushing through his head so loudly he barely heard her last few sentences.

It killed him, seeing how stiffly she held herself, realizing it was the shield she used to show she was strong, that she had risen above her troubles, was capable of handling it all herself.

He needed to protect her, to find a way to fix everything.

He ached to tell her about the buyout possibility. But he couldn't. She'd said it herself, she wasn't an owner, or even an investor. The offer would be made to Jason, and telling her about it beforehand would be, if not unethical, certainly improper.

She stood watching him, chin lifted, only the slight flickering of her eyelids evidence of her emotions.

He searched for something to say, coming up with only, "He's in jail, right?"

"No, but he is under house arrest, and they've confiscated his passport. He's considered a flight risk, since they haven't been able to trace all the money."

"He deserves worse."

One corner of her mouth twitched in a tiny smile. "I agree. But tarring and feathering is no longer acceptable. He could still go to jail, but Elizabeth suspects he's seeking a plea bargain, so he might talk his way out of it yet."

"And what about you?"

"I'm no lawyer, but I'm guessing any charges related to me will be dropped as part of the deal. They'll concentrate on the bigger, corporate crimes." She shrugged. "To add insult to injury, though, he wants me to call him. Elizabeth thinks he's going to apologize, as a show of remorse to strengthen his plea."

"Are you going to? Call him, I mean?" He wished he could take the burden off her, but was helpless to do so.

"I haven't decided yet."

Behind him, Laura babbled incomprehensibly, and he twisted his torso, looking over his shoulder. She subsided into sleep again. He should wake her soon, if she didn't on her own. Otherwise she'd put up a fuss at bedtime.

He focused on Camryn again. "Is there no way you can get your money back? Or get out of paying the credit cards?" Maybe it wasn't as bad as she thought.

"I suppose I might be able to sue him in civil court. But I don't know if I have the energy for that. I just want it all to go away." Giving him a wide berth, she picked up a tea towel lying crumpled on the counter and folded it, meticulously matching the corners. "I'd have to have proof of what he took, and that's not going to happen. After all, who gets a receipt when she lends money to her boyfriend, or pays him for half of the incredibly expensive coffee maker he bought? As for the credit cards, I paid them down as much as I could by selling everything, but I signed the paperwork stating I'd be liable for anything bought on the cards. It was pretty stupid, I guess, but how could I have known?" She kept her face averted, smoothing her palm over the towel again and again.

Her fiercely guarded hurt tore at him, his heart cracking in sympathy. He took the towel from under her fidgeting hands and wrapped his arms around her, folding her into his embrace. She resisted, then, with a tiny sob, allowed her weight to rest against him. He might not be able to fix things for her, but he could offer this much comfort.

"You're smart and strong," he said. "You'll get through this."

"If I had been smarter and stronger," she replied, her voice muffled against his shoulder, "I wouldn't be in this mess."

"Everyone makes mistakes." He was dead certain he was making one right now, not telling her about the buyout, but he bit his tongue. It wasn't his place to tell her. "It's how we grow."

"Then I should be ten-feet tall by now," she said, irritation replacing despair.

He laughed, one hand stroking the skin at her nape,

feeling the soft, short hairs under his fingertips. "If there's anything I can do to help," he said, "just ask, okay?"

Her shoulders rose and fell with her breathing. "How about withdrawing your proposal for Crossroads Corner?"

"Nice try," he said. "I meant anything I can do on a personal level." When he'd started this...whatever it was...with Camryn, keeping business and personal separate had been a lot easier. Now it was getting all ravelled up.

"I had to ask." She shrugged, her breasts rubbing against his chest, triggering a flashback image of her naked on top of him. His groin tightened and he lowered his lips to her hair, breathing in the cucumber-y freshness of her shampoo.

Laura let out a sneeze, followed a moment later by, "Daddy?"

"Right here, sweetie," he said.

"I'm here, too," Camryn said, lifting her head. She didn't move away from him, but raised a hand to cup his jaw.

"I missed the end of the movie," Laura said fretfully.

Naps sometimes made her cranky, and this sounded like one of those times. "I'll start it over for you." He kissed the tip of Camryn's nose and said quietly, "I wish I could start things over for you, too."

"Thanks, but it's okay. I'm smart and strong, remember?" She kissed him back, feathering her lips at the corner of his mouth. His desire was a simmering burn he would have to do something about. Soon.

"Daddy!" Laura's irritable shout stopped any further caresses.

"Hold that thought," he whispered to Camryn, enjoying the spark of battle in her deep blue eyes, then went to deal with his daughter.

Camryn went home shortly after Laura woke from her nap. There was one more thing she needed to do before the night was over, and she needed to do it alone. Will had taken her side against Anthony so staunchly that it had given her the fortitude to take the next step.

Jo's car wasn't in the driveway, and the house was quiet when she went inside. She didn't want to be interrupted, though, so she went to her room and closed the door, just in case. Plumping the pillows at the head of the bed, she leaned back against them and pulled up the text Elizabeth had sent days ago.

The number wasn't familiar. Anthony must have changed his cell after he'd been arrested. Gathering her courage, she tapped the screen.

The call was answered after only one ring. "Anthony Halford."

"Hello, Anthony," Camryn said.

"Who is this?"

Camryn closed her eyes. Is that how little she had meant to him, that he'd forgotten her voice so quickly? "It's Camryn."

"Oh."

Was it possible the pause that came after that single syllable was an indication of his guilty conscience? She hoped so. It would be much easier to forgive him if she believed he regretted what he'd done.

"I asked my lawyer to reach out last week," he said. "After a couple days, I figured you weren't going to call."

"I needed to think about it." Now she was talking to him, all she wanted to do was get it over with. "So? What did you want to say?"

Another pause, this one slightly longer. "I'm sorry, Camryn. For everything."

He *sounded* sincere, but she wasn't about to let him off that easy. "Sorry you stole from me? Sorry you lied? Sorry you tried to shift blame onto me when you knew"—her breath hitched as her heart raced— "you *knew* I had nothing to do with any of it?"

"I could go to jail, Camryn. To *jail*. I am fighting for my freedom."

"And that gives you the right to drag me down with you?" She realized she was yelling into the phone. Damn, it felt *good*. "You gave up your rights when you abused the trust of the company you worked for. When you abused my trust."

"It didn't start out—"

She steamrollered on. "I thought I loved you, Anthony. I thought we were going to get married, have a life together. And the whole time I was just another patsy, someone you could take for everything you could get."

"That's not how I—"

Again, she rode right over whatever pathetic excuse he was planning to use. "I don't care. I don't care what your reasons were. You are a liar, a thief, and a cheat. I'm just glad you're out of my life. I never want to talk to you again."

"Camryn—"

"I mean it, Anthony. *Never.* I don't want to hear from you or your lawyer again."

She broke the connection, her chest heaving, and stared at the phone, willing it to ring. Anthony wasn't allowed to get in touch with her. If he called back, she would be on the phone to Elizabeth the next second so she could add it to his list of transgressions.

It didn't ring. As the minutes went by, her heart rate slowly returned to normal.

A small smile tugged at her lips when she visualized Anthony's face as he'd listened to her rant. She was certain the call hadn't gone anything like he'd planned. He'd never seen her lose her temper, not once in the years they were together. She'd bet dollars to doughnuts he'd thought she'd quietly accept his apology, and he'd be able to report to his lawyer that he'd smoothed things over with her.

Well, she'd spiked his guns, hadn't she?

She laughed out loud, alone in her room, comfortable in her skin for the first time in months.

CHAPTER TWENTY-ONE

Whether it was the catharsis of confession and confrontation, or exhaustion catching up with her, Camryn had the best sleep she'd had since the whole Anthony incident had blown up in her face. Instead of the faintly depressed state she was used to waking up to, she opened her eyes on Monday with an unfamiliar feeling in her chest.

It took her a minute to recognize it. Hope.

As a teenager, she had been diagnosed with mononucleosis. The fatigue, sore throat, and fever had lasted for weeks and it was only after she had fully recovered that she'd realized how sick she'd been. She had that same sense of discovery now. She'd grown so used to feeling off-kilter and out-of-sorts that her current cheerfulness was oddly foreign.

At the office, she greeted Helen with a wide smile.

"Happy Monday! How was your weekend?"

"It was lovely, thank you," she replied with an arch look. "Don't you look chipper this morning?"

"I feel chipper," Camryn said. "Today's going to be a good day, I just know it." She hummed on the way to her makeshift office, regarding the decrepit room with near affection. Even its dinginess couldn't get her down.

She placed her coat on the rack she'd hung over the door, tucking her hat and gloves into the sleeves and draping her scarf over top. With a sense of anticipation, she poured a cup of coffee and opened her laptop.

Her good mood lasted through a check of her emails and her usual troll through the internet looking for potential jobs. Nothing from Charette Architects yet, but it was probably too soon for that. At one point, Mattie wandered in to get coffee, and Camryn smiled a greeting.

"What? What's going on?" Mattie asked suspiciously. "Why do you look so perky?" Then, her expression lighting, she said with hope, "Is it Crossroads Corner?"

"Nope," Camryn said with unconcern. "Just a good day."

She found a couple small opportunities online and whipped up proposals for each of them, sending them off with a decisive tap of the Enter button. She almost wished for the days when proposals would have been sent by snail-mail. It would be much more satisfying to drop a hefty package into the mail slot than touch a small black square.

Pleased with the morning so far, she made a fresh pot of coffee and as she waited for it to drip, poked her head into Jason's office.

"Got a minute?" she asked.

He waved her in, and she took careful roost on the

visitor's chair.

"Anything from the bank yet?"

"No," he said. "Too soon, I imagine. I just wish I knew whether that was good or bad."

In Camryn's new, buoyant mood, she could only see the positive side. "I'm sure he's carefully considering it, which he should, of course. But helping us means helping themselves."

"If he does grant the loan, I think it will come with conditions." He rubbed one hand through his hair, still full and thick and the loveliest shade of silver.

"Then we'll meet them," she answered with determination.

"I think he'll insist we sell."

Camryn felt her smile slip a fraction but pulled it back into place. "They can't do that. Can they?"

"We aren't exactly negotiating from a position of power," he said. "That Roger was right. If we go on the way we are, we'll lose the business. If we sell quickly, we would still be able to get something for it."

It was the same argument he'd presented every time they'd spoken about Roger's suggestion. Camryn's response echoed her previous words as well. "It's too soon to give up," she said, keeping her tone robust. "At least wait until we hear about Crossroads Corner."

Jason's gaze was compassionate, chipping at her feeling of contentment. "We're not going to get that project. I should never have let you even try. You're pinning your hope on a pipe dream."

She could swear she heard the chisel taking chunks out of her cheerfulness, but clung to the enthusiasm she'd woken with. "You can't know that."

"I do," he said, gruff but gentle. "We are not qualified

to lead a project of that size. I know you are only trying to help, but you should be ready to face the truth."

"What I should do is bet you," she replied with a confidence that was slightly less hearty than it had been. "What will you wager?"

He shook his head, although a half-smile played on his mouth. "Where did you girls get this urge to gamble?"

It took a moment for the penny to drop, but when it did, she chuckled. "Well, Mattie's worked out, didn't it?" Several months ago, Mattie had made a bet with Marcus while searching for ways to help Bendixon and Sons out of their financial difficulties. It had turned out well in the end, but Jason had been furious when he found out.

"Once is enough," he said. "There will be no more betting in, around, or about this company."

The phone on his desk rang. Helen answered in the front office, her voice an indistinguishable murmur, and then it rang again.

He picked up the receiver. "Yes?"

Camryn couldn't hear anything from the front office, so Jason must have been connected to an outside line. From his narrowed eyes and tightly drawn brows, whatever he was hearing was not welcome.

Is it the bank? Camryn wondered. She swallowed past the dryness in her mouth. Her earlier euphoria melted away like an iceberg in the Caribbean. She could read nothing from Jason's *yeses* and *I sees*, and metaphorically chewed her nails.

"All right," Jason said, "I'll see you then." He hung up slowly, staring at the phone, expression wary, as if it might attack.

"Was that Roger?" she asked. Keeping her hands out of Jason's sight, she crossed her fingers.

"No." He rolled his shoulders and looked at her. "It was Will Danson."

Just hearing Will's name brought back a little of her earlier jauntiness. *He is such a* good *man*, she thought. Almost good enough to have her believing in the species again. "What did he want?"

"To set up a meeting," Jason said. "He wants to buy Bendixon and Sons."

Will hung up the phone and leaned back in his chair. Jason hadn't sounded surprised at Will's request, or the reason behind it. There had been no blustering or shock, only a polite professionalism.

He had no illusions that Camryn would be as calm when she heard about the offer. How soon would she find out? And when she did, would she ever talk to him again?

Less than half an hour later, he was in Samuel's office just off the main reception area when he heard a small commotion in the lobby, followed by the quick clicking of two sets of heels. Camryn appeared in the doorway, the young receptionist who manned the desk right behind her.

"You!" Camryn said, spitting out the syllable. Her normally pale face was flushed, hot patches of red staining her cheeks and throat, blue eyes hard and cold in contrast.

He straightened from where he'd been leaning over Samuel's shoulder, the better to see the computer screen. "Let's go to my office."

"There's no need. I only came to tell you what I think of you. It won't take long to call you a—"

"Stop." He circled the desk, aware of Samuel's fascinated gaze. At least he was keeping his mouth shut. "You're not mad because I made the offer. You're mad because I didn't tell you first."

"Damn right."

"Then it's personal, and we'll do this in private." He grasped her elbow and she yanked it out of his hold, quivering with tension, inhaling and exhaling rapidly. "I am not discussing this in front of a crowd."

"Don't mind me," Samuel said, putting his chin in his hands and widening his eyes. Will glared at him.

As if suddenly aware of their audience, Camryn said, "Fine," and strode past the hovering receptionist, back stiff, hands fisted at her sides.

In his office, he closed the door. She paced to the window, then spun on her toes to confront him.

"You're planning to buy Bendixon and Sons."

He didn't think pointing out it wasn't him, personally, would help his cause, so restrained himself to a simple, "Yes."

"And I thanked you. *Thanked* you for not taking advantage of my slip last week. How could I be so stupid? You'd think after Anthony I would know better."

Will stiffened. "You're comparing me to a thief and embezzler?"

"I trusted him. I trusted you. And you both used me."

"The decision to make an offer for Bendixon and Sons was made days before you told me Jason's thoughts on the idea."

She didn't seem to hear him. "Damn it, Will." His name caught in her throat, but she kept her gaze levelled on him. "I told you things last night I haven't even told my family. And you hid this from me? *This?*"

Beneath the anger, he saw the hurt. He hated he'd put the pain in her eyes. "I couldn't tell you. It has nothing to do with you."

She sucked in a hissing breath and turned away from him, staring out the window. It was late afternoon and the November sky was already dark, small lights flickering in the elms surrounding City Hall.

He winced. "I mean," he said, "that it's Jason's company. You told me so yourself. It was only right he hear about the offer first."

"I played right into your hands, didn't I?" She spoke quietly, still facing away from him. "Thanks to me, you knew Jason is open to the idea. It obviously doesn't matter that *I* am against it. So, you jumped right in."

"I know you think you need Bendixon and Sons, that you'll never get a job anywhere else. But this thing with Anthony will die down, will be forgotten," he said. "Nothing's been decided yet, but if you have to, you'll get another job, and it won't be slinging burgers at McDonald's like you seem to think. It's way too soon to worry about that, though."

She looked at him over her shoulder, her profile limned against the heavy dusk outside. "You're meeting with Jason Wednesday morning. Privately."

"If you mean, without you, then yes." Will let a little of his exasperation bleed into his tone. "It's his company, Camryn, not yours. If he wants to bring you in on this he will. But that's not up to me. Don't blame me for something that's not my fault."

She turned fully toward him, slim and tall and elegant in her heeled boots and tan overcoat. Didn't she have something warmer to wear? She'd never make it through winter with that.

"You're right," she said. "It's not your fault."

He regarded her warily. "This isn't meant to hurt you. It's strictly business."

"It's not your fault," she repeated. "It's mine."

His uneasiness increased. "What do you mean?"

"I didn't want this relationship," she said. "I said it was a bad idea from the beginning. I was right." She took two strides toward the door.

He blocked her way. "Don't do this, Camryn. Don't give up on us."

"I can't give up something I never really had," she said, eyes shiny but mouth firm. She stepped around him and vanished out the door.

He stared at the empty space, stunned by how it had all fallen apart so quickly. Before he'd drawn two breaths, Samuel appeared.

"What was that all about?" he said, eyebrows raised to his hairline.

"Nothing." Will turned his back on the other man and took refuge behind his desk, dropping into his chair and wiggling the mouse to turn on his computer screen.

"I take it she knows about the buyout." Unfazed by Will's attempt at dismissal, Samuel approached closer, standing behind the visitor's chair and smoothing the back with his hands absently. "But what did you mean, she's mad because you didn't tell her first? That it's personal?"

Will leaned back in his chair and closed his eyes. Samuel wasn't going to let this go. His tenacity made him an amazing employee, but an uncomfortable friend.

"Camryn and I have been seeing each other. Socially."

"Well, duh. I knew that."

Will's eyes flew open. "You did?"

Samuel smiled and shrugged smugly. "You should know by now I know all."

"Why didn't you say anything?"

"It was none of my concern. I trusted you to keep business and pleasure separate."

Will laughed bitterly. "Well, I did. And now I've hurt a person I care very much about."

Samuel dragged the visitor's chair closer to the desk. He sat, leaning forward and folding his elbows on the glossy surface. "And she must care about you, too, to be so upset."

The words were cold consolation.

CHAPTER TWENTY-TWO

On Wednesday morning at 11:45, she sat next to Mattie, facing Jason across his desk. He had just returned from his meeting with Will.

"It's a good offer," he said. Despite this, he didn't sound happy. "I think we could do some negotiating and bring it up a bit, but Will's done his homework, got the values right."

"I can't believe you're praising him," Mattie said with resentment. "Ever since he came to town, he's been undermining our business. And now that he's worn us down, he wants to finish us off."

Camryn kept silent. Mattie was closer to Jason. Maybe he would listen to her when he hadn't to Camryn.

"You girls know I want to pass this business on to family. I named it Bendixon and Sons, after all, hoping your father or uncles would be a part of it. That didn't pan out, and I started thinking your generation might be the one. But I don't want to saddle you with a broken-down horse."

"This is your life, Jason." Mattie stood and leaned her fists on the desk's scarred wooden surface. "It's *my* life. I don't want to let it go."

"I know you don't, honey." Jason rubbed his hands on his face, his expression worn and tired. "I heard from the bank today."

The despair permeating Camryn's mind crystallized in her lungs. "They refused the loan, didn't they?"

"Yes and no. There's a condition."

She could hear Roger's voice in her head, listing all the reasons they should put Bendixon and Sons up for sale. "They'll give us the money but only if we start looking for a buyer."

Jason nodded.

"Can they do that?" Mattie demanded.

"It seems so."

She dropped back into her chair, sawdust puffing out of the creases of her overalls. "Is there anything we can do? We don't want to sell, which means we can't get a loan. If we can't get a loan, we can't run the business. Is there another way to get the money? Another bank, maybe?"

The glimmer of an idea tickled the back of Camryn's brain.

"If the bank I've done business with for decades won't loan us money, I can't see any others wanting to risk it," Jason said.

"Not another bank," Camryn said slowly. "But what about another company? The Kohlenburg Group wants to take us over. What if we find another investor, one willing to buy in, but not buy outright?"

Jason and Mattie stared at her. "You got someone in mind?" Jason asked.

"I do," Camryn said, feeling energized for the first time since learning of Will's betrayal. "Let me make a call."

Charette Architects took up the top two floors of one of the only high-rise buildings in Prince George. The building itself was many years old, including an elevator that creaked and groaned as it carried Camryn to her meeting with Abel Quinson, but when she stepped out into the lobby she could tell immediately that extensive renovations had been done to the interior, at least on these floors.

The reception desk was a long, arching expanse of smoky glass, and the woman who asked for Camryn's name matched it for sleek, glossy elegance. The area directly behind was a large, open space, with drafting desks in gleaming white and chrome, stainless steel filing cabinets and an atmosphere of busy creativity. Men and women hunched over thin, modern laptops or manned keyboards in front of multiple monitors filled with complicated lines that twisted and turned as the view was manipulated.

"Camryn!"

She turned to her right. Abel approached down a wide hall lined with glass walls. He wore yet another eye-popping tie with his dark blue suit, and his thinning hair look recently shorn.

"Thanks for seeing me on such short notice." She'd called him immediately, before she lost her nerve, but even so had been taken aback that he could fit her in that afternoon. She had thought she'd have more time to prepare.

"My office is right this way." He led her to a corner suite with a view over downtown, facing south toward the sandy cutbanks that lined the Fraser River. The chrome and glass theme continued here, although Camryn assumed the curved, transparent chair he offered her was made of something safely durable.

Instead of moving behind his desk—more black glass—he took a seat next to her. "Now, how can I help you?"

He waited expectantly, his eyes open and friendly, with that hint of admiration she'd seen before. The admiration she was counting on.

Now that she was here, nerves clutched at her belly. She hadn't told Jason or Mattie who she was going to see, but the look of hope on their faces had placed another burden on her shoulders. "I have a proposition for you," she said, willing herself to look competent and professional.

His eyebrows rose and he leaned forward in his chair. "What kind of proposition?"

There was nothing lecherous in his attitude, and Camryn suppressed a squirm of guilt. She was skating the edge of professionalism, and it was making her queasy, but desperation was a strong motivator.

She took a deep breath. "Has Charette Architects ever considered branching out into different areas of construction and design?"

The look of interest in Abel's eyes faded to puzzlement. "I can't say we have. But expansion and acquisition aren't my responsibility."

"Bendixon and Sons is a respected, established

company. Like many construction companies over the last year or so, we have seen a slowdown. But we've also had a number of wins." Since her hands were in plain view, she crossed her ankles at this slight fudging of the facts. "You, yourself, liked our focus on accessibility enough to include us in the dental office project. We've continued to make that a focus in our proposal for Crossroads Corner."

"You understand we can't talk about that."

She reassured him. "No, I understand. I'm just trying to showcase our benefits."

Abel frowned. "Your attitude to accessibility is one of the reasons we're considering your bid. But I still don't understand why you're here."

"Like many businesses do from time to time, we find ourselves needing to restructure our finances. Bendixon and Sons is looking for an investor, and I immediately thought of Charette Architects. We are a small, private company, and we're open to joining forces with another firm in order to secure our future." Not to mention her own. Will was wrong. He said she didn't need Bendixon and Sons, that she could be a success elsewhere, but she knew now that had only been a sop to ease his own conscience.

She didn't want to think about Will.

"I'm flattered you thought of us," Abel began. Camryn could hear the *but* coming and prepared herself to convince and cajole. "As I said, I'm not privy to any plans we may have in that direction. If you like, though, I can mention it to the people who make those decisions."

She'd been so certain he was going to blow her off that she just sat there for a moment, stunned. "You will?" she managed to say, a huge smile stretching her cheeks. Realizing how gauche that must sound, she tried to recover. "I appreciate it. If they have any questions at all, they are more than welcome to call me directly."

"I'll let them know." Abel rose and Camryn followed suit, lightheaded and wobbly with relief.

He walked her back to the reception area. "I'll be in touch," he said, his smile polite and perfunctory.

His attitude was so different from when he'd first greeted her that she wondered if his promise to mention her idea to the powers that be was only a strategy to get her out of the office. She had to make sure he would do what he said. Ignoring the curling tendrils of unease snaking through her belly, she asked, "I don't suppose you'd like to get a drink some time?"

He hesitated, long enough that she wished she'd stayed silent. But then the lines around his mouth lifted. "Why not?"

Her writhing gut tightened further, but she was committed now. "Great. How about tonight? Or is that too short notice?"

"Tonight's fine."

They settled on a time and place and soon she was riding the elevator back to the main floor. Camryn had the odd sense that she'd watched another woman make the date with Abel. She'd never used her looks to manipulate a business deal before, and it made her feel ill.

The memory of Mattie and Jason's stricken faces firmed her resolve. People were depending on her, and Abel was a grown man. He could look after himself.

CHAPTER TWENTY-THREE

Will thought the meeting with Jason had gone well. He wasn't sure whether that was a good or a bad thing.

The older gentleman had appeared interested in the proposal. Yet it was obvious what he wanted most was to protect his granddaughters.

"What would their roles be if this were to take place?" he'd asked.

Will had to be honest, but that didn't mean he couldn't give some hope. "In part, it would depend on what they wanted to do. Mattie has an excellent skill set and experience. We want to diversify our workforce, especially when it comes to women." He'd then paused to gather his thoughts, responding slowly. "Camryn may be more difficult to find a position for, but we would do our best. You must understand, though, that I can't guarantee anything, of course. These situations are fluid."

It probably wasn't the answer Jason wanted, but he'd accepted it and they'd moved on to discuss other details. He'd promised to have an answer within a few days. If it wasn't an outright refusal, he would more than likely counter. Jason was an astute businessman. The whole process could take weeks to complete.

Will had no intention of waiting weeks to see Camryn again. He understood she would need time to make peace with the deal, and it was probably best to learn what Jason's formal response was before attempting to get in touch, but that was as long as he was prepared to let the issue simmer.

That evening, after a Corinne-prepared dinner of soft-shelled tacos, one of Laura's favourites, he cleaned the kitchen while she worked on her homework—clay sculptures of different shapes—at the table. Will's laptop was set up on the counter, and it dinged with an incoming Skype call.

"Laura, it's your mom," he said, drying his hands on a towel before swiping the touch pad to answer the call. "I'll bring the computer over."

"Mommy!" she squealed, wiggling on her chair and pushing her supplies out of the way to make room for the laptop.

"Hello, Laura," Elizabeth said, cool as usual. "What are you up to?"

Laura answered while Will went back to cleaning. Since Elizabeth's return to Vancouver, she hadn't let more than two days go by without getting in touch. In most cases, she talked only with Laura, but a couple of times she'd called after Laura was in bed. Will had been leery of that, but she'd only apologized for calling too late to talk to Laura, had made innocuous small talk for a few minutes, and let him go.

It was all very odd.

Tonight, however, she spoke with Laura for a few minutes and then he heard her say, "Laura, I need to speak with your father. Do you mind going to your playroom for a little while?"

"I'm not done my homework."

Will said, "I'll set you up on your table so you can finish. If you get stuck let me know and I'll help when I'm done talking with your mom."

He transferred Laura's packets of clay and the tray she was putting the finished pieces on to the playroom. Returning to the kitchen, he tilted the laptop screen to a more comfortable angle. "What do you need, Elizabeth?" he asked.

"I'm fine, Will, how are you?" She raised a sarcastic eyebrow.

He frowned. "Are you still at the office?" Behind her, a wide glass expanse revealed the upper levels of other office towers.

"I'm heading to a business function in half an hour. There was no time to go home." She leaned into the screen. "I wanted to talk to you about my next visit."

"I thought we'd decided Christmas."

"That's six weeks away. I want to start coming up for a few days every month. Which means I'd like to come in the next two weeks or so."

In the time Will had known Elizabeth, she had never spent more than a long weekend away from work, other than for Laura's birth and the few traumatic days when she'd been ill. "I didn't think you could spend that much time out of the office."

"I'm a partner. I can arrange my own schedule." He

wanted to say *Then why haven't you done so before this?* but kept quiet. "It is possible for me to work remotely for short periods of time." She nodded with decision, her black hair swinging against her jaw.

While he had to give her credit for her consistency and attentiveness during the last few weeks, he couldn't help but be suspicious of this new, friendly, family-oriented Elizabeth. "What's your end goal, Elizabeth? What are you hoping to achieve with these visits?"

"Isn't it enough that I want to spend time with Laura? I know you think I gave up that right, but you promised I could see her whenever I want."

He had made that promise, and was a little ashamed to realize that he'd made it partly because he was certain she wouldn't hold him to it. "Do you plan on spending time with Laura in a hotel room? That doesn't seem very appealing."

Elizabeth's gaze flicked away from his, then back in a rare display of uncertainty. "I had hope that, maybe, you'd let me stay in the house. In the spare room," she added in a hurry, obviously reading his expression correctly.

"I really don't think that's a good idea. That would definitely give Laura the wrong impression." Not to mention Camryn. Although whether that still mattered was obviously up in the air.

Elizabeth answered his spoken objection. "Not if we explain it to her."

"How do you explain to a five-year old that her parents are not getting back together, even though they are living in the same house?"

"She's smart. She'll understand."

"Hell, Elizabeth," Will said, "*I* don't understand. Why

this sudden interest in being with Laura? Why now, after all these years?"

Elizabeth had never been expressive. During their best—as well as their toughest—times together, she'd maintained a calm facade. When her brow crumpled and a sheen of tears filled her eyes, Will knew it was bad.

"What is it?" His fingers went numb.

"It's nothing," she said, blinking quickly and lifting her chin. "The doctors assure me of that."

The chill spread to his gut. "Doctors?"

Her smile was pale and faded. "In early October I went in for my regularly scheduled mammogram. The scan discovered a mass in my left breast. That's not unusual—these scans often pick up anomalies that in ninety-five percent of cases turn out to be nothing. I went in for an ultrasound. The decision after that was to do a biopsy."

"Damn it, Elizabeth. Why didn't you tell me?" She must have been terrified, probably still was. She couldn't stand it when things were out of her control.

She shrugged. "It wasn't your concern. There didn't seem any huge urgency on the part of the medical team, which I took to be a good sign, so when they scheduled the biopsy for the beginning of November, I arranged to visit Laura prior to the procedure."

If she had arranged one trip because of a health scare, and was now asking to come again so soon... "Do you have the results yet?"

"I received them today." She sounded like she was talking about a package from Amazon, not a potential life-threatening report. "I'm told the mass is benign. I have to go back for check-ups, of course, but all is well at this point."

"That's excellent news," he said with complete sincerity. "You must be relieved."

"I am." This time, her smile held more of its usual power. "So, about my visit this month. What day would be good for my arrival?"

He now understood Elizabeth's sudden urge to reach out to him and Laura, but she had to realize it didn't change anything between them. Trying to be gentle, he said, "I'm sure you've been very worried, and am sorry it took something like this to bring you back into Laura's life. But I want to be perfectly clear. This does not go beyond your relationship with our daughter. We are not a couple, Elizabeth. We are Laura's parents, and that's where it ends."

He thought he saw disappointment flit across her features, but Elizabeth only looked at her watch, a narrow, silvery band. "I have to go soon. We'll talk more later. Please bring Laura back so I can say goodbye."

Giving up for the moment, he nodded and went to fetch their daughter. She was the living, breathing, smiling, dancing reason he and Elizabeth were forever connected. But that didn't mean he wasn't entitled to a woman in his life who loved him for who he was.

Whether that woman was Camryn remained to be seen.

Camryn met Abel at Kask, a wine bar in downtown Prince George. He was waiting for her in the tiny lobby when she arrived, and while he wasn't wearing a suit tonight, he still sported a colourful tie. They were seated at a high-top table and, after a short discussion with the server, chose a selection from the tasting menu, including three wines and small trays of snacks to accompany them.

"Thanks for suggesting we come here," Camryn said, surveying the dimly lit room with appreciation. Artwork made from corks lent a touch of whimsy to the space, and the atmosphere was vigorous and buoyant. "I'm out of touch with what's available in Prince George."

"It's new. I was invited for the opening. We did a little work for them," Abel said, tone modest but proud.

He'd given her the perfect opening. She could compliment Charette Architects, and by association Abel himself. Charm him and flatter him and flirt with him just enough to be enticing but not enough to be obvious.

She could casually mention how much saving her grandfather's company meant to her, how grateful she'd be for any help, with just a hint of shyness and embarrassment to keep it believable. Use only a fraction of the cunning Anthony had used to bilk money out of her.

The server brought their wine, and she watched Abel chat with him, his expression open and sincere. His eyes crinkled as he laughed at something the server said, and he turned to her, welcoming her into the joke.

I can't do this, she thought in despair. She'd believed she could do anything to keep Bendixon and Sons going, but she couldn't use Abel this way. He was too nice a man to treat shabbily. Bendixon and Sons would have to survive, or not, as it always had—on its own merits, not through any chicanery or trickery.

"You look lovely, by the way," Abel said after the server left their table. "I guess I should have said that before." He smiled.

"Thank you," she said, and took a sip of her strawberry-rhubarb wine. She needed to make sure the rest of the night stayed professional and hoped what she said next would clarify any mixed signals she might have sent. "Tonight is on Bendixon and Sons. It's our way of saying thanks for the opportunities you've provided us, and of showing our gratitude for your patience in hearing me out today. I know the idea came out of the blue."

Abel regarded her, his head tilted to one side. "I appreciate the gesture, but now that you've mentioned it, I don't want you to think I came here under false pretences." He met Camryn's gaze directly. "I discussed your suggestion with our Vice-President. He was intrigued by the thought, but wanted me to pass on our regrets."

"I see." Camryn's toes curled in her high-heeled pumps. It was ridiculous to feel resentment that all her angst about manipulating him had been for nothing, but between that and the crushing disappointment she had to hold her breath for a moment to regain control. "Well, thanks for asking." She sipped her wine again, giving herself another moment to regroup. "We've been exploring other avenues, of course. But I wanted to give Charette Architects the first option." There. That sounded calm and professional. Even if it was a lie.

"I'm sorry I don't have better news."

"That's all right," she said brightly, "we still have the potential to win Crossroads Corner, after all. Securing that project would be an amazing step forward for Bendixon and Sons."

Abel's expression remained polite and attentive, but his eyes dropped from hers and his fingers began toying with his glass.

"What?" Camryn said, feeling her heart pumping as if she'd been doing yoga for an hour. "Has a decision been made?"

Abel's neatly manicured nails tapped a rapid tattoo on

the stem. In the second of silence before he answered, hope flared in her chest, so hot it ached. Then the significance of his averted eyes, his nervous fidgeting, registered.

"I really can't say anything."

He didn't have to, though. She could read the decision in his face.

The urge to get up and run, to escape, was overwhelming, but she couldn't. No matter what, Abel was still a business associate, and she needed to act appropriately. Even though she felt like screaming.

Smiling around clenched teeth, she said, "All right, I won't tease you anymore. I'll wait for the official notice." Lifting her glass, she said, "To future successes."

"To future successes," Abel echoed.

The server chose that moment to bring their appetizers, and Camryn silently blessed him. It gave her much needed time to get her emotions in order. They were so close to the surface these days.

According to Abel, the savoury smoked salmon was a surprisingly delightful pairing with the sweetness of the fruit wine, and reminded him of a tasting he'd done while on a bicycle tour of California wine country. To Camryn, the wine might as well have been water, and she listened to the anecdote through ears stuffed with cotton balls. Everything was muted and flat, crushed under the weight of her failures. She tried to console herself with the fact she'd stayed true to her ethics, and avoided sinking to the same lows as Anthony, with no success.

It was a long evening.

CHAPTER TWENTY-FOUR

Camryn lay in bed the next morning, mourning the loss of positivity she'd woken with only days before and trying to gather the energy to get up and head for the office.

She'd made it through the evening with Abel, but it had taken every ounce of grit she had to appear lighthearted and interested. She didn't regret treating Abel with the respect he deserved—yet a tiny part of her wished she'd been ruthless enough *not* to. No matter what she did, no matter how hard she tried, doors were closing around her, forcing her down a path she didn't want to follow, and she could see no way out of the maze.

She felt so alone, so isolated. What made it worse was the one person she wanted to rant to, wanted to lean on, was the one person she *shouldn't* want.

Pulling the covers over her head, she gave in and

thought of Will. If nothing else, last night's business disaster had served to distract her from the debacle that was her personal life. But she was too tired to block him out now, and she let her thoughts drift to their night together—the feeling of connectedness, of intimacy. Even given the fact they'd nearly been interrupted by her sister, she still remembered the sense of freedom and joy she'd experienced. It wasn't only the passion she missed. The days she'd spent with Will and Laura were some of the best memories she'd made in months, if not years.

He'd be damn near perfect if he wasn't standing in the way of Bendixon and Sons.

She tossed back the covers in a sudden fury and strode to the bathroom. Enough wallowing in self-pity. She wasn't giving Will or Abel or Anthony or *anyone* the satisfaction of beating her. She just had to try harder.

Less than an hour later, she arrived at the office, pulling up at the same time Mattie arrived in her big, black pickup. She slid out of the cab, her petite frame dwarfed by its bulk, her ubiquitous overalls hidden under a heavy parka, her usual ball cap replaced with a pink toque.

"It's only November and I wish winter was over already," she said as they hurried inside.

"In Vancouver things would still be green." Camryn glared balefully at the leafless branches of the trees lining the parking lot, their grim, grey limbs matching her mood.

The front office looked forlorn without Helen behind the desk. She'd started coming in only from ten to two, saying it was her way of winding down to retirement. Camryn suspected it had more to do with helping the company save on wages.

Mattie headed to the warehouse in the back to check the supplies she needed for the one small renovation project they'd managed to secure since Camryn's return. While even the most menial of jobs were welcome, it might not make a difference in the long run.

She hung up her coat and scarf in the break room. Hearing Jason's voice next door, she squared her shoulders and went to tell him what she'd learned last night.

He put down the phone as she entered. "Morning," he said.

"Hello." She settled in the cracked and broken visitor's chair. God, she hated that piece of furniture. It was a physical manifestation of everything that was wrong with her life. "I have bad news."

He didn't look surprised. "Charette Architects turned down your proposal."

She resented that he was so quick to reach that conclusion, but—"Yes." Yesterday she had told Mattie and Jason her plans while still in the first bloom of hope. Now, she wished she'd kept her mouth shut—especially since she wasn't done confessing.

"I have other bad news. It's not official yet," she said, "but last night Abel told me something else."

Jason swung his chair from side to side, his expression neutral. "We didn't get Crossroads Corner."

"No." She squeezed her eyes shut briefly, clenching her fingers against the humiliation. "I don't know what else to do," she blurted. "I'm trying everything I can think of, but nothing is working."

"I appreciate it. You need to know that." He came around the desk and sat in the chair opposite. He smelled of sawdust and Old Spice, and a wave of nostalgia swept over her, taking her back to childhood, to camping trips to the lake and making snowmen in the backyard.

"I'm not doing it for you," she said. He quirked his thick eyebrows and she hastened to explain. "Not just for you, I mean. I want it for Mattie, too. And for myself."

He leaned his elbows on his knees, clasping his hands. "There's more going on than just that jerk ruining your career, isn't there?"

A hard lump swelled in her throat at the kindness in his eyes. She swallowed around it and nodded. "Yes. But it'll be okay. We just need to get Bendixon and Sons back up to snuff."

"If you need money—"

She cut him off. "I won't take your money. I got myself into this mess, I'll get myself out. I was just hoping the solutions we need could be combined. An all-in-one answer. But I don't think that's going to work anymore."

Thankfully, he didn't press her further. "I've been thinking about the Kohlenburg Group's offer."

"Me, too." She sighed. "I think you should take it."

"You do?" He cocked his head to one side. "What changed your mind?"

A piece of cracked plastic dug into the back of her thigh. She shifted, careful not to tear a hole in her slacks. "It's the best decision for you and Mattie and Helen. You'll get the equity you need, maybe choose to gift some of it to Helen to help her out in the short term. I'm sure Mattie will find a place in the new structure. It works out for everyone."

"What about you?"

She smiled, although panic bubbled in her stomach, making her queasy. "If the Kohlenburg Group doesn't want me"—*Fat chance of that,* she thought—"I'll look elsewhere. I've got a good degree and excellent experience. I'm sure I'll find something." She'd have to stay in Prince George, as it was cheaper to live here than in Vancouver. As well, fewer people would know of the scandal in her past. Maybe she wouldn't be reduced to working in fast food, as Will had accused her of thinking, but at this point, a pay cheque was more important than a career.

Jason leaned back and studied her. "You were always a tough little kid," he said.

She chuckled. "Me? I was the one who wore dresses and had tea parties and hated to get dirty. Mattie was the tomboy, and Jo"—she shrugged and smiled—"well, Jo has always played her own tune."

"I don't mean physically tough, although you were no wuss, either." Elbows propped on the arms of his chair, he steepled his fingers, his hands lean and ropy with age. "When you set out to do something, you did it. You've been told you never crawled, right? Went straight from sitting to walking. And I've never seen a kid work harder at school. If there was a bonus assignment or extra credit available, you did it. No grumbling about it, either. If you didn't understand something, you were even more determined to learn. I always knew you'd be the one to fly out on her own. You left home at eighteen and never looked back."

Stunned at his view of her, she could only stare for a moment. When she found her voice, she said, "I didn't know you'd paid that much attention."

He ducked his chin in abashed acknowledgement. "Just because you didn't want to come to dirty construction sites and learn how to use a circular saw doesn't mean I didn't pay attention."

"Well, thank you. It's nice to know I impressed you with something." She hadn't realized until now how much his praise would mean. She had long known Mattie was his favourite—and why wouldn't she be? She'd followed in the footsteps his sons had rejected. But now, a tiny kernel of jealousy she'd been harboring dissolved. "I'm sorry I haven't been able to keep up the tradition. I'm afraid trying hard isn't going to be enough to save your company."

"I don't know about that."

Camryn looked at him sharply, alerted to something in his tone.

"You know who I was talking to when you came in?" he said.

She shook her head.

"It was the chief maintenance supervisor with the School District. Seems Bendixon and Sons answered a request for proposal for work needed at a few of the older elementary schools."

Camryn recalled the project, something she'd applied to her first week home. "I told you about that, didn't I? They needed a contractor to renovate bathrooms and entrances, due to accessibility issues. It was like what Mattie told me you'd done for Gateway Crescent."

Jason nodded. "Yes, but on a much bigger scale. I hadn't even known they were looking for a contractor, hadn't heard about it through my usual channels. You found it online and squeaked your proposal in under the deadline. By then they'd already received many others, of course."

The spark of hope she'd felt sputtered and died. He was letting her down easy, she could feel it. "I'm sorry I couldn't get it in sooner. I put it together as fast as I could. I needed you to approve the values before I sent it in."

"Yes, I remembered that when the supervisor

confirmed them with me."

"Confirmed the values?" Camryn frowned. "Why did he need to do that if we didn't get the job?"

"Because we did," Jason said, a beaming grin lighting up his face. "We are to start as soon as possible."

For a moment, Jason's image wavered, as if heat waves danced in the air between them. Camryn's fingernails bit into her thighs as she held herself steady. "We got it?" she whispered.

"The first payment is being transferred as we speak, and they are emailing the plans. They want us at the first school by the end of the week."

"We got a job? A big, long-term job?" After all the battering her brain had taken in the last few days, it was having trouble accepting the good news.

"We did. And if it hadn't been for you, we wouldn't even have bid on it."

Camryn's head felt like it was floating. Relief flooded her, and her cheeks tingled like she'd had too much to drink. "I can't believe it."

"Believe it," Jason said, "but don't get too relaxed. We're not out of the woods yet. You have a lot of work to do to get us back to solid ground."

"But we have breathing room."

"Yes, we do. We have breathing room. All thanks to you."

"Okay, then." She rose, slightly unsteady on her feet. "I guess I should get back online, see what else I can find."

Jason rose with her and kissed her gently on the forehead. "I knew you could do it," he said. "The little girl I saw grow up wouldn't give up, and the woman she became won't give up either."

Will's desk phone, a direct line, rang. He reached out, his hand hovering over the receiver, noting the call display. *Bendixon and Sons.* His heart thumped hard, then resumed its normal pattern when he realized it wouldn't be Camryn. She wouldn't be ready to talk to him yet. Not that he was going to let that stop *him* from talking to *her.* He'd give her a couple more days, then it would be time to get them back on track. She was stubborn and melodramatic and elegant and exactly what he wanted. He just needed to convince her of that.

The phone rang again. He withdrew his hand and stared at the device.

He'd just been informed by Abel Quinson that the Kohlenburg Group had been awarded the Crossroads Corner project. He should have been elated—it was what he'd wanted, after all. But work and personal had become muddled, as embodied in his relationship with Camryn, and he hadn't been able to celebrate the win as he'd wanted to, knowing how crushed she'd be at the news.

The phone rang a third time, and he finally answered. "Will Danson."

"Jason Bendixon here."

Even though he'd known it wouldn't be Camryn, it didn't stop disappointment from stabbing him under his ribs. "How are you today, Mr. Bendixon? Anything I can help you with?" It had to be about the buyout, but that didn't mean Will couldn't let the other man broach the subject. Losing Crossroads Corner would make Jason's decision to sell easier and harder, all at the same time.

"I wanted to thank you for your offer, but we will not be accepting it."

That made Will sit up straight and plant his feet flat

on the floor, his chair rocking at his sudden movement. "You aren't?" Realizing he sounded so shocked it might be insulting, he took a quick breath and added in a more professional manner, "I'm sorry to hear that. We thought you'd be a good fit with us. Can you let me know the reason why?"

"We've always been an independent, family-run company and we prefer to stay that way. There are signs business is turning around and we feel our chances of securing new projects are good."

Will thought hard and fast. He couldn't be talking about Crossroads Corner, could he? Charette Architects wouldn't have given notice to unsuccessful bidders yet, as nothing formal had been signed.

While it wasn't his place to tell Jason the news, he couldn't let him decide about the buyout under the mistaken impression they were still in the running. "I can understand how you feel," he said, picking his words carefully, "but you know as well as I do that having bids out is no guarantee of success. Are you sure this is the best thing to do? I can't promise we'll make another offer in future."

"We understand that. But at this time, we feel this is the right step to take."

Did Will hear the echo of Camryn in that statement? "I assume your granddaughters approve of this decision?"

"What do you think?" A soft chuckle rolled down the line. "It is still my company, but day to day operations will be handled by Mattie and Camryn very soon. They were definitely a part of this process."

Will searched for another argument that might persuade Jason to change his mind, but came up with nothing. Keeping the frustration out of his voice, he said,

"I appreciate you letting me know. Best of luck."

"Have a good day." A quiet click signaled the end of the call.

Will tapped his fingers restlessly on his desktop, disturbed and worried. Could Camryn and Jason both be deluded about their chances of getting Crossroads Corner? They had to see that it was too far beyond their reach. Not that they weren't capable people. But the scope of this project was huge—ten times bigger than anything they'd ever dealt with before.

He should go and tell Samuel the deal to purchase Bendixon and Sons was off. Instead, he grabbed his cell and called Camryn. She answered after a single ring.

"I just got off the phone with Jason," Will said without preamble. "It's not too late to get him to change his mind about the sale."

"Why would I do that?" she said.

He rubbed the back of his neck. "Look, I shouldn't be telling you this. But we got the Crossroads Corner bid. It will be official just as soon as we sign the papers."

"Congratulations."

Her tone held none of the coolness he'd expected. If anything, he heard suppressed excitement. He replied with wary confusion. "Thanks?"

"I'm sure it will be a great success. If that's all, I'm in the middle of something."

"Wait. Don't hang up." He was missing something and needed to figure it out. "I got the impression from Jason that you were confident about winning a big project. If not Crossroads Corner, what was he talking about?"

"You're not the only one who received good news today. We just secured a substantial contract with the School District for extensive renovations at a number of schools." Now he realized what he could hear in her voice. It was triumph. "The paperwork is coming through as we speak."

The relief he felt was followed by an immediate rush of pride. "Well done," he said sincerely. "That's great news."

"Thank you." It was easy to discern the satisfaction in her voice. She deserved it.

Seizing the moment of amity, he said, "You understand the buyout was nothing personal, right? My job is to help the Kohlenburg Group succeed, and they had decided an acquisition was what they wanted."

"I've told you, it wasn't the offer. It was the fact you hid it from me."

"Can't we get past that? I've explained why I couldn't tell you, not before approaching Jason."

Silence hummed between them. He held his breath, waiting.

"I've missed you," she said.

Air whooshed out of him in a gasp. He was caught off-guard by a sudden swell of emotion. "I've missed you, too."

"I've also missed Laura, so don't get too cocky."

He grinned, picturing her nose in the air, eyebrows raised, expression matching her brash tone. "I won't. But fair warning, knowing you missed my daughter clinches it."

"Clinches what?" she asked with suspicion.

"An offer for dinner. Want to come over tonight?"

"I really shouldn't. Thursday is the night all the Bendixons get together to Skype with my parents while they're travelling, and I missed last week when I took you and Laura out for dinner."

His heart dropped in disappointment.

"Oh, they'll be home soon enough," she said. "What time should I be there?"

CHAPTER TWENTY-FIVE

Camryn offered to wash the dishes and clean the kitchen while Will helped Laura with her homework. Oddly, the domestic scene sat comfortably on her shoulders. She'd never aspired to the two-point-whatever children and suburban home dream, instead relishing her career and the sophisticated life she'd built for herself. Which was why tonight seemed both right and wrong at the same time.

Nothing like a little white-collar crime to get you re-examining your values, she thought, rinsing suds off a saucepan. *That must be it.*

That didn't, however, explain the glow in her chest as she watched Will and Laura, dark heads close together, working on math homework. Laura had brought a bin full of blocks from the playroom and dumped it on the table. Will was choosing different amounts and placing them in front of her, and then she had to find the correct number on the Braille pad. His patient instruction and her bright determination made for a sweet scenario that had Camryn's heart aching with an emotion she didn't want to name.

The ache stayed with her after homework and chores were done, when they all walked to a nearby park. It was dark out, of course, given how early the sun set at this time of year. Camryn realized with an odd start that the darkness meant nothing to Laura. The cold, however, was another matter, hovering below the freezing mark, chilly enough for everyone to bundle up.

Laura loved to swing, and as she arced to and fro, feet pumping and hair flying, Will and Camryn stood and watched. It was the first private moment they'd had since she'd learned of the buyout offer.

"Want to sit?" Will said, gesturing at a concrete bench a few feet away.

Camryn shuddered, imagining the icy stone under her. "No, thanks."

"We won't be long. It's good for her to get some fresh air before bed, but she'll want to go home soon."

"I'm fine."

Silence fell between them. Camryn wondered if Will felt the way she did, that they were tiptoeing around each other like polite strangers. She needed to break through, help them find their way back to the intimacy of last weekend.

"I didn't think this would be so awkward," Will said.

"Oh, thank god," Camryn said on a relieved gasp. "I thought it was just me."

"Maybe this will help. Come here." Will looped his arm over her shoulders and pulled her in close. The slippery material of his jacket felt frosted with cold against her cheek, but she didn't care. She wrapped her arms around his waist, tucking herself into his lean strength from shoulder to hip.

"You're right. This is better," she murmured.

His chin grazed her skull, protected by a woolly toque she'd borrowed. "Yes, it is."

Words seemed unnecessary in the minutes that followed. Camryn stood, her eyes on Laura and her head on Will's chest, desperately conscious of the man holding her. Much of what came next in their relationship depended on him. But whatever happened, Camryn would accept it.

Laura stopped pumping and dragged her boots on the hard ground beneath the swing, slowing her momentum. "My hands are cold."

"Must be time to go," Camryn said, lifting her head and taking a step back. Not wanting to overstay her welcome, she continued, "I suppose I should head home, too."

"Daddy!" Laura called.

"Be right there." Will lifted Camryn's chin, his hand encased in a sleek leather glove, yet she still felt heat seep into her skin. Despite the streetlamps surrounding the park, the evening dim deepened the brown of his irises to black. "Don't go. Come home with us." His gaze intensified. "I'll put her to bed as quick as I can."

He didn't have to say more, the glow in his eyes telling her everything she needed to know. The ache she'd carried most of the evening softened, and a tingle spread through her limbs, her belly.

"All right," she said.

It was turning into the kind of evening Will had never expected to have. It had always seemed like asking too much.

Even at first, when Elizabeth had been closely involved in Laura's life, they'd never spent time together like a family. It had been a series of meetings to pass the baby, not quiet dinners or simple excursions or a sharing of chores.

He'd certainly never experienced the low-grade fever that sweet anticipation built, not like he was experiencing tonight.

"Let's get those teeth brushed," he said to Laura, resisting the urge to skip straight to a bedtime story. Thank goodness it wasn't bath night. He didn't think he could wait that long to get back to Camryn.

Her mouth full of foam, Laura burbled something he couldn't understand.

"Spit," he instructed. "Then speak."

She spat into the sink then raised her head, her lips still covered in bubbles. "Can Camryn read my story tonight?" Her hand unerringly found the cup he had filled with water, which he placed in the exact same spot every night, so she could rinse.

"I can ask her if you like."

Laura nodded. "Yes, please."

"Okay. You get to your room. I'll go see."

Camryn was seated on the couch in the family room, feet tucked underneath, scrolling through her phone. The main lights were off, and the table lamp illuminated her short blonde hair. She was a beacon, shining just for him. His heart thudded with need.

She looked up. "Done already?"

The hopeful tone in her voice pleased him no end. As did the gleam of disappointment when he shook his head. "Not yet. Laura is hoping you'll read her bedtime story."

Her eyes widened. "Me?"

"It's a great honour. You are not allowed to say no." A fleeting look of panic crossed her face, and Will swallowed a sudden chuckle. "I'm just teasing. You don't have to, but she'll be disappointed if you don't."

"I imagine I can handle it." Camryn rose, leaving her phone on the coffee table. "I don't think I've read out loud to anyone since my last babysitting job," she said, adding with what sounded like horrified wonder, "almost twenty years ago."

"It's quite simple. She'll tell you which one she wants. Just make sure to read every word. She has most of them memorized so you can't get away with skipping pages."

"All right." She went to move past him and he put his hand on her hip.

She wore a thin sweater of some ultra-soft fabric in blue, a colour he noticed she wore often. He didn't mind. It made her eyes even more alluring. "For luck," he said, and kissed her.

Her lips immediately softened and his fingers tightened, drawing her closer. But before he had a chance to get too lost in the embrace, a small voice called down the hall.

"Daddy? Is Camryn coming?"

With a sigh he stepped back. "You're being paged."

A mischievous grin transformed Camryn's face. It was an expression he'd never seen on her before, and he couldn't tear his eyes away. "I'll try and make it quick. Don't go anywhere."

She disappeared into Laura's room and for a moment

he just stood there, taken aback by the hunger rising in him. Going to the kitchen, he rummaged in the junk drawer to find the plain white candles Corinne had stuffed in there after a craft project, collected a stack of the small plates he and Laura used for toast in the morning, and headed down the hall. He paused to listen to the soft cadence of Camryn's voice telling the story of a goose girl and a handsome prince, then continued to his bedroom. Inside, he did a quick tidy, tossing clothes onto the chair on the corner and pulling the bedspread up over the sheets, giving the illusion he'd made it in the morning. Then he created a puddle of melted wax in the centre of each plate, anchored the candles upright, and placed them in clusters on the dresser and nightstands.

Surveying his work, he nodded. It wasn't a room at the Four Seasons, but it looked warm and romantic, the amber glow of the candles flickering on the basic beige walls and box-store furniture, softening and transforming them.

The murmur of Camryn's voice ceased. He crept down the hall and peered around the door jamb. His daughter was out like a light, snoring gently, Mr. Rabbit secure under her arm. Camryn slipped out of the bed, moving with the deliberation of a bomb disposal technician around a live fuse, and leaned down to brush her lips to Laura's brow. His heart clutched.

Before he could analyze his reaction, Camryn saw him. She held a finger to her lips. He smiled and tiptoed past to give Laura his own goodnight kiss. Her cheeks were rosy, her forehead warm, and he pulled the comforter below her shoulders to cool her off.

In the hall, Camryn took a step toward the kitchen, but he stopped her by taking her hand. Walking backward, he tugged her gently toward his bedroom. She followed, leaning back against his hold as if they were dancing. At the doorway, she spun, drawing his arm with her, her back resting against his chest for a tantalizing instant, then spinning away again, causing him to release his grip on her hand. She came to a breathless stop at the foot of the bed.

He closed the door and leaned against it, marvelling at the bright gold of her hair, the sweep of her cheekbones, the rise and fall of her breasts.

"Shouldn't you leave it open a bit?" she said, "so you can hear Laura if she needs you?" She grinned, a dimple popping up in her cheek. "I'll be quiet."

He didn't want her to be quiet. He wanted to make her scream and shout and beg for more. But her concern for his child, which she'd shown in so many ways tonight, staggered him, tipped him over the edge. He'd been teetering for days and wasn't surprised when the ground suddenly gave way. *Falling in love isn't that hard,* he thought, in dazed, lustful stupor. *Not with the right person.*

He could only hope she might feel the same someday. He was content to wait. Right now, however—

She stood, hands clasped at her waist, still except for the flexing of her fingers, waiting for his answer.

"She'll be fine." He approached and raised his hand, cupping the back of her neck, caressing with tiny touches of his fingertips the hollow at the base of her skull that intrigued him so much. She sighed, her arms dropping to hang lax at her sides, the restless motion of her hands ceasing.

He stepped even closer and was enveloped by her scent, her heat. With a hand on her lower back he pulled her in, her hips arching into his. He was hot and throbbing, his erection unmistakable. She didn't seem to mind, rubbing against him with a purr low in her throat.

She met his stare boldly, with confidence. A flare of desire lit their depths, like a jewel caught in the last rays of the setting sun.

"Kiss me," she said, and closed her eyes.

He happily obeyed.

CHAPTER TWENTY-SIX

Her mouth was hot and wet and welcoming. Her tongue danced with his, teasing and tempting. She strained closer, her arms slipping under his and stroking his back from shoulder blades to buttocks. Her fingers pressed hard and he felt her touch like a brand.

She didn't seem to notice when he rucked up her shirt and undid the clasp of her bra, her mouth busy on his, nipping and tasting as if he was a feast to be devoured. When he pulled away her frustrated moan would have made him grin if he hadn't been so focused on ridding her of her clothing. Soon she stood before him, naked. She gave no hint of self-consciousness, instead planting her hands on her hips and jutting out one knee in a demanding pose.

"Fair's fair," she said, pointing with her chin. "Off with them."

He shook his head. "Not yet." He needed the small buffer his clothing provided if he didn't want this to be over as quickly as last time.

She opened her mouth, but he forestalled whatever she might have been going to say by dropping to the floor and pressing his face to her belly. She smelled of lemon and herbs and the unmistakable aroma of female arousal. He was glad he was already on his knees, as her scent would have put him there anyway.

Her hands fluttered on his scalp, not quite touching, not quite directing, but conveying she wanted more, needed more. He was willing to oblige. He slid his hands up the backs of her legs, from her calves to her thighs, and placed an open-mouthed kiss just above the neat triangle of hair. She gasped, her legs trembling, and he held her tighter.

"Hold on to me," he muttered against her skin, and her hands clamped onto his skull.

It took only a few strokes of his tongue before her knees buckled. She fell backward onto the bed and he hooked her legs over his shoulders, driving her relentlessly up and up and up until she gave a strangled shriek, her body stiffening with tension, then collapsing as if all the bones in her body had evaporated.

He rose from the floor, moving carefully, excruciatingly aware of his cock pulsating behind the zipper of his jeans. He stripped off his clothes, hissing in relief, and crawled up the bed until he could lean against the headboard.

Reaching forward, he grasped Camryn under the shoulders and dragged her up with him. She gave him no help, sliding languidly on the slick sheets. "Give me a minute," she slurred.

He greatly enjoyed her sated limpness, but he wasn't about to let her drift off to sleep. Rolling her to her side, he spooned her from behind, his erection pressing between her thighs. His hand found her breast and he fanned her nipple with his palm, raising it to a hard bud, while he licked and nibbled her nape.

"I love the back of your neck," he whispered. He loved more than that, but didn't think she was ready to hear the whole truth.

She wriggled, nestling closer to him, and moaned deep in her chest, all of which he took as encouragement. Working his way from her neck to her ear, with a small side trip to the curve of her shoulder, he teased and tempted them both.

"What do you want me to do?" he whispered, his lips brushing the shell of her ear. "Where do you want me to touch you?"

"Anywhere," she panted, her hips circling, his cock squeezed between soft, wet flesh.

He took his hand from her breast and reached down, tapping her kneecap. "Here?"

She squirmed. "No." She lifted her leg, stretching it over his thigh, opening herself.

"Aaah," he said, his breath lifting wisps of hair off her temple. "Maybe…here?" He poked a finger in her navel.

She jerked. "No," she said on a sob. "You know where. Please. Touch me."

"I should make you say it," he said, torturing them both a little longer.

"Will!" she said, and he took pity on her.

When she was once again sprawled as if she would never move again, he slipped on a condom and slid into her, slowly, gently, relishing every sensation. Her lids fluttered up, revealing eyes slumberous and dazed.

"Hold on to me," he told her again, and she wrapped her arms around his torso, her calves hooking into the bend of his knees.

They moved in rhythm, without the haste of their first time. He didn't want it to end, and yet at the same time moved harder and faster, until he reached that moment when the world ceased to exist and all that was left was him and the woman he loved and the frantic pounding of his heart.

Camryn woke with a start. She stared at the wall opposite, disoriented, wondering how her curtains had changed from pastel seashells and starfish to navy and blue stripes while she slept. Voices behind her brought her fully awake and she rolled over, pulling the sheet up to conceal her nakedness and shifting up on one elbow to see Will's side of the bed.

Will's side of the bed, she thought with dazed wonder. Had she already made a claim to *her* side?

Bedazzled thoughts of making love with Will were pushed aside the moment she caught sight of Laura's pale, unhappy face as she stood next to the bed.

Will swung his feet to the floor, keeping his lower half covered with the comforter, and scooped her up onto his lap. "What's wrong, sweetie?" he said, his voice hoarse.

"I don't feel well," Laura said, and even though Camryn could no longer see her face she could hear the tears. She glanced over Will's shoulder to the clock on the nightstand. It wasn't yet midnight, even though she felt like she'd slept for hours. Snagging Will's T-shirt, which had been discarded on the floor near her, she slipped it on and crawled across the mattress.

"Does your tummy hurt?" she asked Laura, stroking the hair out of the little girl's eyes.

Laura shook her head, nestling closer to her daddy. "I'm cold."

Will dragged the bed cover over Laura's shoulders, tucking it around her slight body, and then laid his wrist on her forehead.

"She's got a fever," he said to Camryn, his voice calm, his eyes anxious.

Meningitis started with a fever. Could a child get meningitis twice? She had no idea. Fear struck a blow below her ribs.

"Do you have a thermometer?" she asked.

Will cuddled Laura close. She had dropped into a sudden doze, but made fretful noises, wriggling as if trying to escape her discomfort. "The ensuite. Left-hand drawer. While you're in there, bring the Children's Tylenol from the medicine cabinet above the sink."

Camryn clambered off the bed, tugging Will's shirt down to cover her butt. Not that Laura would notice, but it seemed wrong to be exposed with a child in the room.

It took her awhile to find the thermometer, as she was looking for the thin tube she remembered from her own childhood illnesses, and instead discovering something that resembled a white electric razor—a handheld unit with a flat, rubberized pad on its head. Snatching the medicine from the cabinet, she hurried back to Will.

He had laid Laura on the bed and pulled on his robe. Taking the thermometer, he placed it on Laura's forehead. "Thirty-nine point five."

Camryn had no idea what the proper body temperature should be. "Is that bad?" she asked, not caring if she revealed her ignorance. It was more important to know.

"It's been this high before," Will said, never taking his eyes off Laura, even as he took the pill bottle from Camryn and twisted the cap. "Only once since then." He didn't elaborate, but she knew when he meant. "But that was during the day and she seemed pretty good otherwise, so I waited it out."

Camryn wondered at the courage it took *not* to rush to Emergency every time your child was sick. Especially one like Laura, one that had already been through so much. "Do we just wait, then?"

"We'll give her the medicine," he said, and her heart thumped at the *we*. "Then I'll take her temperature in half an hour or so."

After he'd woken a cranky Laura enough to get her to chew the tablets and helped her wash the taste out with a sip of water, he settled her into the big bed. She looked so tiny, barely making a bump under the covers.

He sat next to her, one hand absently rubbing his daughter's back. Not exactly sure what to do, Camryn settled beside him.

"Thanks for your help," he said.

It wouldn't be the first time he'd had to deal with Laura in the middle of the night. And normally he'd be alone. Camryn was glad she had been with him this time. "No problem."

"Kind of a rude awakening, isn't it?" The skin around his eyes crinkled as if he was smiling, but his lips remained serious. "As good as you look in my shirt, you probably want to get going. It's early enough—you can still get a decent night's sleep before work tomorrow."

It had been a crazy week, and there was one more day

to get through. Not that the weekends had given Camryn much respite lately. She'd spent a lot of her time studying the industry, refreshing herself on business laws and taxes, anything that might help her save Bendixon and Sons. But she found herself reluctant to leave.

"Even if the medication eases Laura's fever, you won't want to send her to school," she said. "Will you call Corinne to come?"

"No. I'll work from home. I've done it before." He swept the back of his free hand on her cheek, the caress making her want to curl into him, while her heart gave another odd little kick, thinking of him dealing with a sick child alone.

"I'll wait a little," she said. "I'd like to know if the medicine helps."

"That's nice, but not necessary. We'll be fine on our own."

"I know." She shrugged, a little nonplussed at his determination to send her home. "I'd still like to stay, if that's all right."

If he told her to go home again, she'd leave. As much as she wanted to make sure Laura was okay, she couldn't force herself on them. After a pause, he quirked one corner of his mouth into an apologetic grin. "When she's like this, I let her sleep in my bed with me. That way I know how she's doing, and if she wakes up I'm right there for her. Did you want to bunk down in her bed? Or on the couch?"

Now that he was allowing her to stay, she had no intention of being relegated to the status of guest. "It's a big bed," she said. "Don't you think there's room for all three of us?"

That earned her a soft chuckle, and she felt inordinately proud that she lightened his mood even that much. "You've obviously never slept with a child before," he said. "You have no idea how much space they take up."

"I'm willing to give it a try. If you are," she said.

He led her to the other side of the bed and climbed in, so he would be nearest Laura, then lifted the covers for her. "Come on in," he said, "but don't say I didn't warn you." His eyes were teasing as he said it, and she relaxed, certain she was doing the right thing.

CHAPTER TWENTY-SEVEN

By Monday morning, Laura was recovered and fit to go back to school. As Will helped her get ready, his mind couldn't let go of the thoughts and feelings he'd been trying to digest all weekend.

Three mornings ago, lying in bed with Camryn on his right and Laura on his left, he had wondered how he could possibly feel so content while his daughter burned with a fever. The word alone had the power to throw him into a panic, but that night the desperation tinged with terror hadn't taken a hold of him as it usually did.

It was easy to figure out why. Camryn had been there. He hadn't been alone.

He hadn't realized how isolated he was, how solitary, until she filled the empty space he didn't know was there.

As planned, he'd stayed home with Laura the next day, after sending Camryn off to work. Her reluctance to leave both amused and touched him, and he'd kept that warm feeling with him throughout the weekend, even when a petulant Laura tried his patience, which was often. He took her grumpiness as a sign she was getting over whatever had thrown her into the sudden fever, but that didn't mean he enjoyed it.

Camryn had called to see how things were going but hadn't come to visit. He had the impression she was waiting for an invite, but he hadn't suggested it. While her support that night had been welcome, the last thing he wanted to do was frighten her off by exposing her to a bad-tempered child. Better to ease her into that sort of thing, if he wanted to convince her to become Laura's stepmother.

He dropped Laura off at school and headed for the office, mulling *that* thought over. He wanted to marry Camryn, that much had become clear to him in the last few days.

Too bad he had a nasty suspicion she wasn't in the same place. Not at all.

"Morning," Samuel greeted him as he entered the office. "How's that little sweetie of yours?"

"Much better, thanks." Will unwound the scarf from his neck and headed down the hall, Samuel on his heels. "Thanks for holding the fort on Friday."

"No worries." He made himself comfortable in the visitor's chair and waited as Will took off his coat and opened his laptop. "You got my email?"

Will resisted the urge to reply he had gotten *all* of Samuel's many emails. But since he knew which one he was referring to, he simply said, "I don't know what Wayne wants us to do. Jason turned down the offer. It's not like it's a publicly traded company and we can go in and snap up shares."

Wayne had not been happy to learn of the failed deal. Samuel had done too good a job pitching him Bendixon and Sons, and once Wayne had an idea in his head, he was difficult to budge. It made him a successful businessman, but a tricky boss.

"You tell him that," Samuel said. "He'll be calling any minute."

Prophetically, the desk phone rang. Will connected the call, putting it on speaker so Samuel could hear. "Good morning, Wayne."

"Explain to me again what happened with Bendixon and Sons."

Will raised his eyebrows at Wayne's brusque tone. This sounded like more than simple disappointment. "There's really little I can say. I made the offer, Jason thought about it, he decided not to accept."

"He didn't make a counteroffer?"

"No," Will said patiently. "He told me they'd just signed a good contract and wanted to keep the status quo, see if things would even out for them."

"He gave no hint that he might be in discussion with another company? That he was playing us against someone else?"

Will glanced at Samuel, who gave a puzzled shrug. "No, nothing like that. What's this about, Wayne? We gave you two other possibilities. Why not move on to one of those?"

"Believe it or not, those possibilities are no longer options. While they may have been our second and third choices, they were the first two choices for Jepsen Contracting."

Samuel's mouth dropped open. Will was equally stunned. Jepsen Contracting was the Kohlenburg Group's biggest competitor in the Lower Mainland. "Since when are they even looking at Prince George? We've heard absolutely no hints of that up here." Samuel would have known if there had been any rumours, Will was certain of it.

"Obviously, we are not the only ones who have seen the potential in Northern British Columbia." Wayne's tone was grim. "Our early arrival may have given us the edge for a while, but as of now we've lost whatever advantage we had. Jepsen will be able to step right in, picking up contracts already on the books for their new acquisitions, and it won't take long for them to move on new projects, either. We should have thought of this expansion sooner."

Will's brain tumbled as he tried to assimilate the news and decide their next steps. "There must be other companies we can look at."

Samuel shook his head. "The rest are much too small, or so new they don't have a solid core of contracts. I know Bendixon and Sons is struggling right now, but they have one of the best reputations in town. If Jepsen picks them up, we'll really be behind the eight ball."

"Get them," Wayne said. "I'm willing to up the offer. I'll email you the details right away. We have to block Jepsen from Bendixon and Sons if we want to solidify our stake in the market."

This is bad, Will thought. It had been difficult enough to offer Jason the first deal, knowing how intensely Camryn wanted to make the family firm a success. But now his career with the Kohlenburg Group might rest on it—his thoughts shied away from the logical conclusion.

He owed Wayne Kohlenburg for giving him the opportunity to grow and succeed. The company had supported him in the first terrible months of Laura's blindness, and trusted him to open the new branch. He couldn't let the Kohlenburg family down now.

But he couldn't let Camryn go, either.

Doing what was right for the woman he loved shouldn't be tearing him apart. But how could he jeopardize Laura's security when he didn't even know how Camryn felt about him?

Camryn put her phone down slowly, staring at the wall before her without really seeing it.

Will had sounded…she searched for the right word and the best she could come up with was *odd*. He'd asked for a meeting with her and Jason, and Mattie if she was available, as soon as possible. That obviously meant his out of character-ness had nothing to do with Laura, which had been her first thought at hearing his voice. Now, the only reason she could come up with was he wanted to re-open the discussion about selling Bendixon and Sons. If so, she could have told him to save his breath. She had called Roger Roswell at the bank and told him about the School District contract, which had soothed his worst fears. He'd assured her the paperwork would go through immediately and they'd have the short-term funds they needed. The hesitant optimism she'd felt last week glowed once more.

After speaking with Jason, she texted Will back, setting up an appointment within the hour. She wasn't going to get any work done while wondering what he wanted, so getting it over with seemed best.

Shortly before the appointed time, the draft of cold air that heralded the opening of the front door swooped down the hall and into the break room. Without waiting for

Helen to call, she went to reception.

Her heart gave a joyful twist when she saw Will. He wore his leather coat over dark jeans, his only concession to the colder weather a navy-blue scarf draped loosely around his neck. His slightly too long hair was flecked with white from the light snow she could see falling past the large window behind him. He looked...*right*...chatting with Helen, standing in the familiar office that was so much a part of her family.

She stepped closer. He looked at her and she couldn't help the smile lifting her lips. It faded quickly, though, when he didn't return it, and worry poured back in.

"What's going on, Will?" She bit the inside of her lip to stop more questions from streaming out. *Is it bad news? Why are you here? Why do you look so grim?*

"Where are Jason and Mattie? It will be better if you all hear it at the same time," he said.

This was sounding worse and worse. "This way," she said, and started down the hall, Will's footsteps behind her raising the hair on the back of her neck. She rolled her shoulders, trying to shake off a sense of doom. *You are making too much of this*, she scolded herself. *It's just another business meeting.*

It didn't help.

Jason rose from his chair and reached across his desk to offer his hand to Will before gesturing to one of the visitor's seats. Camryn stood at Jason's shoulder, shifting her weight from foot to foot.

"All right, then," Jason said. "What's so important that it couldn't wait another minute?"

Will surveyed the room, his eyes shuttered. Camryn couldn't tell what he was thinking. That in itself was frightening. "Is Mattie coming?"

"She's on a job," Jason said. "We'll pass on your news later. If you ever get around to telling us what it is."

Will gathered himself, pressing his hands on his knees and leaning slightly forward, his glance flickering between Jason and Camryn. "I've come to make another offer for Bendixon and Sons."

Camryn's shoulders drooped in disappointment. Why couldn't he just move on? "We've already declined," she said, watching Will through narrowed eyes. "What's the point of asking again?"

He flared his nostrils, opened his mouth and closed it. When he finally spoke, he directed his words to Jason. "If I ask you a question, will you answer it honestly?"

Camryn saw Jason's jaw harden. "If you have to ask for honesty, what's the point of the question at all? Sounds like you won't believe me no matter what I say."

Will closed his eyes for a moment. When he opened them, a new determination shone in his expression. "I'm sorry. That was poorly done of me. What I'm hoping you'll tell me is this—have you received any offers to buy your company, other than mine?"

"Of course n—" Camryn began, but Jason lifted a hand to stop her.

"Not that it's any of your business," he said, "but since you seem to think it's so important, there was one, a few weeks ago." He twisted his neck so he could look up at Camryn. "It was before you came home. Didn't think it worth mentioning." He turned back to Will. "Some outfit called Jepsen Contracting."

Will nodded, a quick jerk of his chin. "You only spoke to them the once? Nothing since then?"

"Well, we had more than one conversation at the time, but nothing since then, no. I have to admit, I was tempted—" He broke off at Camryn's startled movement and looked up again. "It's my job to consider what's best for the company. Don't tell your sister, though. She'll take a strip off my hide." Turning once more to Will, he repeated, "I was tempted, as the offer was a good one, but there was something about the fellow I just didn't feel comfortable with. In the end, I walked away."

Taken off guard by Jason's revelation, Camryn stepped back and perched on a small table pressed against the wall behind his chair. He'd considered selling even before she'd come home? The thought made her dizzy. Life wasn't exactly secure, but at least she had her family around her. If he'd agreed to a sale before she'd returned, where would she be now? Still struggling to find another job in Vancouver?

And what about Will? She would never have met him or Laura if she hadn't come home. A chill chased the dizziness away and she shivered.

"What's all this got to do with you coming here today?" Jason asked.

Once more, Will took his time answering, tapping his fingers on his knees. "Jepsen Contracting is our biggest rival in the Lower Mainland," he finally said. "We didn't think they had any interest in Prince George, but we just found out they've bought two local companies."

"Which ones?" Jason asked, and Will named them. They meant nothing to Camryn, but Jason's expression grew thoughtful. "Good companies," he said. "That'll make an impact in the market."

Will nodded. "It means my boss is even more serious about controlling the opportunities here. He really wants Bendixon and Sons. He's authorized me to add fifteen percent to our initial price."

Jason puckered his lips in a soundless whistle, looking impressed.

No, Camryn thought. *He wouldn't.* Out loud, she said firmly, "We're still not interested."

"It's an excellent offer," Will said.

He had trouble meeting her eyes, and a treacherous sympathy bubbled inside her. She squashed it down. How could he sit there and tempt Jason like this, when he knew how important this was to her?

"We don't need to sell," she said. "We're getting new financing and I signed up another job just today." And that didn't count two very promising phone calls she'd fielded recently. All those hours sending out bids and proposals were finally paying off.

If anything, her revelations made Will look even more miserable. "That's just going to make you more attractive. I'm willing to bet Jepsen Contracting will be back with another offer soon." He met her gaze squarely for the first time. "This is my job, Camryn. My boss has told me to make it happen. What do I need to do to get the deal?"

CHAPTER TWENTY-EIGHT

Will waited for an answer. Jason's expression was polite and thoughtful, which gave him some hope. But he shied away from Camryn's cold, frozen face. He really didn't know what he'd hoped to achieve by confronting Jason and Camryn like this. But there was no way he was going to sit around the office dithering about the situation. If it had to be dealt with, it might as well be now.

Knowing he was pitting grandfather against granddaughter, he said, keeping his gaze straight at Jason, "It's an extremely generous offer. And my former comments still stand. Mattie is certain to find a position within the Kohlenburg Group, and I'll do my best to keep Camryn on as well."

"I don't need your pity, and Bendixon and Sons doesn't need your money," she said, her tone scathing. "I have only been home a few weeks, but I've made a difference, made changes that are going to improve the business." She stepped forward, turning her back on Will and speaking directly to Jason. "We've turned a corner, I know we have. If you give me a chance, give Mattie and me a chance, we'll prove it to you by working harder than ever to make sure your company is a legacy you can be proud of."

Jason looked at her with a steady blue gaze. "You don't know what you're getting into. Sure, things may be looking up, but that's today. This is a fickle industry, and it's wearing on the spirit, riding the boom and bust."

"I should be going," Will said. He shouldn't be around for this discussion. "You can call me with your decision."

Camryn spun toward him, eyes flashing, chin lifted defiantly. "We'll give you our decision now. The answer is no."

Jason rose and put a hand on her shoulder. "We should at least get Mattie's take."

"Jason." Camryn's voice trembled, the vulnerability flaying Will's soul. "Don't do this."

"We'll talk more later, with Mattie." Nodding at Will, he said, "Camryn will walk you out."

She stiffened, her face bleak, as if he'd asked her to face a firing squad. Then she turned and marched past Will to the door. He followed her out, noting the tight set of her shoulders and jerky walk. Cold radiated from her, chilling the air.

The older lady who'd greeted him when he'd come in was not at her desk. Her chair was tucked neatly underneath, the computer screen off. Camryn stepped to the side to allow him to reach the front door.

He couldn't leave her, not like this. If there was a better time to beg, he couldn't think of one.

"I know you're angry, but listen to me, just for a minute." He stood close, braving the icy armor she wore. Her gaze lasered past his ear, but he took her silence as consent and continued, keeping his voice low so Jason couldn't hear. "This is part of my job. I tried to talk my boss out of it, but he's set on buying this company. He deserves my loyalty and my dedication. Please, try to understand."

She met his gaze then, the ferocity in their blue depths almost knocking him to his knees. "What about me?" she said in a furious whisper. "Don't you owe *me* something? I could have loved you, you know. It wouldn't have taken many more days with you and Laura, many more nights in your bed. I was starting to trust you, to believe that maybe, just maybe, all the crappy stuff that happened in the last few months was worth it, because it brought me here, to you. But if your job means more to you than I do, I guess I was wrong."

He couldn't breathe. She'd been falling in love with him? It was more than he'd hoped for, so early in their relationship. But then the rest of what she said exploded in his brain. "It's not that my job means more than you"— *nothing means more than you*—"but it matters. Everyone there has supported me for years. You've only been with Bendixon and Sons a few weeks. I can't jeopardize what I've built through more than a decade."

As soon as the words were out of his mouth, he knew he'd made a mistake. Camryn pointed at the door.

"Out," she said.

"I didn't mean my career was more important than yours."

"And yet, that's exactly what you said. Get out, now."

He stared at her, searching for the words to fix this, to

fix everything, and finding none. So, he left. What else could he do?

The cold outside had nothing on Camryn's frigid bitterness.

Camryn's soul had taken such a beating in the last few weeks she wasn't sure she'd ever be the same. Especially when, just as she thought she might be on the mend, Will had betrayed her. Again.

She scowled at the empty wine glass she clenched in her fist.

"Here, have some more." Jo refilled her glass.

"I think it'll take more than alcohol to loosen her up," Mattie said from her post, curled in the corner of the couch.

The three of them were in the family room of their parents' house. Camryn wasn't sure how it had come about, but shortly after she'd arrived home, Mattie had shown up, followed almost immediately by Jo.

There was something wrong about Jo being here at this time. "Don't you have class this evening?" she asked. The words felt like rough-edged marbles in her mouth, her thoughts sluggish.

Jo shrugged. "I've got a buddy taking notes for me." She perched on the coffee table in front of the couch, folding her legs up underneath her.

"Why are you skipping it?" Camryn's gaze slipped from Jo to Mattie and back again. "Why are either of you here?"

Jo tipped her head to one side, her dark-lashed eyes brimming with sympathy. A sympathy Camryn didn't want, and probably didn't deserve. No one should feel sorry for you when it's your own fault you've been an idiot.

"Mattie told me what happened at work," she said. "We figured you might need us."

Camryn frowned. "There's nothing wrong. You shouldn't be missing school."

"For Pete's sake," Mattie said, "for once let us take care of you, Camryn. It won't kill Jo to miss one class, and right now you do need us, whether you admit it or not."

Shocked out of her stupor by Mattie's uncharacteristic outburst, Camryn felt some of the fog in her brain lift.

"You're acting like something horrible happened today," she said.

"From the expression on your face when I got back to the office at the end of the day, something did," Mattie said. "Even before Jason told me about Will's offer, you looked ill."

"Then she told me what happened, and we decided to keep you company tonight." Jo reached under the coffee table without getting off and pulled out a bag of pretzels from a basket on the lower shelf.

"It isn't that big a deal. I overreacted. After all, it's just business." Maybe if she kept telling herself that, she'd grow to believe it. *Just business.* That's what Will had said.

So why did it feel so personal?

Of course, she'd as good as told him she loved him. That was fairly personal, wasn't it? She hadn't known the words were there, waiting to burst out, until they'd left her lips. And instead of acknowledging what she'd said, giving her any indication that her love would be welcome, he'd belittled her.

"Since when do you sleep with a guy if it's only

business?" Jo said.

Mattie uncurled abruptly, dropping her feet to the floor. "You slept with Will?"

"I almost caught them at it," Jo said, grimacing. "Let me tell you, that was a close call."

"Whether or not I slept with Will has nothing to do with why I'm upset." It was obvious her sisters weren't going to believe she was all right, so she might as well tell them at least part of the truth. "I'd be upset no matter what. He knows how I feel about making Bendixon and Sons succeed. And he keeps trying to undermine us."

"I don't want to sell the company either," Mattie said. "But you don't see me staring into nothingness and working my way through a bottle of wine."

Defiantly, Camryn slugged back a large gulp. "Things were just starting to look up. I was really hoping the worst was behind us."

Jo noisily picked through the bag of pretzels. "Jason said no once. Why doesn't he just say no again? It's not like he can be forced to sell the company, is it?"

"Of course not. But this second offer is a really good deal, financially speaking. Even I can see it makes the most sense," Camryn said miserably. "And if he does say no, what about Will? He's been told to do this. What happens to him if he can't do what his boss wants and expects?"

Mattie and Jo looked at her in surprise.

"What?" she said.

"Are you worried about Will?" Jo said. "I thought it was just the company."

"It's all a mess." Camryn leaned her head back on the couch. "Someone's going to lose, one way or the other. There's no way we can both come out of this on the plus side."

"Surely they won't fire him over it." Mattie leaned forward, her elbows on her knees. "He must be a valued employee, to be put in charge of the branch here."

Camryn tilted her head toward Mattie. "You're right," she said slowly. "Even if he did get fired—which I don't think they can do, I mean, it's not exactly a cause for dismissal—he's a smart guy. He'd find another job." He'd said the same thing about her, hadn't he? It was disconcerting to see it from the other side.

"I wonder if he's ever thought of running his own business," Jo said, nibbling a salty twist. "From what you've told me, he's only forcing the issue because he's been told to, not because he thinks it's the right decision. Maybe it's time for a change."

Out of the mouths of babes. Camryn stared at Jo. "Maybe that's it," she said.

"What?" Mattie asked.

"Maybe Will needs a change."

CHAPTER TWENTY-NINE

Will put Laura to bed while on autopilot. She had to remind him to remind her to brush her teeth, which would have been funny if he'd thought about it. He left her after one story, standing steadfast against her entreaties.

"Not tonight, sweetie," he said, brushing a kiss on her forehead. "I'm too tired. I think I need some alone time."

"Ah, alone time." She nodded soberly, her hair making a shushing sound against her princess pillowcase. "That's what my teacher tells Jordy he needs when he's being bad. Then she makes him sit in the quiet corner for a little while. Were you bad today?"

Will wanted to laugh at her earnestness, but her innocent question hit a little too close to home. "Goodnight," he said once more, and tucked the covers more securely around her narrow shoulders. "Go to sleep. I'm going to my quiet corner."

He poured himself a small shot of whiskey, an indulgence he rarely allowed himself, then dropped onto the squashy couch. Turning on the TV, he clicked between channels without seeing what was on the screen, his thoughts once again with Camryn.

He'd really screwed up today, and could only hope an apology would set things right. The tricky part was how exactly to word it without making things worse. After all, he wasn't sorry about what he'd said, just how he'd said it.

A soft rapping interrupted his dismal thoughts. It took him a moment to realize it was someone knocking at the door, a sound he rarely heard. Since even a door-to-door salesperson was better than sitting alone and moping about Camryn, he put down his drink and went to the door.

He opened it to a gust of chilly wind, a random scattering of snowflakes—and Camryn.

"Hello," she said.

"What are you doing here?" he replied, dazed and stupid with relief and confusion.

She flinched and took a step back. He grasped her wrist before she could escape.

"I can't seem to say anything right these days," he said. "Please, come in. I was just surprised to see you." To put it mildly. She was the last person he'd expected to find on his front step tonight.

He closed the door behind her. She stood in the hallway, slim and straight, the tip of her nose slightly reddened from the cold, the fringes of her bright hair peeking out from under a blue wool hat.

"I didn't want to ring the doorbell," she said, "in case Laura was sleeping." Her fingers, encased in wine-coloured leather gloves, twisted together.

"I just put her to bed." His heart beat faster just looking at her. "I'm sorry," he said, all plans for a carefully worded speech forgotten. "I expressed myself badly this afternoon."

She hunched her shoulders, the fabric of her coat rustling. "It's possible I overreacted. I may be a little irrational when it comes to my livelihood these days."

It killed him to see her so lacking in confidence. The first few times he'd met her, she'd been brimming over with ideas and schemes and determination.

"I didn't come here because of our argument," she continued. "Well, not completely. If you have time, I'd like to talk to you about something."

"I was just having a nightcap," he said. "Want to join me?"

"Why not."

"Let me take your coat."

Under the enveloping garment—finally one designed for winter weather, he was pleased to see—she wore slim-fitting jeans and an ivory, chunky knit sweater that slipped off one shoulder, revealing the graceful line of her collarbone. She readjusted it and he felt a momentary sense of loss as she covered the smooth skin.

She accepted a small glass of port—a gift from an appreciative client that he had yet to open. Instead of taking a seat next to him on the couch, she settled on the overstuffed chair opposite, her feet flat on the floor, hands clasped around her drink.

"What did you want to talk to me about?" he asked, when a few moments had passed in silence.

Her gaze flickered nervously about the room, and then settled on his. Drawing a deep breath, she said, "I think you should buy Bendixon and Sons."

Her statement shocked him even more than her sudden appearance had. He inhaled the sip of whiskey he'd just taken, choking as it burned his lungs.

She waited patiently for him to regain his composure, no hint of amusement on her features. "You're serious, aren't you?" he managed to say between coughing fits. "What made you change your mind? Why would you be willing to accept the Kohlenburg Group's offer now?"

"I'm not," she said, her eyes steady. "I don't want *them* to buy Bendixon and Sons. I want *you* to."

Camryn hoped the blank look of shock on Will's face was a good sign, but didn't wait to find out. She dove in with further explanation.

"You said it yourself, you don't agree with what your boss is asking you to do. Do you want to be in the same sort of situation in the future? With your experience and resume, I think it would be easy to get financing. You'll do what you're good at—finding jobs, preparing quotes, getting things done. I've had some success with that, but it's not what I'm trained for. I can handle the financial side. Helen, who does all that now, won't be around long after Jason retires, she's already said so. I'll take over the office, send out invoices, pay bills. That's what I'm good at. Mattie will be your crew chief, of course, and do what she does best, the actual construction."

She could see it so clearly. The future glowed before her like the sun rising in the morning—crisp and clean and hopeful.

"You want me to leave the Kohlenburg Group and take a risk on a business that's in financial difficulties?" Will's voice rose at the end, both in pitch and volume.

She swallowed. "We're on our way out of the woods," she said, trying to sound optimistic not defensive. "The bank is demanding we find a buyer, but a new investor would suit us better. Jason and I have talked about it. It will show the bank we're making changes, will improve our standing with them, but the family will still have control."

"If the family has control, what about me? Not that I'm considering this crazy scheme, but why would you expect anyone to buy in if he'd be a minority owner?"

His brusque tone more than the words he used shattered Camryn's glittering excitement. "What do you mean, crazy scheme?"

Will pulled no punches. "If you want a new investor, you'll have to look somewhere else," he said. "This is not the sort of risk I'm willing to take. I have a child to care for. Staking her future on a failing business is not the smart way to go."

Heat flushed Camryn's cheeks and her palms tingled. "Failing business?" She felt like she was in a dark room, windmilling her arms, searching for the way out. This wasn't how she'd envisioned the conversation going.

He leaned forward and placed his glass on the table between them. The clink sounded like the locking of a door. "I'm sorry if I gave you the wrong impression," he said, his tone gentler. "I was upset when my boss told me to offer for Bendixon and Sons again. But that was because I didn't want to cause you more grief, not because I don't agree with him. I know you don't want to sell, but I have to be honest. It's probably the best move for Jason right now."

She closed her eyes briefly, needing a respite from the pity in his expression. "You don't think we can do this," she said. "You think we should give up, sell out."

"The world is changing." Will rose and came to sit on the arm of her chair. He brushed a fingertip on the shell of her ear. She wanted to lean into his touch, wanted his comfort, but what good would that do? They were obviously on different sides of a barbed wire fence. He sighed when she tilted her head away. "Every day is a struggle for smaller companies like yours. Why put yourself through that?"

Why indeed? She had at least one reason. "I can't bear to start all over. Not again. It was hard enough, losing what I'd worked for because of Anthony's deceit. Hard enough to admit I was a failure and come home, practically a charity case." She stood up, her thoughts crystallizing even as she spoke. "I didn't want to be here. I only returned to Bendixon and Sons because I had nowhere else to go." Her pacing steps took her to the kitchen island. She spun to face Will. "But it's mine now. I've put my heart and soul into that company the last few weeks, and I won't give up now."

Later that night, lying sleepless in bed, she heard her own words echo back at her like a fading war cry. Was she being unrealistic to continue the fight? Was she simply delaying the inevitable, and in doing so throwing away everything she might have had with Will?

What was the right thing to do? And did she have the courage to do it, whatever it was?

CHAPTER THIRTY

"I'm sorry, Wayne," Will said into the phone. "Bendixon and Sons isn't for sale. We'll have to come up with another plan." After he'd cooled down from Camryn's visit, he'd thought of one, but he needed to broach the idea carefully.

"What are they thinking?" Wayne's exasperation travelled clearly through the speaker. "It's only a matter of time before they get pushed out. Why not take a good offer now?"

It was only what Will had said to Camryn last night, but hearing it from Wayne gave him a hint at what Camryn had felt. "They're thinking they'd rather be independent and fail than admit defeat. It's a forty-year-old company. There's a lot of history there. The family doesn't want to give it up." He pushed to his feet and stood next to the window overlooking City Hall. The room was warm, but a brisk chill emanated from the glass.

Behind him, Wayne's disembodied voice answered. "Pride has killed many a company. What do you think about sweetening the deal a little more? We could go up another percent."

"They're not looking for a buyout." His breath misted the glass. *Here goes*, he thought. "If you were interested in investing, they might look at that."

"Really?" Wayne's tone turned thoughtful. "Is that rumour or certain fact?"

"It's fact." Will turned from the grey, blustery scene outside, leaning back against the window. Cold seeped through the cotton of his shirt. "They know they need an infusion of cash, but they don't want to lose control. They approached me with the idea."

It was Wayne's turn to pause. "Jason Bendixon asked the Kohlenburg Group to invest?"

Will took a metaphorical step onto a tightrope. This was the tricky part, but he'd always been honest with Wayne, and he wasn't changing now. "No," he said, "the offer came from Camryn Bendixon, his granddaughter. And she didn't ask the Kohlenburg Group. She asked *me*. With the idea I would leave here and join them."

The silence over the speaker was long. Will's palms began to sweat.

"Is that something you've thought of before? Striking out on your own?" Wayne's voice held no censure, only curiosity.

Will let out a pent-up breath, but didn't fully relax. "No, I haven't." Not until Camryn had broached her harebrained idea. Now he was having trouble getting it out of his mind. "I need stability for Laura. I can't give that up for the uncertainty of my own business."

Wayne grunted acknowledgement, but whether in agreement or not Will didn't know. "Maybe we have been looking at this the wrong way."

"What do you mean?" Will wasn't certain he trusted Wayne's tone.

"Maybe we can all get what we want."

Will's rejection last night could have crushed Camryn. She'd sensed the weight of it hovering over her head, ready to slam down and finish her off. Instead, she rolled it aside, and used its momentum to push her determination into a new gear.

She didn't need Will's money. She didn't need his experience or his skills or his network. She'd do just fine without him, and had proven that by signing off on two new contracts just this morning. Mattie was making calls to some of the guys they'd let go earlier in the year, seeing who could come back, before they started looking for new crew members. It had been a great day.

She didn't need Will. No siree, Bob!

God, she *needed* Will.

This final dissolution of their relationship was like the ocean's seventh wave. Most of the time, her misery lapped gently at her feet. But every so often it overwhelmed her, the undertow dragging her down until she didn't think she'd ever come to the surface. But somehow, she did, and would paddle for a little longer, before the next wave took her under again.

Helen had gone to the bank to make a deposit, so when the front door opened and a rush of cold air swept down the hall, Camryn dragged herself to her feet to greet the visitor. When she saw who it was, she about-faced and started marching back to her dingy, stale-smelling room.

"Don't go," Will said. "Please, Camryn."

She halted, one hand braced on the wall. "We have nothing to say to each other," she said, staring down the hall, refusing to look at him.

"You don't have to say anything. But please, will you listen?"

She closed her eyes, gathering strength. The deep bass rumble of his voice rolled through her belly like thunder, warming her, setting off shocks of lightning along her nerves. What did it matter if she listened? She couldn't hurt any more than she hurt right now.

Turning slowly, she faced him. "Talk, then."

He shoved his fists into the pockets of his leather jacket. His cheeks were stained with red, whether from the cold or emotion she couldn't tell.

"I told my boss, Wayne, that you'd asked me to invest. That you'd asked me to quit the Kohlenburg Group."

She sucked in a breath on another flare of pain. If she'd needed any further proof of where his loyalties lay, there it was. As she concentrated on breathing through the crushing misery, she missed his next words.

"What?" she said.

Will repeated himself. "Instead of buying Jason out, Wayne is willing to consider investing. The Kohlenburg Group will infuse new capital into the business, and in return become a minority owner."

Her emotions took a rapid swing and she shook her head as if that would realign her swirling thoughts. It couldn't be that simple. "Just like that? What changed his mind?"

"He figures something is better than nothing. And he really wants to erase Jepsen from the equation." Will rolled his shoulders. "He does have a condition."

"Of course he does." Camryn's thoughts finally caught up with the conversation. She knew what Will was going to say.

"I take over running the business."

"He's willing to be a minority owner, yet he wants you in charge. How is that any different from buying us outright?

"I wouldn't work for Wayne. Not if you agree to this deal."

She frowned. "I don't understand."

"He wants to give Samuel more authority. Samuel would take over my duties, and they'd bring a new person up from Vancouver to assist him. My focus would be completely Bendixon and Sons. Yes, we'd ultimately be responsible to the Kohlenburg Group. But we'd bid for our own contracts, be completely in control of our own jobs. As a sister company, we'd also be counted on to support them on their larger projects. You'd take over Helen's responsibilities, just as you suggested. Mattie would continue in her role."

The strength went out of Camryn's knees. She wobbled her way to Helen's chair and dropped into it. "We'd still be our own company."

"It's exactly what you asked for last night. Except for where the money is coming from."

He hadn't moved from his post by the door. His hands were still pressed into his pockets, and he regarded her warily.

"What about Laura?" she asked. "What about all the reasons it wouldn't work last night?"

He took a step closer. "It's still a risk, but with the Kohlenburg Group behind us, not so much of one. I'm comfortable working hard—I just couldn't gamble with my own money."

She was beginning to believe they'd finally found a solution. "It sounds too good to be true."

"Well, you would get saddled with me." Will rounded the end of the desk and pulled up another chair. Sitting in front of Camryn, he reached for her hands, clasping them in his. "What about Jason? Do you think he'll go for this new structure?"

Camryn nodded slowly. "I think he believed selling was the best option. But he didn't want to disappoint Mattie and me, and he didn't want to see four decades of pride lost. This is perfect. I'm sure he'll agree."

"I have something else to offer you."

Already anticipating the looks of joy and relief on Mattie and Jason's faces, she asked absently, "What?"

"My love."

Her eyes widened and her hands clenched his, seeking an anchor, dizzy at the abrupt switch in direction. "Pardon?"

He leaned closer. "I know this is probably the worst timing in the world, but I have to tell you now. I love you. If I need to leave the Kohlenburg Group to keep you, I will. But I can't stand anymore of this back and forth. I know I'm the one who said we could keep our personal and professional lives from interfering with each other, but it's too late. You've wound your way into all parts of my life, and I don't want to unwind you."

She shouldn't be feeling this way. She was probably on the rebound still, probably giddy with knowing she'd secured Bendixon and Sons' future. But she couldn't keep the grin from stretching her lips. "I told you yesterday, I wasn't far from falling in love with you already. I lied."

His gaze twinkled, secure in what she was about to say. "You did?"

"Yes. I'm not far from it at all. I'm right in it. I'm in love with you. I don't care that it's too soon, that we can't possibly know each other well enough, that we've done little but argue and compete for weeks. I love you, and I don't want to miss another minute with you."

His lips touched hers, warm and soft, heating to fiery and demanding in moments. He dragged her out of the chair, wrapping his arms around her, breaking the kiss only long enough to let her breathe.

"Does this mean you accept my offer?" he muttered, nibbling along her jaw.

"Yes," she said, not sure which one he meant, but too dazed to care, and more than eager to accept them both.

EPILOGUE

Camryn stood next to Mattie and listened to Jo and Luke exchange their vows. The scent of evergreen from her bridesmaid bouquet mingled with the aroma of candle wax and incense that permeated Sacred Heart Cathedral.

Jo's voice rang clear and true, without hesitation or doubt. Her dress was demure, as befitted a church wedding—long-sleeved, high-necked, with ivory Brussel's lace over an ivory satin bodice. But the skirt was very Josephine—layers of floating chiffon in a pale forest green. Luke's mother had made a comment or two about brides who didn't have the right to wear white and Jo had chosen to interpret that in her own unique way.

Camryn let her gaze wander past Luke—handsome in a charcoal grey suit with dark green cummerbund—out into the pews, where the congregation was seated. Even with a guest list limited to family and close friends, there was still a crowd of more than one hundred and fifty people. That didn't stop her from easily finding the one person she was looking for.

As if he'd known she was searching for him, Will met her gaze immediately. The connection made her toes curl and she ran her tongue along her bottom lip. Heat flared in his warm brown eyes, unmistakable even at this distance.

Without taking his eyes off her, Will reached down and lifted Laura to his hip. He whispered in her ear and her face lit up in a wide smile as she waved energetically in Camryn's direction.

Her heart thumped in a completely new way. Before Will, before Laura, she hadn't spent much time thinking about being a mother. Now, she couldn't imagine her life without this child in it. She was in love with both father and daughter.

With an effort, she dragged her concentration back to Jo and Luke.

Soon the newly married couple was being kissed and hugged and fêted in the narthex of the church. It was a perfect December day—bitterly cold but bright and blue—and each time the door opened for departing guests a chill wind gusted in, swirling at the ankle-length hem of her deep-green gown. She slipped to the back of the crowd and waited.

Finally, Will and Laura appeared, the little girl still perched in her father's arms. Instead of heading to Jo and Luke, Will veered directly toward her.

Again, she felt that thrill of connection. *Would it ever fade?* she wondered. Somehow, she knew it wouldn't.

Conscious of Will even with her attention on his daughter, she said, "Laura, you look beautiful. Did your Daddy do your hair?"

The little girl beamed. "Do you like it? I love how it feels." She reached up to stroke her brown tresses, twisted and woven into an intricate design. This skill with braids was just one of the many fascinating things she'd recently learned about Will.

"It's lovely," she agreed.

"So are you," Will murmured, dropping too quick a kiss onto her lips. And that was something she'd recently learned about *herself*. She couldn't get enough of Will's kisses.

"Still consorting with the enemy?"

Marcus appeared beside Will. Since they had revealed their relationship to the family, the three men the Bendixon sisters had chosen had bonded over insults and bantering. Luke and Marcus had been friends in high school, so that wasn't surprising, but Will slipped so seamlessly into their partnership it was almost scary.

"As of the first of February, you won't be able to say that anymore," Will replied easily.

Jason and Mattie had agreed to the Kohlenburg Group's proposal, as Camryn had been certain they would. Everything was working out so well she pinched herself once a day to make sure it wasn't a dream. After so many weeks of panic and stress, having the weight of responsibility lifted from her shoulders made her feel like she was floating inches off the ground.

"Can I show you guys something?" Marcus asked. "It's a surprise, so you can't tell anyone, okay, Laura?" She nodded solemnly. Casting a sidelong glance at Mattie, who was chatting animatedly with Jason and Lorraine, Marcus shifted his body so his back was to her and pulled a small blue box out of his trouser pocket.

"No!" Camryn said.

"Yes." Marcus nodded as he opened the box and revealed a white gold band sparkling with princess-cut diamonds.

Will whispered in Laura's ear, letting her in on the secret.

Marcus stroked the ring, an odd mix of certainty and anxiety on his usually serious face. "I know she probably won't wear it to work, but just in case I chose one with a channel setting so it can't get caught easily. What do you think?"

When Camryn remained speechless, Will said, "It's perfect. Well done."

"I hope so." Marcus closed the box carefully. "I don't want to upstage Jo and Luke, so I'm going to ask her at Christmas. But I'm afraid to leave it in the house in case she finds it by accident, so I've been carrying it around for days." When he was in town, Marcus lived with Mattie in her little bungalow.

Since he'd returned from his world tour, he'd made a couple of short trips to Vancouver, but Camryn knew he had a longer one planned in February. The frequent separations seemed to work for Mattie and Marcus, but Camryn came to the sudden and surprising realization that she wouldn't want that life for her and Will. She couldn't imagine not seeing Will and Laura for weeks on end. Just the idea caused her breath to hitch.

"It's time to get going for photos," Mattie said, popping up at Marcus' side. She didn't seem to notice his guilty jerk as he shoved the box back into his pocket, but something in Camryn's face must have looked odd. She asked, "Are you okay?"

"I'm fine." Camryn turned to Will and Laura before her sister could query her further. "I'll see you tomorrow, Laura." Corrine was looking after her for the rest of the day, leaving Will free to attend the reception. To him, she said, "I'll see you later."

Will reached out with his free hand—Laura was still balanced on his hip—and caressed the nape of her neck, rippling shivers across her skin. "You bet."

Hours later, after photos and dinner and speeches and the first dance, Camryn, Mattie, and Jo clustered in the lounge area of the bathroom at the hall rented for the reception.

"I think I can finally relax," Jo said, collapsing onto the bench, her skirts floating around her. "I've been in a panic all day that Luke's mom would make a scene of some sort. The worse part was during the ceremony. I kept waiting for her to jump up and object."

Mattie sat down next to Jo and patted her thigh. "You don't have anything to worry about. I swear she almost smiled during Luke's toast to his bride. I think you're growing on her."

"I can only hope."

"I'm lucky in Lorraine. I know she's not my mother-in-law"—the hint of wistfulness in her voice had Camryn biting her lip to keep Marcus' secret—"but it's so great we get along."

Camryn had yet to meet Will's parents, though they had talked on the phone. As Elizabeth was coming to Prince George for Christmas, they'd decided to make a visit in the new year. She had the feeling they didn't approve of their granddaughter's mother, which only added to her anxiety. What if they didn't approve of her, either?

"I have something to say," she announced. She took a deep breath. "Anthony drove a wedge between us, and that's my fault. But I just want you to know that, no matter what it was like when I first came home, I am so glad to be here now, with both of you."

"Don't make me cry," Jo said, sniffing. "I haven't cried all day, and I refuse to start now."

Mattie stood and wrapped her arms around Camryn. "I think it is great Anthony was a crook," she said, surprising a laugh out of Camryn. "If he wasn't, you'd still be in Vancouver, and Bendixon and Sons would still be in trouble. You saved us, Camryn. You must know that."

It was Camryn's turn to sniff. "Okay, enough mushy stuff." She hugged Mattie, then bent to hug Jo, too. "We'd better get back out there before Luke thinks you've run away."

In the hall, Camryn left her sisters and joined Will at one of the long, rectangular tables. She hadn't had a chance to snatch more than a minute or two with him all evening, and was embarrassingly hungry for his voice, his touch. She lowered herself carefully onto the uncomfortable metal chair next to him.

"Are you done?" Will asked. He reached down and clasped her ankle, lifted her foot onto his lap, slipped off her high-heeled sandals and started to massage her instep.

"Oh, god, that feels so good." She let her eyes drift close for a moment. "Yes, I am done. Everything went so well. It helps that Jo is the most relaxed bride I've ever seen. She just let all the little things that go wrong slide right off. I don't think she's stopped smiling all day."

"Maybe that's what happens when you know you're making the right decision."

Camryn quirked an eyebrow. "She is, isn't she? Making the right decision, I mean. I've known Luke most of my life, and I don't think it ever crossed my mind he'd make a match with Jo. But they really are happy together. And it's a *solid* happy—not a high-strung, fairy-tale happy. You just get the sense that things will work out for them, no matter how tough it gets."

"And now Marcus is going to propose to Mattie."

Camryn sighed. "Yes." The couple were dancing in the open space in front of the stage, where Luke's brother's band played. Mattie laughed as Marcus spun her around and dipped her before planting a robust kiss on her lips. Every time Camryn saw Marcus, he was less starchy and formal. Mattie was good for him.

"You sound less certain about them than you do Jo and Luke." Will replaced her shoe and switched to her other foot.

She readjusted in her chair so he could keep up his good work. "I think they'll have a tougher time, that's all. Marcus is too prominent a musician to stay in Prince George, so they're going to be separated often. I just hope Mattie knows what she's getting into."

"I'm sure they'll be able to work it out." His thumb pushed hard into her instep and she couldn't hold back a moan. "Sorry. Too much?"

"No. Don't stop."

He rubbed her foot in silence for a few moments. "I talked to your dad while you were busy helping with the cake. He told me a few more stories of their trip. Sounds like they had quite the adventures."

Will had met Camryn's parents when they had arrived home a week ago. What with one thing and another, she hadn't found her own place to live yet, so for the last few days it had been like old times, with Jo, herself and their mom and dad living in the same space. Mattie had spent most of her free time there, too, helping with last minute wedding prep.

"He says Jo's moved all her stuff to Luke's already,"

Will continued.

"She didn't have much, but yes."

"They must enjoy having you home."

Camryn snorted. "I don't know about *enjoying*. They don't mind, of course—they'd never turn any of us away. But I'm pretty sure they're hoping I'll move out soon. They got used to being on their own during their year away."

"If you're serious about moving out, I have an idea."

Camryn held back a yawn. She was exhausted, and Will's hands on her foot felt *sooooo* good. "Of course I'm serious. I just have to find something I can afford that isn't a total dump." While her financial future looked rosier than it had in months, she was still digging out of debt. Elizabeth had been right, and Anthony was negotiating a deal that would keep him out of jail, but as Camryn had suspected, it didn't include making restitution to her. The official focus was on recovering as much of Rosin Interiors' money as possible.

"You could move in with Laura and I."

"That's sweet, but my parents aren't in that much of a rush to kick me out. I don't want to have to move twice."

"Not for the short term, Camryn. For good."

She yanked her foot out of his grasp and sat up straight in the hard metal chair. "What did you just say?"

He met her gaze directly, although small creases at the corner of his eyes hinted at a nervousness his words belied. "I know we haven't been together very long, but what I said about Jo, how she's so calm and relaxed because she knows she's doing the right thing?" He tapped his chest with his fist. "I feel the same about you. I love you, Camryn. I want you to live with Laura and me."

Camryn gasped out a lungful of air. "I wasn't angling

for an invite," she said in a whisper due to lack of oxygen. "If that's what you thought when I talked about moving. I wasn't."

"I know. To be honest, that kind of ticked me off."

Camryn's eyes widened. "It did?"

He leaned towards her so all she could see was him. "I want you to come to me when you need something. I want to help you, want to take care of you. And if that's not enlightened enough for a 21st century woman, I'm sorry. But when I love someone, I want to be there for them. And I love you."

"I love you, too," she said. "I just never dreamed—" She bit her lip, then said what she had to. "What about Elizabeth?"

Some small, evil part of her delighted in the confused expression that crossed Will's face. "What about Elizabeth?"

"What will she think if…" She trailed off, not wanting to give away how much she wanted to accept his offer. It twinkled and glittered just inside her reach, but she was afraid to grab it, afraid it would disappear if she held onto it too hard.

"Elizabeth does not come into the equation at all," Will said firmly. "Yes, she'll be in Laura's life, but that doesn't make a difference to us." His thumbs rubbed the back of her knuckles and his knees brushed hers. "You should also know, before you make any decision, that I talked it over with Laura, and she is very excited. She can't wait to have you come live with us."

Tears burned at the back of Camryn's throat. "I am honoured. But she can't understand—"

"Maybe she doesn't have the adult awareness of what living together means, but she knows you would be a bigger part of our lives. And that's what she wants. What we both want."

If Will had proposed to her, she'd probably have bolted, still gun-shy over Anthony. But living together… While her head knew it was only a degree removed from a proposal, her heart was relieved she was being asked to take this smaller step first. Because a wedding was in her and Will's future, she knew it. She just wasn't ready for it yet.

Somehow, Will understood her feelings. Knew she needed time to adjust. And that made the decision easy.

"I would love to move in with you and Laura," she said. "Is tomorrow too soon?"

Thank You!

Thanks for reading *Crossroads Corner*. I hope you enjoyed it!

Reviews are a great way to help other readers learn about new authors. I encourage you to publish your honest review at the retailer where you purchased your copy.

I'd love to connect on social media! You can find my links on my website, www.brendamargriet.com. And while you're there, you're also invited to sign up for my newsletter. It's a great way to keep up with new releases, promotions, and contests. And just for joining, you'll receive a free copy of my short story, The Life She Had Before.

Other books in the Bendixon Sisters Series

ALLEGRO COURT
(March 2019)

Marcus Temple escaped his despised birthplace, driven by his passion for music. Now a sophisticated, world-class cellist, he must return when his mother suffers a severe stroke. Going back also means dealing with the woman whose heart he broke when he left—Mattie Bendixon.

More comfortable in overalls than orchestra seats, Mattie's childhood dreams were simple—working for her grandfather's construction company and building a life with Marcus. His ambitions forced her to abandon one goal, and now her beloved company is also under threat.

Mattie thinks she sees a way to save Bendixon and Sons—if she can convince Marcus to stay in his hated hometown for one month. All she has to risk is her heart.

GATEWAY CRESCENT
(June 2019)

Jo Bendixon loves to sing, enjoys working in a coffee shop, and is secretly teaching herself to code. If only she could find a way to combine her varied interests into a career her sisters would approve.

Luke Donwell's Catholic faith is the bedrock of his life. For as long as he can remember, he's contemplated a vocation to the priesthood. Now it's time to make a final decision about taking his vows.

When Jo and Luke end up working together, neither of them is prepared for the heat blossoming between them. Luke begins to doubt his calling, but Jo encourages him to continue seeking the truth. Her heart will break when he leaves her, but how can a girl compete with God?

About the Author

Brenda Margriet writes contemporary romances with heroes you'd meet at the grocery store. And by that she means real-life men – sexy, smart, and looking for the love of their life. Her heroines are bold, savvy and determined to accept nothing less than the man they deserve. A voracious reader since she was old enough to hold a book, Brenda's idea of the perfect holiday involves a comfortable chair near the water (ocean, lake or pool will do), a glass of wine, and a fully loaded e-reader. She lives in Northern British Columbia with her husband, various finny and furry pets and has three grown children. Discover more about Brenda and her books at www.brendamargriet.com.

www.ingramcontent.com/pod-product-compliance
Lightning Source LLC
Chambersburg PA
CBHW030603180626
46816CB00005B/1654